Having pulled your boy and found him
to be a prince, you might want to
kiss him twice . . . just to be sure!

Stealing Princes

THE CALYPSO CHRONICLES

by Tyne O'Connell

BLOOMSBURY

Published by Bloomsbury Publishing, New York, London, and Berlin
Distributed to the trade by Holtzbrinck Publishers

Library of Congress Cataloging-in-Publication Data
O'Connell, Tyne.
Stealing princes / by Tyne O'Connell.
p. cm. (The Calypso chronicles)
Summary: Back at her elegant English boarding school for another term,
Californian Calypso Kelly continues her pursuit of Prince Freddie with style.
ISBN-10: 1-58234-992-4
ISBN-13: 978-1-58234-992-3
[1. Interpersonal relations—Fiction. 2. Fencing—Fiction. 3. Boarding
schools—Fiction. 4. Princes—Fiction. 5. Schools—Fiction. 6. England—Fiction.
7. Humorous stories.]
PZ7.O2168St 2005   [Fic]—dc22   2005040537

First U.S. Edition 2005
Printed in the U.S.A.
1 3 5 7 9 10 8 6 4 2

Published in the U.K. by Piccadilly Press

Bloomsbury Publishing, Children's Books, U.S.A.
175 Fifth Avenue, New York, NY 10010

Typeset by Hewer Text (UK) Ltd, Edinburgh

All papers used by Bloomsbury Publishing are natural, recyclable products
made from wood grown in well-managed forests. The manufacturing processes
conform to the environmental regulations of the country of origin.

To my divinely regal, wildly intelligent, stunning daughter, Cordelia, because she is my role model and the most inspirational muse any writer could wish for.

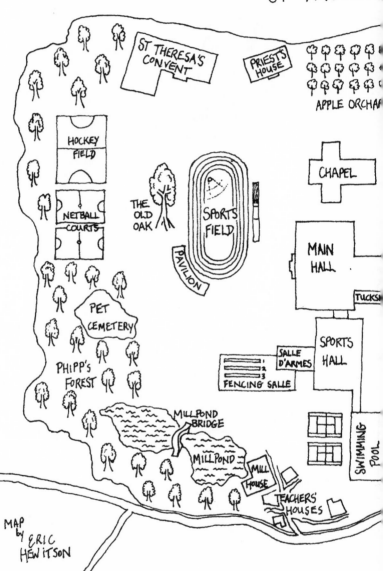

ST AUGUST[INE'S]

ST THERESA'S CONVENT

PRIEST'S HOUSE

APPLE ORCHA[RD]

HOCKEY FIELD

NETBALL COURTS

THE OLD OAK

SPORTS FIELD

PAVILION

CHAPEL

MAIN HALL

TUCKS[HOP]

PET CEMETERY

PHIPP'S FOREST

SALLE D'ARMES

SPORTS HALL

1
2
3

FENCING SALLE

MILLPOND BRIDGE

MILLPOND

MILL HOUSE

SWIMMING POOL

TEACHERS' HOUSES

MAP by ERIC HEWITSON

SCHOOL FOR LADIES

NUNS' CEMETERY

PULLERS' HILL

PET SHED

CLEATHORPES

BURSAR

AUGUSTINE'S
MAIN
BUILDING

LIBRARY

BLUEBELLS

PULLERS' WOOD

TO EADES

QUAD

INFIRMARY

SCIENCE LABS

6ᵗʰ FORM

SHORTCUT TO STATION

THE MARSHES

FRONT GATES

MAIN ROAD

N

E

W

S

LOWER COMMON

RAILWAY STATION

ONE

The Agony and the Txt-acy of Flirt-Txting Two Boys at Once

I was standing in the en garde line, wired to the electrical recording device which would register hits (should I be lucky enough to get any). I saluted my opponent casually and focused. Well, I focused as best a girl can when she's about to fence one of the fittest boys in all the world.

Eades is the grandest of grand boys' schools in England, and they know it. Royalty, the good, the great and the madly wealthy of the world all send their sons to Eades to be educated in the art of effortless charm and entitlement. I suppose they teach them hard sums, Latin and a bit of Greek too, but then so do other schools. It's the effortless charm and sense of entitlement bit that sets them apart – and the fact that each and every Eades boy is distressingly fit. I suspect that their entrance exam includes a fitness test.

Billy Pyke, captain of the Eades sabre team and the boy I was about to fence, isn't a bit grand, though. Well, his family is ridiculously rich and he speaks in the grand way all Eades boys do, but he's actually from the East End of London. His father runs the country's largest limo sale and hire business, but being ridiculously rich doesn't necessarily make you grand. In fact, it can work against you and earn you the term *nouveau*, which is worse than being a pleb. Most boys from Eades can point to their name in *Debrett's Peerage and Baronetage* or, if European, the *Amanach De Gotha*. At the very least your people's money has to go back hundreds of generations for it to be respectable in the high-stakes world of English boarding schools. Billy's family money only goes back one.

'Better to be titled and poor as a church mouse than rich and common,' as they say here. Which is especially tragic for me because my parents aren't titled and they aren't rich, even new-money rich. They struggle to send me to Saint Augustine's because they are obsessed with giving me the best education money can buy, which according to my mom isn't available in LA. Also, she's English and went to Saint Augustine's, and she thought it was 'super.'

Apart from the new-money thing, Billy is distressingly fit and cool, and tall, blond, blue-eyed and dashing. And did I mention older? He's seventeen. Older is always a plus. So clearly it was pretty tricky to focus my mind on combat, knowing of the gorgeousness that lurked beneath the tight white fencing gear and the electrically conductive metal mesh mask he was encased in.

The fencing master called 'Play,' and I advanced swiftly down the piste, preparing for an attack. Usually boys are a bit hesitant to hit girls on the chest. When I say hesitant, I'm speaking in nano-milliseconds. Obviously they still hit you, and just as hard! Nevertheless, their hesitation often gives a girl an advantage, because that's all you need in sabre to grab the point. One second – less, even.

Billy was renowned for not being the least bit hesitant when it came to hitting girls. Actually, he was the most aggressive fencer I've had the privilege to be rinsed by. Sabre is all about speed and concentration, and the attacker always has priority, as long as the opponent's target (anywhere above the leg) is continually threatened. I won my first point and after that I made sure that Billy's target area was continually threatened for the rest of the bout.

If I say so myself, I was unbelievable. My mother, Sarah, often says that false modesty is artless, so all modesty aside, my footwork was faultless. Honestly, I was shocked by my own talent as each lunge sent the electrical recorder lights flashing and buzzing. I was a veritable Olympian. I was indestructible, and what's more, I didn't even feel the few hits Billy *did* manage. And in sabre that is something because it's not like the graceful fencing you've probably seen in James Bond films or on ads for hair products. It's brutal and you get bruised and sore and seriously sweaty.

At the end of the bout, I triumphantly tore off my mask; but instead of the usual spray of sweat and mucky hair, my unruly blonde mane came out like . . . well, like hair-commercial hair. *Incroyable*, as my French teacher would say.

The applause was deafening, but all I cared about – as the V was chalked onto the board and I strode towards Billy to shake his hand – was snog-aging him. Not that I would be allowed to, obviously. Single-sex boarding schools like to keep intergender activities strictly lips-off. 'There must always be a balloon distance between boys and girls,' Sister Constance likes to chant.

Time moved in slow motion as I stretched out my hand to shake his. I watched his hand begin to remove his mask, tugging the chin guard upwards, revealing inch by inch not the features of Billy, but Freddie, as in HRH – you know, Prince Freddie, heir to the British throne.

'You have to put your seat belt on now,' the flight attendant warned as she woke me. 'We'll be landing at Heathrow in a moment.'

Okay, it was only a dream, but it was kind of spooky actually because all summer I'd been txt-flirting with Freddie and Billy. I know it sounds bad, but you can't blame me. We are talking about two wildly fit boys here – even by Eades standards – and after taking so long to pull a single boy (fourteen years), I now had two boys txt-flirting me. What girl is going to resist that? How was I ever going to choose between Freddie – heir to the British throne –

and Billy, captain of the Eades sabre team, who had rescued me from the jaws of a girl-eating attack dog before we broke up for summer?

My two best friends, Georgina and Star, both found the txt relationships of my summer hugely entertaining. I forwarded them every txt, even though a part of me wanted to keep some of them all to myself. Like the one where Freddie said his parents wanted to meet me.

Me, Calypso Kelly, a complete nobody from America! No title, no money – not even new money – and yet the king and queen of the United Kingdom and all its other territories wanted to meet *me*. I could have swooned with the excitement of it all, only then Freddie went on to say how of course he'd never put me through that, because apparently it would mean spending a weekend at Bardington with his gran's Labradors, who are elderly and quite nippy.

I sent a txt back telling him that I wouldn't mind being nipped to bits by royal Labradors. I was madly restrained, in fact – deleting the bit about how I'd happily be mauled by them if it meant staying a weekend in one of his family's castles.

Freddie sent back a txt saying:

ha, ha, ha! Freds x

You see, my fear of dogs is legendary at Eades ever since news got out about my attempted escape from school to go clubbing one night last year. I was chased up a tree by one of the school's attack dogs. That's how I met Billy. He had helped me down while the girl-eating dog licked his hand.

Freddie knows all about my shameful stuck-up-a-tree experience, though he doesn't know about the wobbly feeling I felt in my tummy as Billy helped me down and held me in his arms. And he definitely doesn't know I've been txt-flirting Billy all summer.

I'd already pulled Freddie, but everything between us got complicated because Honey O'Hare, the most toxic psycho-toff ever, sold a camera-phone snap of us kissing in the bushes to the tabloids. It all ended in a bit of a messy misunderstanding, which is why I got mixed up and started flirt-txt-ing Billy.

Only now Billy's txts were getting progressively steamier, and I knew I couldn't go on flirting with two boys from the same school without it all blowing up in my face. So while my predicament may have made my holidays in LA and the prospect of returning to Saint Augustine's exciting, I was going to have to sort my feelings out by the end of the week when I faced them both on the fencing piste. It was that or – *quelle horreur!* – risk having no boy txt-ing me at all! Just like the old days.

Even as my taxi dropped me at school, the thrill of having two fit Eades boys txt-ing me was beginning to feel more like pressure than a flattering thrill. And guess what? Mental telepathy really does work because no sooner did this thought flash through my mind than my txt alert sounded:

Can't wait to see your navel piercing . . . Freddie x

I txt-ed him back immediately!

Can't wait to rinse you at sabre x Calypso

I didn't really feel like confessing that I'd been rinsed by my parents, Sarah and Bob, and made to remove my navel ring. I quite fancied the idea of Freddie thinking of me as this madly cool, wild-child American girl who did her own thing and made her own rules. Sadly, nothing could be further from the truth.

TWO

It's Hard Teaching Your Parents Where Their Dreams End and Yours Begin

I will turn fifteen on the fifteenth of December. Just ten days before Christmas. This explains a lot about me. Firstly, it means my parents are Catholic and didn't practise birth control. They've never admitted this (the lack of birth control thing), but I ask you, what sort of unfeeling parents would purposefully elect to bring their child into the world at Christmas? Who do they think they are, Mary and Joseph?

Secondly, it explains why I am quite cynical. By the age of ten, I knew that when people said, 'I just opted for One Big Present for Christmas rather than two small presents,' they were *definitely* lying. What they were really opting for was the economy of one regular-sized gift.

That's where my third skill comes in handy – my precocious gift for being able to keep my disappointments to myself – because you can't really challenge people about the One Big Present Lie without sounding ungrateful, can you?

But that's okay because cynicism and the ability to suppress disappointment help you survive the single-sex boarding school system of England. And those two aspects of my character are what I relied on the first day back at school as I scanned the dormitory list to discover with whom I'd be rooming.

My cynicism prevented me from hoping that I would be sharing with someone lovely and fun. And cynicism soon gave way to suppressing the disappointment that I didn't have a valet to lug my seven-thousand-ton trunk up the ancient, narrow, dimly lit, winding stone staircase that leads to the dormitory rooms.

My parents, who insist I call them Sarah and Bob (what can I say, they still listen to Bob Dylan and eat tragic brown food), live in LA and had long since given up accompanying me back to school each term. Now that I was about to turn fifteen, they thought they were off the hook.

That's the other thing. I was almost a full year younger than anyone else in my year – Year Eleven – something my parents took a sick pride in. They are always bragging to their friends about me, as if being the youngest, most physically immature girl in my Year is something to boast about. They weren't the ones having to stuff their bra with toilet paper throughout Year Nine. By the end of that year I was even lying about having my periods so that when I finally started to menstruate and discovered that I had blood on my white fencing breeches, I was so relieved I forgot to be embarrassed.

This summer I sat my parents down and said, 'Look, Sarah, Bob, I know you love me, and you know I love you, but you have got to stop living vicariously through me!' Star put me up to it, although she suggested I just say 'get a life' because Sarah and Bob still think I should have the same aspirations I had when I was six and wanted to be the next Marie Curie. Actually, let me put that more accurately: *they* wanted me to be the next Marie Curie, and I went along with it so they'd make a fuss of me.

My best friend, Star, always says, 'It's hard teaching your parents where their dreams end and yours begin.' Although as far as I can see, her parents, Tiger of Dirge and Tracey the commensurate Rock Star Wife, are perfect parents – mostly because they're always stoned, I guess.

There was no sign of Star's or Georgina's friendly faces in the mad scrum of toff parents, toff valets, guardians and girls (all dressed in the tragic Saint Augustine's uniform of maroon pleated skirt and green ruffled shirt) clustered around the notice board. I scanned the lists of dorm rooms, hoping I'd be sharing with Arabella or Clementine, two of my other friends. But instead a cold band of fear tightened around my heart as I read the name on the list with mine for the Saint Ursula room: Honey O'Hare.

I was literally shaking as I backed my way out of the braying adults and girls squealing with delight or groaning with disappointment. As I turned around, I slammed straight into the culprit herself – or rather, the culprit's new manservant.

'Watch out, you American Freak!' Honey shrieked in her special shrill way as she stepped out from behind the man. The poor fellow stumbled a bit under the weight of her heavy Louis Vuitton trunk and other assorted designer luggage, including a mauve Prada pet carrier no doubt containing her designer pet of the term.

'I'm sorry,' I apologised, trying in vain to make eye contact with the poor guy I'd bumped into. He was two hundred and ninety if he was a day.

Then Honey added darkly, 'If you damage my manservant, your parents can buy me a bloody new one and pay to have him shipped out and processed through immigration.'

Honey is your *classic* psycho toff. In other words, she has all the characteristics you might imagine spoilt aristo-girls – also known as Daddy's Plastic Girls – to have, only thank goodness for me they usually don't. But Honey does. Unbridled, unrestrained horribleness exudes from the tips of her platinum card–breaking, Nicky Clarke-personally-coloured hair to her designer French soles. And mostly her horribleness is turned on me, who as an untitled, ordinary American is a classic sitting duck.

Last term she laced my dinner with laxatives and as I

mentioned sold a photograph of me kissing Prince Freddie to the press, which almost destroyed my life. It created such an international brouhaha that my parents flew over from LA to be by my side. Actually it was Sarah and Bob who discovered that Honey was the culprit, for which Sister Constance had her rusticated for a week.

Even when she returned to school and realised how evil everyone thought she was, she was totally unrepentant. All she said was 'Soz,' which is Sloane for 'sorry' and translated in Honey's case to 'So sorry your misery has impacted my life.' Because you see, horribleness comes naturally to Honey, a bit like photosynthesis comes naturally to plants.

The other name on my room list was Lady Portia Herrington Briggs. Of course she didn't go about referring to herself as *Lady Herrington Briggs*. That would be considered vulgar at Saint Augustine's. Naturally all the girls and teachers were fully aware she was the daughter of an earl and treated her accordingly – apart from the nuns, that is, because they think the only title of merit is 'Saint.'

I *sort* of knew Portia, but not as well as I should, given that she was on the sabre team and I was the captain. I suppose 'enigmatic' would be the word for Portia. I love the word 'enigmatic.' I've tried to be enigmatic all my life but I can't seem to stop this awful habit I have of blurting things out. Portia would never blurt something, in fact the word 'blurt' probably isn't even in her vocabulary.

In the past I'd been more interested in her talent on the piste than in her grand ancestors, and to be fair she'd never pointed those out to me. But I could well imagine that with Honey in our room, my American-ness and lack of pedigree would go against me.

Honey isn't titled – well, she is an Hon., thanks to her new stepfather, but not a real one. It really grates on her that of all the men her society It Girl mother has married, none of them has done his duty in bringing a truly grand title to the marriage table. Her latest stepfather is a lord but he's only a life peer, so while she gets to be an Hon., she'll never assume the title she *really* covets, that of Lady. However, on the plus side, her new father gave her Oopa, a manservant to fetch and carry after her.

At Saint Augustine's School for Ladies you get to request the girls you want to share a room with. I'd opted for Clemmie and Arabella. But as our head nun, Sister Constance, is always remarking, 'There are no guarantees in life, girls!' I'm cynical about that too because there *is* one guarantee; if you share with someone one term, you won't be sharing with them the next. This policy is meant to tackle bitchiness but all it really does is stick you with people who have the capacity to make your life miserable. I wished I was sharing with *exactly* the same girls as last term, my best friends Georgina and Star.

The people you share a room with at boarding school define your term. Popular, fun people = popular, fun term. Anything else is *merde*, as our ghoulish French teacher would say. If she hears us say how *merde* her French class is, though, she showers us in blues.

Most of my terms at Saint Augustine's have been *merde*, but last term was the exception and I honestly thought my popularity had turned a corner. I was finally out of the cul-de-sac of loneliness and isolation that had marred my previous years in England.

The reason my school life got so much better during that term of Year Ten was that I'd been roomed with my best friend, Star, who is rock royalty, and the Honourable Georgina Castle Orpington and her opinionated teddy bear, Tobias. Yes, we are talking about a teddy with his own custom-made miniature Louis Vuitton trunk in which he stores his designer teddy bear wardrobe. Even madder, Georgina's father actually pays full fees for Tobias to attend Saint Augustine's! I used to think it was just a rumour, but it soon became clear that it was true, which is probably why the school adores Georgina so much.

Despite being friends with Honey, Georgina turned out to be far less grand than I'd always imagined. Star and Georgina and Tobias had even come to Los Angeles and spent two weeks of the summer holidays with me – although Tobias couldn't go out in the sun because he burns easily.

My parents were horrified when Georgina told them about Tobias being a full fee-paying student. My mother declared it tantamount to a bribe. Georgina told her not to be so mad and explained that Tobias happened to be exceedingly bright and what's more did ALL his course work *and* hers. She said it with such conviction that Bob and Sarah didn't know how to respond. Even living in LA, they'd never met anyone as self-possessed and truly grand as Georgina before.

'Besides, Sarah,' Georgina had added sweetly. 'You've been lovely enough to set a place for Tobias at dinner every evening during our stay so you must see how special he is.' This was true, and Sarah and Bob were forced to acknowledge that Tobias was no ordinary bear.

Sarah and Bob were completely different people when Star and Georgina came to stay. Despite threatening to wear love beads and show my nudie baby photographs, they behaved themselves beautifully. Well, as beautifully as parents can be expected to behave.

Basically, they let us hang out at the mall, just like real teenagers, and drive ourselves recklessly about the studio lot where my mom works on those little golf cart thingamees.

They even agreed to allow me to go to my very first ball, the La Fiesta Ball, this term. La Fiesta is one of the Capital VIP balls that the posh schools all attend. Capital VIP run several balls and parties a year, including the Mistletoe Ball and the Valentine's Ball. They have really cool bands and famous DJs and pop stars perform. All the boys go in black tie (Americans call them tuxes), which makes them look even *more* distressingly fit, and girls get to wear achingly cool clothes.

Previously, Bob and Sarah had barred me from attending any of the balls, despite the fact that *Tatler* declared them 'the most exclusive teenage parties in the world.' I had even smugly directed them to the parent section of the

Web site where it states: 'For £40 ($70) we promise you that your daughter will be followed by jailors all night, besides which, we hardly let any boys in anyway unless they're royalty or arrive by helicopter. Also, we totally guarantee to shoot on sight anyone caught with alcohol or drugs or attempting lip-attachment manoeuvres.'

I'm paraphrasing, but you get the idea.

Bob and Sarah said they thought these balls sounded 'a bit too risky.' Then again, brightly coloured cereal is 'a bit too risky' for my parents. It's granola all the way with them. But even that all changed when Star and Georgina were staying. We had Oreo O's cereal (miniature chocolate biscuits) and Lucky Charms. The Lucky Charms were a favourite with Georgina and Star, who thought the cereal shapes were madly rude – actually comparisons with testicles were made – and even then all Bob and Sarah did was laugh.

So there it was. In two weeks Georgina and Star triumphed with my parents where I had failed for the past fourteen years. Everything they spoke of or suggested was met with delight. 'What super fun these VIP balls all sound!' Sarah announced one evening as we were drinking wine in the courtyard. Yes, even alcohol (in moderation) was given the green light by S and B while my friends were staying.

'But you always said . . .,' I began.

But Sarah dismissed my interruption. 'Of course you must go, Calypso, don't be such a stick in the mud!'

My eyes almost sprung out of their sockets. They even

gave me extra money so we could all buy our outfits together at a trendy shop on Robertson Boulevard. We were all going to wear sleeveless cashmere tops with beading and sequins, tiny, tiny mini-skirts and pointy-toed kitten heels – in different colours, of course.

I was soooo excited, though obviously I acted madly blasé about attending my first ball. Prince Freddie often attends them. I'd already txt-ed Freddie and Billy to say I would be there, which meant I would have to choose which of them I fancied the most because I didn't want them to think I was a slut. Besides, I'm not a slut. Honestly.

I was certain that as soon as I laid eyes on them at fencing I'd instantly know which of them I fancied properly, but at the time all I could think of was the excitement of it all. I'd been listening enviously to the other girls going on and on about these balls and all the fit boys they've pulled for the past three years. This time I would be going to the ball myself! Thanks to the influence of my two best friends on my parents.

Star and Georgina kept saying, 'Your parents are soooo cool, Calypso,' and by the time we waved my friends off at LAX I had even started to believe it myself. Maybe my parents really *were* cool?

THREE

Okay, So Maybe It Did Get a Little Bit Septic . . .

Thank goodness I am cynical because my parents went back to their Draconian ways as soon as the plane was out of LA airspace and they noticed that I'd had my navel pierced. Being cynical and capable of harbouring secret disappointment doesn't help you avoid crop-tops in the heat.

The three of us had decided to have it done in a shop near the Beverly Center in Beverly Hills. Star said it was like having friendship rings, only more painful. But actually it was all madly hygienic, and the guy who did it was, like, *soooo* fit, we were all swooning so much that we didn't even feel the pain.

It's true that mine *had* gone slightly septic and pussy, which admittedly was fairly nasty, but Bob and Sarah *totally* overreacted the way only Liberal Parents can. First they made me take it out, and then they marched me, yes *marched* me (I blame all the Save Our Environment marches they went on before I was born) to the shop where I'd had it done. There's nothing Bob and Sarah like more than a good march.

Everyone in Los Angeles – give or take a few million people – were staring at us as we entered the shop, which also did a bit of tattooing. I hadn't noticed that on the sign, but Bob and Sarah did. Initially I refused to get out of the car, but of course that failed and S & B made this hugely embarrassing scene, which I am so ashamed about that I haven't even told Star.

Star has no idea what American parents are like because her dad is usually so stoned he doesn't even remember who she is. She claims the reason he calls her 'darling' all the time is because he forgot her name in the early nineties. Her mom is just really chilled. She even has a pierced navel herself.

Anyhow, Sarah and Bob kept asking the poor guy (who'd been really, really, really, really nice to us and was so fit it was untrue) questions that they'd then answer themselves.

Bob asked, 'Do you know how old she is?'

The guy went to open his mouth, but Sarah replied for him, 'A minor!'

To which Bob added, 'Do you know what would happen to you if we were to get the police involved?'

I went bright red and tried to shrink so I could hide

behind Sarah's skirt as she answered, 'You'd be closed down, and very possibly incarcerated, that's what.'

For a couple of old hippies, Sarah and Bob can be quite quick to call in the forces of law and order. All in all it was possibly the most embarrassing scene in Sarah and Bob's long history of embarrassing scenes.

But that's okay because I had my outfit. I was going to the ball.

FOUR

The Fine Line Between Honey and Hell

I came across Oopa a second time as I was lugging my trunk up the damp, narrow, winding, dimly lit stone stairwell of the main building. The main building is the oldest building at Saint Augustine's, apart from the chapel and the convent, of course. I'm not big on man-servants myself, but I felt sorry for Oopa when I heard one of the vertebrae in my own spine cracking as I struggled under the strain of the steamer trunk on my back. I was also carrying my wheelie hand luggage, and sabre kits aren't exactly light.

The main building is so ancient, there is always a renovation program in progress, which means the place is always covered in scaffolding. This provides a handy escape route at night, according to the Upper Sixth girls who'd been housed here the year before, but it also makes it very dark and dingy. The only light filters through a stained glass window depicting Our Lady of Perpetual Succour.

Oopa looked like he needed some succour. He was buckling under the weight of Honey's heavy trunks and bags, and my American sense of fraternity couldn't help exerting itself. The English call it wading in where I'm not wanted.

I was worried he was going to have a seizure and collapse because, seriously, he was gasping for breath and swaying about dangerously.

Honey was skipping ahead of him, totally oblivious to his struggle and chatting away loudly on her mobile about how she was sharing with a freak that term and how she was *so* going to have Mummy's PA speak to Lord Aginet about speaking to his lawyers. 'Honestly, darling, it's outrageous that I should have to share with an American Freak. You should hear what she does to her vowels. My ears ache every time she opens her mouth. It's beyond plebbie even. It's disgusting.'

'Erm, excuse me, but do you need a hand?' I asked Oopa, about to reach out the hand holding my sabre kit to help support the enormous LVT trunk on his back. It was a really cool old steamer that Honey's grandmother had owned – you know, the ones that open up with drawers and hanging space? Cool as they are, they must be really heavy.

Oopa was not impressed by my offer to help. At first I thought he must still be bearing a grudge about my bumping into him earlier, because he went totally bonkers and started yelling at me. All the other guardians, parents, valets and girls stopped and stared at me too, like I'd just set fire to someone or something.

I realised in that moment how blatantly stupid I'd been to offer assistance to anyone associated with Honey. My French teacher has always told me that I do a great line in *faux pas*.

I didn't have a clue what he was babbling about because he was shouting at me in his native tongue, which I think might have been something Asian, but I couldn't be sure. He was definitely quite cross with me, though.

Honey turned and looked me up and down in that clever nasty way she has. 'Honestly, you Americans are soooo insensitive. How *dare* you question Oopa's ability to carry multiple heavy objects up a dimly lit stone staircase!'

Well, she didn't actually say that, but her dismal look said it all, and what's more the mood of the crowd seemed to be with her.

Predictably, halfway up the stairs Oopa did tumble down, but this time I wasn't insensitive enough to look, let alone comment or help. I decided just to carry on towards my room while Honey yelled at Oopa to stop embarrassing her or she'd report him to immigration.

Finally I arrived at my prettily decorated room to find Portia lounged cat-like on one of the three beds, reading *Tatler*. She'd already smothered her pin board with magazine pages and photographs. I noticed a really fit boy in the magazine pages who had his arm around her in a society photograph. On her bedside table there was a photograph of her family. There was also one of the school's ancient oil paintings above her bed. It was of Saint Ursula, the patron saint of virgins. Above another bed was an oil painting of Saint Augustine, the patron saint of our school.

My focus was on the best bed though, the one against the window overlooking the chapel with a view across to Pullers' Wood, where the leaves were already beginning to turn various shades of orange and gold. There was no painting above it, but there was a radiator running along the side.

I watched Portia's very English valet quietly yet purposefully unpack his mistress's trunk. All I could think was, how very odd that Portia hadn't grabbed the best bed, the one by the window with the radiator.

'Hi, Portia, do you mind if I take this bed?' I asked cautiously. Every girl at Saint Augustine's dreams of having the bed against the radiator in the winter term and it was beyond me why anyone would pass it up.

For a second, a paranoid thought that a practical joke was being played on me flashed through my mind, but then Portia looked up from her copy of *Tatler* and smiled what seemed to be an actual genuine smile. 'Oh, hi, Calypso. Take whatever bed you want darling, I don't give a toss frankly. As far as I'm concerned, dorm rooms are all an endurance test any way you look at it.'

How cool is that? I was thinking as I dumped my

trunk beside it and tossed my fencing kit on top of the coveted bed. I was still rubbing my arm to try and get my circulation going when it got even better! Lady Portia tossed her *Tatler* on the floor, climbed off her bed, walked over to me and embraced me, saying, 'Darling, I'm so pleased we're sharing, especially with the British National Fencing Trials coming up this term! I was worried I'd have no one to stress out with!'

'I know, me too. It's, erm, nice isn't it,' I agreed. Why do I say these things? *Nice?*

'But anyway,' she continued, 'how was *your* summer break? I want to hear all about it. Did Star and Georgina really go out to LA? Has Freddie been txt-ing you? I'm soooo jealous.'

Portia, the quintessential Saint Augustine It Girl, was jealous of *me?* I mean, I know pulling an HRH might be the height of cool to some, but for the girls of Saint Augustine's the world of royals was their natural pulling ground. 'Yaah, totally cool,' I replied, automatically falling into the use of 'yaah' rather than my Californian 'yeah,' which I knew from experience would result in a piss-take of my American-ness.

I was just about to tell her about my fantastic summer and how Star and Georgina and I had spent the whole time shopping and how Freddie and Billy had *both* been txt-ing me. But then Honey strode in with Oopa limping behind her.

FIVE

My Favourite Mad House Spinster Ever!

I'd always hated Honey and she had always hated me, but at least in the past I'd had the buffer of a wall. Now she would be sleeping in the same room, sharing the same air, the same bathroom, the same wardrobe, and there would be no respite.

I watched her – the ultimate psycho toff – snapping her tiny and cuter-than-thou bejewelled mobile shut with a sharp *clack*. I watched as she flicked her long, artistically streaked blond locks over her skinny golden shoulders. I watched her violet contact-lens-covered eyes as they surveyed the prettily decorated room with its breathtaking view of the old oak woods.

Last year we'd been housed in rickety rundown Cleathorpes, but this year we were in the main building, which had been newly redecorated and now had lovely marble bathrooms. I'd had a peek when I'd deposited my Body Shop Specials in the bathroom cabinet. We all decant vodka into empty shampoo and conditioner bottles. That's how we disguise alcohol so house mothers don't catch us. Getting sprung with alcohol usually means a gating – not allowed out on weekends – but it can even lead to expulsion if you're discovered revoltingly drunk. Anyway, the marble bathrooms were divine and included a separate shower and a bath!

'Oh, isn't it dismal, darling,' Honey groaned, pressing her French-manicured hand against her Botoxed brow. 'Isn't it all just soooo *evil!*'

I accidentally responded, blurting something tragic, like 'At least we have new mattresses this year.' As I said, I am marvellously gifted when it comes to the art of the blurt.

She glared at me. 'Excuse me? Was I speaking to *you*, American Freak?'

I looked over at Portia but she was immersed in her *Tatler* again. Honey pointed at my fencing kit, grimaced, and instructed Oopa to remove it from the window bed. Predictably enough, she ignored me when I muttered something ridiculously pointless about how I'd grabbed that bed already.

'Oopa, will you stop panting,' she scolded as he wheezed and limped his way about the room. 'It really gets on my nerves,' she warned, pressing her fingers against her temples as if warding off a migraine. 'I don't want to have to call Daddy and have you sent back,' she warned.

I cringed as I witnessed fear flash across Oopa's face. I might not know precisely where Oopa was from, but if it was worse than working for Honey it must be grim. I looked over at Portia, hoping she'd concur with a raised brow, but she remained immersed in her *Tatler*.

'You are soooo NQOC,' she whispered in an aside to me before turning away and leaning down to Portia for an air kiss. 'But darling,' she drawled in her OTT toff voice, 'at least I'm rooming with *you.*'

'Yaah darling, really looking forward to it,' agreed Portia mildly as she flicked a page of her magazine, which slightly annoyed me because if she were my friend Star, she'd say something pointedly cutting like, 'I'd rather chew through my own cheek than share a night in the same room as you.'

Rock stars' daughters don't take crap from the likes of Honey, you see. Then again, Honey would never even *pretend* to be glad to share with Star. She hates her almost as much as she hates me. In fact, if Star's father wasn't Rock Royalty and the richest father in our year, I suspected Honey would hate Star *more* than me.

I watched with horror as Honey roughly threw her mauve Prada pet carrier on her bed (the one by the window that had briefly been mine). Her rabbit was still inside and I was wondering if I could get away with rescuing the poor thing. But Portia put my mind at rest by asking, 'Oh Honey, is your rabbit in there? Can I hold it?'

I really wished Georgina would get here so I could cuddle little Dorothy Parker, the black rabbit we shared. Georgina looked after Dorothy on her grand country estate during half terms and holidays. Star was always the last to arrive, but surely Georgina would be here by now and she'd want to find where I was roomed . . . wouldn't she?

Honey picked up her dyed-mauve rabbit, which was wearing a blue Tiffany collar and large diamond hoop earrings. They might well have been real diamonds, as she boasted, but I was more worried about how very big they were. The poor rabbit's ears were dragged down by their weight. She passed Absinthe, as she referred to the poor little thing, over to Portia with disinterest. Then she started calling people on her phone again to tell them about the hell of her journey, the shoddiness of her manservant and the evil American Freak she'd been landed with.

'Bless,' said Portia as she stroked the rabbit. 'Do you want me to take her down to the pet shed for you, Honey?'

'No, I'll sort out my packing first,' replied Honey as if she was doing it herself.

I set about unpacking my own trunk, fighting for what little space I could find in the wardrobe allocated to my inferior bed. As I swung open the door I noticed a few designer jackets already hanging.

'So sorry, darling, I simply didn't have room in mine, hope you don't mind?' Portia asked, making a face of what looked like genuine shame and regret.

Portia was very beautiful, with long hair – albeit raven instead of the more typical blond of Saint Augustine girls – a willowy figure and the peach-coloured skin of the English aristo. Her most significant feature was her aloofness. I don't mean aloof in a madly superior way because that would have been unbearable and marked her out for secret hatred. No, Portia was aloof in a quiet, self-contained way that you couldn't really challenge. Nothing ever fazed her. Her hair was never mussed or sweaty, even after games. When I took off my fencing mask I had fluffy little bits that crowned my face like wet horns, but when Portia took off her mask and shook out her mane of long, dark hair, she looked like she'd just come from the salon.

I was about to tell Portia that it was fine to steal my precious wardrobe space – which it *was*, really, because quite honestly my clothing allowance is pretty meagre compared to the other girls – when I was distracted by the sound of clapping.

We all turned. A four-foot-nine hunchbacked woman stood leaning on a cane in the doorway of our room. She announced in a loud, screechy Essex whine, 'Hello, girls, my name's Miss Bibsmore. I'm your new 'ouse mother. Now, I don't want any trouble 'ere, so don't you go getting ideas! Just because I'm short and hunched doesn't mean I'm ignorant, understand?'

'Yes, Miss Bibsmore,' Portia and I replied in the Saint Augustine chant of perceived obedience. That's the rule with house mothers. You just let them rant on and hope they don't try to hug you, and eventually they leave you be. House Spinsters, as we called them, love to wield their power so you definitely never cheeked them, which was effectively what Honey was doing as she totally ignored Miss Bibsmore and loudly bossed Oopa about, telling him where to put her designer outfits and shoes while she stroked poor shivering Absinthe.

That was another thing. Pets weren't allowed in rooms,

and if she'd been anyone other than Honey, she'd be trying to conceal Absinthe from Miss Bibsmore, not openly stroking her!

Miss Bibsmore entered the room with a series of awkward little steps and shuffles, her eyes glinting with the suspicion of a woman who can see inside a girl's soul. Finally she was looming over Honey's bed. Honey looked up at Miss Bibsmore as if she were a mad witch – which of course she was, because all house mothers are mad, although perhaps Miss Bibsmore took mad to a new level. She had a jutting-out chin and messily arranged teeth. Her grey hair had been loosely gathered together in a bun that was doomed not to hold despite the net around it. Last year's house mother, Miss Cribbe, seemed virtually normal by comparison. And Miss Cribbe had a beard!

'I'm not here to pick up after you nor nothing neither, so don't you go giving me none of your airy graces, madam, because I won't 'ave it, 'ear?'

Honey sneered at her. Honey is the queen of the sneer. Actually she's sneered so much that she's upset the balance of collagen in her lips so that the sneer side has a permanent nasty swelling on it.

'Did you hear me, madam?'

Honey ignored her. 'Oopa, I said in the top drawer! Are you deaf, because if you are I'll complain to Daddy,' she screeched.

'I mean it, madam. I'm not like the likes of 'im, that fellow there. I'm not 'ere to doff my cap to no one,' she warned, making to prod poor Oopa with her cane.

But Oopa, like his mistress, sneered as he avoided Miss Bibsmore's prod. Honey snapped, 'Oh shut up and leave my manservant alone, you mad old witch.'

Portia and I looked at one another, both of us equally uncertain as to whether we should do or say something to defuse the tension between Honey and Miss Bibsmore. Then Portia raised an eyebrow in Honey's direction so I knew that she was as appalled as I was at the way Honey had just slacked Miss Bibsmore down. Arousing the wrath of a House Spinster at this early stage of the term would mean misery for all of us. And that made me feel better, like maybe Portia was on my side and actually quite cool. Even her valet with his impeccable manners raised a brow. Portia nodded at him and he made a slight bow and departed.

Miss Bibsmore glared at Honey. Her eyes actually flashed. 'Right, that's it. Off 'e goes. Go on, git out!' she shrieked, hustling a confused Oopa out the door with her stick. The poor fellow looked terrified, but soon he was gone and Miss Bibsmore had Honey in her sights again. 'There'll be no bowing and scraping 'ere, madam. Grandee or not, I'm warning you now, I don't like the cut of your jib. You'll be treated like anyone else while you're in my dormitory, understood?'

'Don't be ridiculous,' Honey shrieked back at her. 'Do you know who I am? Daddy sued the last person who threatened to treat me like anyone else, and he won't think twice about doing it again.'

I looked over at Portia and our eyes met again in a look

of shared disbelief, but the rest of her face was concealed behind the magazine. I suspect she was hiding her suppressed giggles – the same ones I was trying to suppress by applying my lip-gloss.

Miss Bibsmore grinned. 'He can sue 'imself sick far as I'm concerned. I is what I is. I spent the first nine years of my life in a pram! If I wanted to see the light I 'ad to peer out from under the canopy. No footman, no butler, no servant for me, just a pram and an old tartan rug that kept falling off. Then, when I was well enough to get out of the pram, they put my legs in these braces.' With that, Miss Bibsmore hiked up her skirt and stuck one of her metal-encased shins athletically up in the air. 'So if you think I'm afraid of your father setting a pack of nancy fancy lawyers on me, you'll be disappointed.'

'Well, perhaps the school will feel differently,' Honey began mildly, but there was an obvious threat there.

I looked at Portia and Portia looked at me. We were struggling to stop our eyebrows riding up our foreheads by this point. Neither of us knew what to say.

Honey, on the other hand, was far from stuck for words. '. . . when my lawyers shower them in litigation suits for allowing an insane old witch like you to care for me.'

Miss Bibsmore's eyes were glinting gleefully as she asked, 'Insane am I? Well then, you had better watch out all the more, 'adn't you?'

Portia rose imperiously from her bed, clearly deciding enough was enough. 'Thank you, Miss Bibsmore, I think we're all clear now and we wouldn't want to keep you from your rounds.' She spoke with a calmness of one whose family traced its roots back to the Domesday Book and had survived the Catholic purgings of England with their title and lands intact.

Miss Bibsmore seemed to concede Portia's suggestion. That is, she stuck her lower lip out and humphed. One thing was certain, though: she was on the warpath and Honey had been marked down as Enemy Number One.

'I am *so* complaining,' Honey muttered under her breath. Then she turned to Portia. 'I'm calling Daddy *now*.' She began to punch numbers into her phone, but Miss Bibsmore snatched the tiny little gem of a mobile from her, popped it in the pocket of her long skirt and shuffled out of the room. 'And you can take that poor creature down to the pet shed an' all. No pets in rooms or I'll have you rusticated.'

Miss Bibsmore didn't officially have the power to rusticate girls, but the fact that she even used the word proved she wasn't to be messed with. I was definitely going to regret the thought running through my mind, but as I watched Honey's mouth open and close in uncharacteristic helpless shock, I couldn't help admiring Miss Bibsmore's style. I was beginning to think I liked the cut of her jib. And as I caught Portia's eye I got the feeling she might even be feeling the same way.

SIX

God's Law
Versus Sod's Law

Within seconds of Miss Bibsmore's departure, Star and Georgina burst into our room in a tumble of long limbs, long hair and laughter. They tripped over my fencing kit, which had been dumped on the floor by Oopa, and landed on the floor in a giggling heap.

'Guess what!' asked Star, untangling herself from Georgina and dive-bombing onto Honey's bed by the window. I looked at Honey, anticipating fireworks, but before she could formulate her put-down, Georgina declared, 'It's the best news ever!'

I thought they were going to mention how we'd all had our navels pierced in the break. I hadn't had the mettle to tell them that Parental Control had made me take mine out. Star pulled Georgina onto the bed and waved me over.

'Please tell me, Star's finally being sanctioned?' Honey hazarded sarcastically.

'We're sharing!' cried Georgina, throwing her arm over Star's shoulder. The two of them started bouncing up and down on the bed, punching the air with their fists.

'Wow, that's soooo cool,' I told them enthusiastically, although really I couldn't help feeling a bit disappointed. I remembered a time when Star and I were considered the school freaks – not that I enjoyed being the school freak, obviously, but it meant we were closer than close. Besides, as far as Star was concerned, Georgina and Honey et al. were the school freaks. She hadn't even wanted to be friends with Georgina initially – that was my idea. Now they were finishing each other's sentences.

Georgina went, 'Calypso! You have *got* to meet Indiamaca . . .'

Pulling a stray lock of her strawberry blonde hair from her mouth, Star added, 'Yaah, she's a new girl, an *actual* princess from Nigeria. Only she calls herself Indie.'

They were still jumping up and down on Honey's bed. I guess Honey probably felt she wasn't in a position to say anything as Georgina was the closest thing she had to a real friend. Even though Georgina knows how toxic Honey is, the two of them have known each other since they were four, when they were packed off to school at Hill House in Knightsbridge. They learnt to ride together, ski together, use Daddy's plastic together and pull together. Plus their biological fathers still attend the same hunt meet, so I guess that gives them a bond that won't ever totally be broken.

Watching Georgina's exuberant bed-jumping, I was quite glad it *wasn't* my bed now. The mattresses at Saint Augustine's are about as comfortable as lying on lumpy porridge because we all jump up and down on them.

'Calypso, she's soooo nice you have to love her and also she's got this amazingly cool limited edition Hermès bag. They covered it in a purple Nigerian fabric just for her. So individual,' Star enthused.

'And loads of vintage clothes, all purple because that's her favourite colour,' Georgina added.

'Oh, how cool,' I said, trying to get into the swing of their enthusiasm for this new girl.

'And she plays guitar! I showed her one of my songs, Calypso, and she *totally* got it,' Star said.

I should explain that Star writes these Gothic anthems about the despair and pointlessness of being a successful rock star's daughter and the miserable privilege of her life in an all-girls boarding school. Love Star though I do, even *I* want to eat my own tongue when she starts playing her minor chord compositions.

'She said she loved my angst. Isn't that gorgeous?'

'I love your angst too!' I blurted for want of something more ridiculous to say.

Thankfully though, Star didn't hear my pathetic suck-up attempt because Georgina had cut in breathlessly. 'She used to go to Cheltenham Ladies', only she said it was too plebbie. She's already pulled loads of Harrow boys.' Harrow on the Hill, known as The Dump on the Hump, was another toffer-than-thou school for boys. There was always a lot of debate amongst the girls of Saint Augustine's about whether it was cooler to pull Eades boys or Harrow boys. Eades was a lot closer to us, which made Harrow seem more exotic, although that was mainly because we didn't pull as many of them and they didn't get to break our hearts as much.

Star went, 'I told her about you and Freddie, Calypso, and she can't wait to meet *you*. We both love her, don't we, George? She's our new best friend.'

'I can't wait to meet her either, she sounds really cool,' I sort of lied. I say 'sort of' because while I was thrilled that my friends were in a great room together, I couldn't help feeling a bit jealous. Okay, make that hugely jealous. Especially about Indiamaca, because if she was their New Best Friend that made me . . . the *old* best friend! And when did Georgina become George anyway?

I looked out over the lawns that trailed into the oak woods with their flaming leaves and wondered how long before the trees would be bare and we'd have snow. I love snow. Star and I used to sneak off up into the woods on our own in winter to make snow angels.

It's a Saint Augustine's tradition to have snowball fights with the new Year Seven girls. Once a year, someone has to throw a snowball at Sister Constance as she steps out for her morning perambulations (that's what she calls her meditative wanders though the school grounds and woods). Sister just laughs these attacks off and throws snowballs back at us – unlike the lay teachers, who, if you hit them with a snowball, shower you in blues.

Once Star was gated for hitting Ms Topler, our evil English teacher. It was not only an overreaction but resulted in Star's parents and every member of Dirge turning up at the school to complain. Star's mad extended family is like a pack of wild things when they're on a mission. All the members of Dirge and their roadies and friends think of Star as a surrogate daughter. It's so sweet when they all turn up for Parent Teacher Day, and the school is infiltrated with long-haired tattooed men and their wildly dressed rock chick girlfriends.

Star says parents don't pay the equivalent of twice the average annual wage in order to have their daughters taught by teachers who have no sense of fun. I think Sister Constance agrees because she overruled the gating and Ms Topler got a telling off.

But now as I sat listening to my friends' excited chatter about their new exotic *friend*, I wondered if maybe Star would prefer to do snow angels with 'George' now, or purple star angels with Indie! So much for Sister Constance's rule about not sharing with the same girl two terms in a row, I thought to myself bitterly.

'So much for Sister Constance and her rule about not sharing with the same girl two terms running,' Honey sneered, eerily echoing my own thoughts.

'Sod's Law, darling.' Georgina shrugged as she air-kissed Honey. 'But anyway, tell me about your summer in Kenya, darling,' Georgina asked airily. I noted the way she pronounced Kenya *Keenyah*. 'Star and I had the *best* time in LA with Calypso,' she told her, grinning at me fondly.

I was always very aware of the way the other girls spoke when I came back from LA. The way you speak defines you, and after four years here, I pretty much sound like them. Even so, my accent still lets me down when I spend too long in LA, which leaves me open to very bad piss-takes of the way I speak. Ironic, given that in LA everyone does very bad piss-takes of my English accent.

'Absolutely terrific,' Honey replied, stroking Absinthe's mauve fur with her mauve-coloured nails.

I wondered what Miss Bibsmore would say about her nails. I suppose Miss Bibsmore hadn't terrified Honey that badly or she would have legged it to the pet shed with Absinthe.

I was looking over at Portia, who had barely said a word. I wondered if, like me, she was feeling left out, or whether she was really absorbed by the magazine she was reading and rereading.

Suddenly Honey dropped Absinthe like a bag of sugar on the bed and started posing in front of the mirror. 'Goffy – that's what we call Mummy's latest husband, Lord Aginet – bought me Oopa, *the* most adorable manservant ever.'

Star and I rolled our eyes at one another, but Honey didn't notice as she played with her expensively long,

Nicky Clarke-personally-coloured hair. 'Portia met him,' she continued. 'Darling, didn't you think him adorable?' she asked rhetorically, not even looking at Portia for confirmation. 'He was a refugee. The luckiest refugee in the world as it turns out. Goffy discovered him in Nairobi and said I could have him.'

'He's a man, not a discovery, Honey,' I blurted before I could stop myself.

'Yes, you really should pay more attention in biology, darling,' Star added, dragging out the word daaaahrling in the OTT way Honey did.

'Oh, what would you know with all your father's plebbie hangers-on,' Honey snapped back, referring to the roadies who hung around Star's family's estate in Derbyshire, where they did a spot of valeting (between spliffs) when the band wasn't touring.

'They're roadies and friends, actually. At least I don't go round referring to people as manservants or exploiting refugees. What century are you from anyway?'

'Yes, darling, how old are you really? Underneath all that surgery of yours?' Georgina teased. The smile on her face didn't do anything to break the chill in the air, though. I had never heard Georgina openly tease Honey. She and Honey, well, apart from the odd falling-out, were always civil to one another.

Honey ignored the remark, or at least she appeared to as she began brushing her hair. 'Honestly, Oopa would lay down his life for me and little Absinthe,' she sighed, as if relishing the idea of poor Oopa lying dead in a ditch for the sake of her and her rabbit. 'But enough of me,' she said, speaking directly to Georgina. 'How's *your* padre, darling? Daddy said he had a drink with him at his club recently and invited Koo-Koo and him to join us for Christmas in Saint Moritz.'

No one ever mentions Georgina's father unless she does. Sure enough, I noticed her eyes welling up with tears. Her father divorced her mother a couple of years ago after his second bypass operation. After her mother had nursed him back to health, he had announced that he felt 'suffocated' by her and that if he was going to die in the near future – which looked highly probable – he'd rather do it in the arms of a younger, less intelligent (he actually used the words '*supportive*' and '*less demanding*,' but Star says it amounts to the same thing) woman than Georgina's mother.

Georgina had a bit of a scary brush with bulimia over it and she's still really cut up about it. Catholics aren't meant to get divorced, although Honey's mother does it all the time. Not that all the girls at Saint Augustine's are Catholic. Some parents merely send their daughters here because it's conveniently close to Eades, where their sons and heirs go.

Georgina's father had married Koo-Koo over the summer at what was once Georgina's family seat in Glouster-shire. Georgina used being with me in LA as her excuse not to attend the wedding, and we all took our cue from her and didn't mention it. Koo-Koo is a twenty-nine-year-old and refuses to let Georgina stay overnight anymore. Koo-Koo says, 'It's better for everyone this way.' As a consequence, Georgina barely sees her father now.

Honey knows about all this, of course. She was just mentioning him to get back at Georgina, to be cruel in the way small boys pull legs off bugs or older boys say they'll txt you and never do.

Honey definitely hit her mark. Georgina looked miserable. I tossed her my lip-gloss but she didn't even attempt to catch it, and it just landed on the floor, near her feet.

'Oh my God, what's that, darling?' Star asked, breaking the toxic tension. Picking up a piece of dusty fluff from the top of the radiator, she held it up, pretending to examine it carefully.

'Don't worry,' she announced in mock relief, 'it's just a piece of dust. For a minute there I thought it might be your brain, Honey.'

Georgina bent down and picked up the lip-gloss. She smiled at me as she applied it. Honey sneered, probably to give herself time to think up a sarcastic response, but Star pressed her advantage. 'I always forget, *darling*, you don't actually have a brain, do you, Honey? They sucked it out during the lipo.'

Georgina chucked me my lip-gloss and I started applying like mad. Who knew where this confrontation would end? Okay, so Honey was a walking advertisement for teen cosmetic surgery, but suggesting that she may have had liposuction was suggesting she may have once been fat, a taboo topic at Saint Augustine's, where specialists were on tap if any girl showed the slightest sign of developing an eating disorder. But as everyone knows, Saint Augustine girls are slim – mostly because they feed us inedible grey slops.

Honey smiled evilly. 'Star, you are too, too hilarious. How fortunate your parents are giving you their full support to break into vaudeville.'

Star's response was to pull the lip-gloss out of her pocket and apply it ostentatiously close to Honey's face. 'Wear your pain like lip-gloss' was one of our secret mottos. Lip-gloss is a girl's biggest asset when dealing with difficult situations. When Star and I were out of the cool-loop, we used to use it as a secret sign to show we weren't dealing with something. It made me feel a bit better seeing Star use our special sign language.

And then out of the blue, Portia remarked, 'Oh yes, lip-gloss. What a good idea,' and although she didn't apply any she smiled at me warmly. It seemed significant.

SEVEN

Aloof Demeanours Versus the Scent of *Eau de Parbitch*

Georgina doesn't like to get involved in Honey's issues with other girls. None of us do, really, and so, keen to change the subject, Georgina grabbed the *Tatler* Portia was reading and asked her, 'So darling, what about you? Good summer? Calypso, Star and I had our navels pierced, see!' She and Star both lifted their shirts to expose their rings.

I was about to come clean and fess up when Portia looked Georgina straight in the eye and replied, 'Hardly,' her voice laced in pain.

I suddenly felt really guilty and self-obsessed. I hadn't even bothered to ask about her summer when she'd asked about mine.

'Mummy was killed in a car accident,' she explained flatly and then picked up her magazine and adopted an absorbed look. None of us knew what to say to that, apart from Honey, of course.

'Darling, how absolutely devastating,' Honey remarked breezily, gathering up her rabbit and popping her into her matching mauve Prada pet bag. 'I'm so sorry, but these things do happen.' Her lower lip dropped in a look of regret as she gave the room a little wave. 'I'm just going to take Absinthe down to the pet shed before the hideous Miss Bibsmore returns.' She rolled her big violet eyes at the thought. 'Do you want to come, darling?' she asked Georgina.

Georgina looked up at her but not with the sort of look you could interpret. Star claims that one of the major reasons parents pay exorbitant sums of money to send their girls to Saint Augustine's is so they can develop a poker face – known to the toff parents as an Aloof Demeanour, a sort of non-look. Honestly, if you could buy an Aloof Demeanour, effortless charm and a sense of entitlement on Bond Street, England's boarding schools would be out of business in a day. Nuns are very good at poker faces. They're very good at poker too. Sometimes when they invite us around for tea they cut us in on a game. They always beat us, but we only play for sweets, which they then insist we eat or take with us afterwards, so that's okay.

Honey chose to take the look as a no. 'Well, ciao ciao!' she called as she swept out of the room on a cloud of *eau de parbitch*.

We all turned our attention back to Portia. 'Darling,

what happened?' Georgina asked gently, sitting down on the bed and rubbing poor Portia's back. Star was sitting beside her and so I sat beside Star.

Portia's loss distressed me. The tears were banking up behind my eyes as I tried to think what I might want someone to say to me if anything happened to Sarah.

Portia put down her magazine and replied calmly. 'It was the first day of the holidays. We were shopping, she was walking across Sloane Street, only not at the pedestrian crossing, and this Range Rover ran over her. It was all so fast. I was right there. . . .' Her voice faded, and Georgina took her in her arms and kissed the crown of her glossy raven head.

If it had been me, I would have cried. As it was I was wiping back a tear at the horrible sadness of it all. But I was paralysed by awkwardness and found I couldn't join Star and Georgina in hugging her. I knew I was being inept and I wanted to say something more . . . I don't know . . . ept, I guess, so I got off the bed and sat on my haunches in front of Portia and passed her my lip-gloss.

'Do you want some lip-gloss?' I asked, attempting a smile.

Portia took the lip-gloss, smiled bravely at me and applied liberally as I added, 'I'm really sorry I didn't ask about your break before, Portia. Actually, I mean I'm sorry about your mother and everything else too, obviously, it's so sad . . .'

Portia gave me another brave smile as she passed me

back my lip-gloss. I told her to keep it as I had loads, which was true. 'Honestly, it's so sweet of you, but I've dealt with it now,' she said. 'Honey's right; devastating, but these things happen. It's Daddy I'm worried about, rattling about all alone in that big house.'

By all alone, of course she meant there would still be gameskeepers, butlers, valets and staff galore, but her sadness and concern were real and my heart went out to her. Suddenly my txt alert sounded, and without thinking I dug my phone out of my pocket and read,

Can't get you out of my head.
Freds x

I smiled, mostly because I had invented the nickname Freds. How cool was that; I had invented a nickname for the heir to the throne who couldn't get me out of his head? No one seemed to notice me reading the txt but the inappropriateness of my joy wasn't lost on me, and I shoved the phone straight back into my pocket.

'I met your mother loads of times,' I told Portia. 'She was always lovely to me. She was so tall and beautiful and I loved the way she would always kick her shoes off and fall asleep at the back of the chapel on your father's shoulder during Mass.'

A half-smile broke across Portia's face. 'And snored,' she added. 'She always snored.'

'Well, Father Conran *can* go on,' Star said, which made

Portia laugh, even though I noticed a solitary tear running down her cheek, and then we all laughed the way you do when crying is the only other option and you know tears won't help.

'Thanks,' Portia said, wiping her tear away. 'Since the funeral I've been so miserable and pathetically wrapped up in my own self-pity. I've just stayed in my room and tried not to think about Mummy, but I can't help it. Daddy's lost loads of weight.'

'What about Tarkie?' Georgina asked, referring to Portia's older brother, Tarquin, the Marquess of Eaglemere, who attends Eades in the year above Freddie.

'Tarkie's dealt with it by throwing himself into partying,' she replied. I sensed she was being economical with her feelings about Tarquin's partying in that upper-class English way, which had taken me so long to adapt to. Actually let me amend that; I am still getting used to it. 'He went to Rock with friends straight after the funeral.'

'What? Surfing?' I blurted, shocked at what I saw as Tarquin's callous abandonment of his sister and father.

'Yes, well, it was pretty gloomy in Eaglemere, and we've always spent that fortnight in our house in Rock . . .' She trailed off as if remembering past summers with her family when it was complete.

'But what about you? What about your father?' I asked, frustrated by my own inability to say anything useful and annoyed that I was saying anything at all. It was pretty obvious by the way Portia's head was bowed and her demeanour in general that she didn't want to answer questions or discuss her mother's death more than she had to.

'Daddy locked himself away,' she answered politely, as if I'd asked about the weather, but she was looking at her hands, which were folded neatly in her lap. 'He told me to go with Tarkie. My ghastly grandmother came to stay.'

'Oh,' I replied as if I genuinely thought the arrival of a ghastly relative made everything okay.

Then Portia looked up at me. 'And she told me I should have gone with Tarkie to Rock too, and so I locked myself away from her.'

I could see she was about to tear up again, and I felt bad. 'Boys are different,' Star said, then pinched me in the ribs, which made me squeal, and Georgina pinched me too.

Portia smiled as I beat off Georgina and Star. She was clearly relieved that my probing was over.

'Honestly, Tarquin's been brilliant. He sent Daddy and me a postcard every day. Daddy said he wasn't even sure Tarquin could write before that.' Then a real smile broke across her beautiful features as if she was remembering something happy. 'Actually, do you mind if I *don't* talk about it?' she asked, looking at me almost pleadingly. 'I mean, I can't stop missing Mummy, but it did feel good to laugh again just then.'

'In that case,' Star urged, pulling Portia to her feet, 'you have *got* to come to the pet shed and see Hilda. She's learnt this really cool new trick.'

'You've taught her to talk?' Portia asked teasingly.

Star's always trying to teach her rat, Hilda, and her snake, Brian, to do clever tricks, but all Brian does is slither about and all Hilda does is run herself stupid on her little rat wheel. If you ask me, those two are a lost cause as far as tricks go.

'Almost. She can beg for her little rat pellets now.'

'Ooooh, bless,' Portia said. 'Let's go.'

'Just one sec,' Star said as she rushed off to her dorm room, returning with a can of Febreze concealed inside her blazer so she'd be able to have a fag at the pet shed and spray the smell away.

We all traipsed downstairs and outside across the school grounds. As we passed our old dorm, Cleathorpes, I remembered our last term there, when Star and I had first become friends with Georgina. Soon I was straggling behind, musing about what sharing with Portia and Honey was going to be like this term. My parents told me they had big hopes for me this year as they waved me off at LAX.

This year we'd be sitting our GCSEs, a national exam, which meant the work would be piled on us; but far more important to me were the National Fencing Trials in December. As one of the top sabreurs in the Under Sixteens, Portia was probably focusing on the trials as well, which could bond us on one hand and make us competitors on another. I had to rate in the trials if my big dream to fence in the Nationals was going to come to anything. Freddie's message couldn't have been further from my mind when my txt alert sounded again.

So going to slay you on the piste next week!
Billy xxx

Three kisses from Billy, one from Freddie . . .

EIGHT

House Spinster Alert

It was a very quiet dorm that first night. Hardly a word was spoken as we each took our turn in the pristine luxury of the marble en suite bathroom: showering, brushing our teeth and changing into our winter pyjamas.

Portia appeared gorgeously cool in a pair of black tight jersey shorts with a pink lace frill and a matching long-sleeved, tight-fitting top that showed her athletic figure to greatest advantage.

Honey sashayed out later as if trotting down a catwalk in a flesh-coloured, slinky, lace La Perla nightie that was very grown-up, sexy and see-through. I came out of the bathroom last so that they could witness together my madly un-posh, un-sexy Hello Kitty flannelette pyjamas.

'Oh, bless,' said Honey sarcastically.

I had thought them adorable when I bought them with Star and Georgina at the Beverly Center over the summer, but now realised how tragically babyish they were. My parents might be proud as punch that I was almost a full year younger than everyone else in my year, but they weren't the ones who had to endure the feelings of immaturity that went with it.

I dived into bed and pulled my lovely new goose down double duvet up against my chin, trying to ignore the look Honey was giving me. A nasty look, pregnant with derision and loathing. I thought she was about to say something else, but she merely pulled her mauve silk eye mask over her eyes. I suppose she decided I wasn't worth it.

Portia was reading another magazine, *The Fencer*, this time. I was exhausted from the flight, and I could feel my eyelids getting heavier and heavier as I read Edith Sitwell's *English Eccentrics*. Eventually I turned my light out and began to float off, thinking how different the atmosphere of this dorm room was compared to last term, when most nights held the excitement of a pyjama party. Eventually Portia said 'Goodnight,' to which I responded, 'Sweet dreams.' Honey just ignored us even though I suspect she was still awake.

Lying in the quiet, I almost welcomed the *tap, tap, tap* sound of Miss Bibsmore's stick as she made her way down the corridor in an odd series of little steps and shuffles. I could hear her giving warnings about chatting after lights out to other rooms. And I listened to her dragging bins across bedroom floors to wedge the doors open so that she would hear any late-night chatting that wicked girls might try to engage in.

At ten-thirty, her odd little shape was silhouetted in our doorway. We already had our lights out, which must have been a first at Saint Augustine's because *everyone* always waits for the lights-out rule to be enforced by the House Spinster. And let's be honest, what room of girls would voluntarily turn their own lights out at fifteen years of age? Apart from when it was exam time, maybe.

'Lights out now, girls,' announced Miss Bibsmore in her shrieky voice as she perversely turned our evil fluorescent strip lights back on.

I peeked out from under my duvet and watched as she cast a suspicious eye over our room.

'Wot's that then on the floor by your bed, Miss Kelly?' she demanded.

I leant over and scanned the floor, but there was nothing on it. For once, my area was spotless. 'I don't know,' I told her honestly.

'Don't know!' she screeched, using her stick to lift one of my Hello Kitty slippers into the air with a circus performer's agility, then dangling the offending slipper in my face. It was definitely time to get over my Hello Kitty stage. In three months I would be fifteen, and looking at my little pink slipper as Miss Bibsmore wobbled it on her stick made me feel like it was high time I grew up and got some cool nightwear like Portia.

'It's by *your* bed, madam, so I suggest you acquaint yourself with the item and identify it quick smart!'

'It's a, well, it's a, a slipper. Isn't it, Miss Bibsmore?' I asked uncertainly. I could hear Portia struggling under her duvet to suppress laughter.

'No, it's not a "slipper," Miss Kelly, and well you know it.'

At which point Portia pretended to have a coughing fit to disguise her giggles. Honey was silent, no doubt waiting for a chance to stick the knife in.

I was genuinely stumped. Maybe there *was* another term for slipper that I was yet to learn. As an American, I was always discovering new words for everyday objects. It had taken me all the first term of year seven to work out what vests were, and jumpers had stumped me for a further year. So I asked cautiously, 'Sorry, Miss Bibsmore, we call it a slipper in America.'

'Well *I* call it your classic death trap. I can smell the stench of a dead girl just looking at it. Wot if there was a fire innit? Wot if you had to evacuate at a moment's notice? You'd dive out of bed, blind as a bat, and trip over this so-called "slipper," and knock your 'ead on a bed or the floor. You'd be out cold while the flames licked about your body. A slipper indeed! I've never heard such nonsense.'

This time I heard Honey suppress a laugh – only I think she was laughing at the tantalising thought of me burning to death rather than the absurdity of Miss Bibsmore's rant.

'Sorry, Miss Bibsmore,' I replied.

'Now in the future, I want all so-called "slippers" under the bed. Do I make myself clear?'

'Crystal, Miss Bibsmore,' I agreed obediently.

Miss Bibsmore patted me on the head. 'Right you are, then, sweetie. Off to the land of Nod with you now, little love. Say your prayers.' I stuck my head deeper into my duvet, secretly delighted by her comforting words. 'And sweet dreams to you too, Briggsie,' she added gently.

Using an affectionate abbreviation of Portia's surname and calling me 'sweetie' was a privilege I suspected Honey wasn't going to enjoy.

'Thank you, Miss Bibsmore,' Portia replied.

She patted Portia's head again. 'I'm sorry to hear about your mum too. Sister Constance told me what happened an' all. It can't have been easy for you. I understand she was a proper angel with an 'eart of gold and it's a curse on those like me wot didn't get to meet her.'

'Thank you, Miss Bibsmore,' Portia answered quietly.

'I won't mention her again, mind, but I felt I should say something. It's only proper. I might be stern but I'm not made of stone, Briggsie. As for you, Miss O'Hare,' she added, her voice changing tone as she shuffled back toward the door, 'don't think I'm not on to you, pretending to be asleep indeed. As if butter wouldn't melt in your mouth. I've 'ad a good look at your record, madam, not to mention your sister Poppy 'oo I had up 'ere two years past, so may the Good Lord Jesus Christ and the saints in 'eaven protect you if I ever catch you up to anything.'

'Whatever,' Honey muttered.

'Hail Mary, full of grace . . .,' Miss Bibsmore began, and Portia, Honey and I joined her in a decade of the rosary.

By the time our lights actually did get turned out, it was eleven o'clock and the jet lag was seriously kicking in.

NINE

Secret Disappointments & Less-Than-Secret Hatred!

*A*fter Miss Bibsmore left, Portia expressed what I'd been thinking. 'She's *really* gunning for you, Honey.'

Honey turned on her torch and tore off her eye mask. 'Oh, don't worry, darling. I've already called Daddy on one of my other mobiles and his solicitor is writing a letter as we speak. Her days are numbered, and Daddy said he'll make sure she'll never get a reference.'

Suddenly the fluorescent strip lights flickered on again and framed in the doorway was the ghostly figure of Miss Bibsmore. 'I warned you, Miss O'Hare. I might not be bright but I'm blessed with a nose for trouble, I am, and I'll not have your kind having one over on me. Do you understand?'

With that the fluorescent lights flickered off again.

'Would you kindly allow us to sleep, you mad old witch! It's against the Geneva Convention to wander in and wake us up, you know . . .,' Honey spat, but the *tap, tap, tap* of Miss Bibsmore's stick was already fading away down the corridor.

'Did you get much fencing practise in during the break?' Portia whispered to me once we heard Miss Bibsmore descending the stone staircase. I could see that the stone staircase was going to be a great advantage if our dorm *did* ever become fun. We'd hear Miss Bibsmore coming easily.

'Yaah, a fair bit but it's hard finding decent opponents over there. The standard just isn't as high. Fewer people do sabre in LA so the competition isn't great. I worked on my lunges and footwork though. What about you?'

'Daddy hired me my own fencing master. We've got a piste in the gym at home so I was planning to be practising all the time, but then, after Mummy . . .'

'We'll be back on the piste tomorrow,' I reassured her, not wanting to torture her further over the loss of her mother. She'd made it quite clear she didn't want to talk about it, and I was going to respect her wishes.

'We'll both need to push ourselves with the BNFTs coming up in December. It's such a ghastly time for Professor Sullivan to take a sabbatical,' she sighed.

'Has he left?'

'For a term at least.'

This was an enormous blow to me. Professor Sullivan

had been my fencing master since I first came to Saint Augustine's. I hadn't counted on this turn of events at all. 'You mean we have a new fencing master?'

'Mr Wellend. I doubt he's a Mr Sullivan, but he sounds the business. Olympic silver, quite old but madly accomplished, apparently,' she explained.

'Oh, I'm just surprised Professor Sullivan didn't mention anything.'

'He probably thought we'd make a fuss of him. Besides, he's not gone forever. This Wellend chap used to coach the Eades team ages ago, apparently. I'll go down tomorrow in the break to speak to him and see if he's willing to give us extra lunchtime tuition.'

'Do you think he's unlikely to?'

'If you don't mind, some of us are trying to get to sleep,' Honey hissed.

Portia ignored her. 'Hardly. He's not obliged, but now's the time to ask. Plus it is in his interest for us to distinguish ourselves.'

'Our success being his success, you mean.'

Honey groaned and moved about noisily in her bed.

I ignored her. 'Well, if you don't mind going alone, I'd really like to check on how Dorothy's doing back at the pet shed during break. I really missed her over the summer,' I explained.

Honey switched her lamp on, pulled off her eye mask – which was embroidered with the word HEIRESS – and scowled. Portia smiled conspiratorially at me, blew me a teasing kiss and said, 'Not at all darling. You check on Dorothy and I'll report back.'

'Deal,' I replied, almost delirious with hope that Portia and I were going to be friends or at least get along despite Honey's poisonous presence.

'You two are really annoying me,' she said as she switched her lamp off and groaned again.

A few minutes later, Georgina, Star and a third girl I took to be Indie crept into our room on all fours with their torches in their mouths, which made them look like a pack of pyjama-clad dogs on the prowl. Silently moving the bin and shutting the door, they climbed into our beds. I was pleased that Star climbed in with me.

'My feet are *frozen*. I need socks,' she told me.

'Drawer underneath the bed,' I told her.

She stayed under the covers as she opened the drawer and riffled round for socks.

I watched with mixed feelings as Georgina climbed in with Honey and started tickling her, and the two of them started giggling together. Just like old times – until a voice piped up from the shadows.

'Hi, I'm Indie,' the new best friend whispered as she stood up and shined her torch around our room, finally shining it under her own face so we could see her properly. She was smiling. She was so stunning I was shocked. She looked like Naomi Campbell and she was almost as tall. 'I've heard so much about you all. Especially you, Calypso,' she said in the sweetest, poshest voice I'd ever heard.

'Same,' I replied brightly, determined in that moment to like her and stop feeling jealous.

Portia invited her to jump in under her duvet. Even though it was only September the nights were already quite chilly, especially as they didn't turn on the central heating until November – even if it was snowing!

'Isn't Miss Bibsmore the weirdest?' Georgina asked rhetorically.

I wanted to say I actually quite liked her, but I knew it would only set Honey off.

'Oh, she'll be gone in a week, darling, I've got Daddy on the case. Do you know she even had the audacity to confiscate one of my phones! The pikey way she speaks, ugh! Fag, darling, fag?' Honey suggested.

'I've given up cigarettes,' Georgina told her. 'How about a spliff?'

Even Honey seemed surprised, and Honey doesn't do surprised. It's quite hard to do surprise when you've had as much Botox as she's had, I guess. Still, even in the torchlight I was pretty certain a look of surprise attempted to flash across her feline features.

A moment later, Georgina and Honey opened up the window to the cold night air, stuck their heads out and fired up their joint companionably.

'Should you be doing that?' I asked Georgina when she pulled in after blowing out some smoke and asked if anyone else fancied a puff.

Star pinched me, leaving me in no doubt I'd said the wrong thing.

'Gee, are you sure you should be doing that?' Georgina parroted in a bad piss-take of a hillbilly accent.

Honey stuck her head in, blew some funny-smelling smoke towards me and drawled, 'Oh, go back to LA will you, Calypso! All you Americans are soooo sanctimonious.'

Georgina giggled, just a tiny little bit, but it was a defining giggle.

Honey seized her advantage and carried on. 'Or maybe you could set up an NA group for us, Calypso? You just love setting up little groups and salons, don't you? Would you make Georgina and I confess our wickedness to a counselling group? Would you, darling?'

I declined to reply, consumed by embarrassment and squirming with all the old familiar feelings of being an outsider in their exclusive world with its maddeningly tricky English in-jokes which were so much a fabric of their lives. Here I was again, a foreigner in another world where, despite the deceptive similarities, I didn't really speak the language.

Not that any of that mattered, because Honey was on a roll and anything I said would have only been used as more ammunition against me. This time she sent herself up as a clever way of sending me up. 'Darlings, my name is The Honourable Honey O'Hare, and this is my friend, The

Honourable Georgina Castle Orpington, and we're the most ghastly spliff-a-holics.'

I descended deeper into my spiral of dread. What was happening here? Why was Star giving Honey free rein to go on like this? Why had Georgina suddenly done an about-face and cosied up with Honey again? I waited for the inevitable paroxysms of smothered giggles, but instead Indie's voice came out of the semi-darkness. 'This is getting soooo boring.'

Honey shone her torch into Indie's eyes. 'Oh, go back to fruuping Cheltenham will you.'

Indie shone her own torch straight back into Honey's face, as the room fell silent in this war of torches. 'Hardly!' she said in a madly grand way. 'I left because of a chav toff like you.'

Honey looked around the room for support. Portia had her back to everyone, Georgina merely giggled and Star and I weren't even on her radar. Resigned to the mood change, Honey announced, 'I've got the munchies, anyone have sweets on them?'

I smiled at Indie gratefully and she smiled back. Between Miss Bibsmore and Indie, Honey was going to be facing some stiff opposition this term. I definitely wouldn't want to get on the bad side of Indie. As beautiful as she was, when she'd gone for Honey just then, she'd looked terrifying.

Star stuck her tongue out at me to reveal a new stud in her tongue. She was only doing it to tease in a nice way. I knew that Star would never want to make me feel bad. She winked at me and gave me a cuddle as well, but something had changed between us. Once she would have sent me a txt to announce a step like tongue piercing. It had always been just the two of us, and while I was pleased that Indie had slapped Honey down, I couldn't help wishing it had been Star.

The spliff was finally spliffed out and Star sprayed Febreze around the room and things went back to normal as if a tidal wave had receded. We chatted amongst ourselves, catching up on things generally, and Indie joined in as if she'd always been part of our group. It turned out she knew loads of the boys we knew and shared lots of the same opinions as us about them.

'So Calypso,' she said to me. 'I'm really looking forward to watching you fence. I wish I'd taken it up now; it looks so achingly cool in all those movies and ads on television. I adore the outfits, and all the fit boys seem to fence now.'

'Actually, it's more aching than cool,' I told her, and Portia agreed.

Honey made a sarcastic remark, but everyone ignored her. She was sitting alone on the floor now wrapped up in her duvet, devouring our room's tuck stash with ridiculous abandon, stuffing herself with M&M's and Jelly Babies like there was no tomorrow. I was really glad that Clemmie wasn't there to witness it. She cries when people eat Jelly Babies because she thinks they look like her little brother Sebastian. I watched in disbelief as Honey consumed a term's worth of tuck, while giggling dement-edly to herself and talking drivel. I suppose it was the spliff, although all Star's father does when he's stoned is fall into unconscious stupors. As for Georgina, she didn't seem stoned at all.

When Georgina suggested I bring out my Hershey's Kisses, as Honey might still be hungry, I directed her to where she'd find them in my cupboard.

Georgina ate a few – well, we all did – but Honey demolished most of the bag. Normally she's really careful when it comes to sweets, being obsessed as she is with her figure and complexion. I guess she was more affected by the spliff than Georgina because Georgina didn't appear to have the munchies at all. I'm sure Honey would have grazed on tuck all night if it we hadn't heard the *tap, tap, tap* of Miss Bibsmore's stick on the stone stairwell.

'We'd better scarper,' Star hissed. And then she did it again. Poked her tongue out at me and grinned. If a nun or even a non-nun teacher saw her stud, she would be gated, if not suspended. But as I mentioned, the school was far from keen to damage relations with such a generous donor to school funds as Tiger from Dirge, so they were just as likely to turn a blind eye to Star, I guess.

Georgina air-kissed me and Indie gave me a cuddle before she left.

'It was really cool to meet you, Calypso,' Indie said sweetly.

'Same,' I agreed.

'Good luck with *that*,' she said, pointing to Honey as if she was an unpleasant problem rather than a girl. Honey was still on the floor, wrapped in her duvet and giggling to herself. 'Please tell me she's a one-off?' Indie begged.

'Oh, she's definitely special,' I assured her.

Indie and Portia both giggled.

Then Indie carefully pushed the bin back and slipped quietly out the door.

TEN

The Political Subjugation of Youth

I n the large refectory hall at breakfast the next
morning, the sounds of clattering plates, chatting
girls and squawking kitchen staff were deafening.
There was no noise on god's earth that could drown out
Sandra, though. Sandra, the head of kitchen staff, wields
her power ferociously. Everything about her is fake –
from her peroxide platinum hair to her Saint Tropez tan
and everything in between. Louie Vuitton belt, Versace
t-shirt, Chanel sunglasses – you name the label, she owns
the fake. The only thing genuine about her is her Essex
screech.

Every morning she stands by the milk dispenser, point-
lessly screaming, 'No *cups* of milk, always jugs, girls,
remember! No *cups* of milk, always jugs, girls, remember!
No *cups* of milk, always jugs, girls, remember!'

Not even the Year Sevens ever heeded her, of course.
Between teachers, older girls and our workload, there was

enough to heed without listening to mad dinner ladies trying to ration our milk.

I grabbed a couple of croissants and stood in the queue by the milk dispenser with my cup and watched the teachers at wretched High table. High table is an ancient long, dark oak table around which high-backed, ornately carved Jacobean-style chairs are arranged. The whole affair looms over the ref on a platform under an ancient portrait of the school's founder, Sister Angelo Meed.

The teachers were all chatting away, hatching their plans about how horrible they would be making our lives this term. The nun teachers were with them, but every year there were fewer and fewer teaching nuns, as they were getting older and older. The three sitting at High table now were all napping. Mostly you just saw the nuns wandering about the school grounds hand in hand, saying things like 'Isn't it a lovely day, girls' even if a blizzard was blowing their black robes in the air. We all adored the nuns, who always ignored us if we went up to Pullers' Wood for a fag – not that I smoked, but Star did. Also, they were always telling us they'd pray for us and we loved knowing someone existed just to say little prayers for us.

The non-nun teachers lived in lovely old houses scattered around the school grounds and ate special food, cooked to be edible. The worst part of it all came when they wandered past us during Sunday lunch (having polished off their delicious roasts) and watched over us sadistically as we ate our grey-slop-roasts. They always said things like,

'Doesn't that look scrumptious, girls?' I'm not even sure 'scrumptious' is a real word. Teachers are pure evil.

Finally it was my turn to shove my jug under the milk dispenser. After snatching a couple of sachets of chocolate, I joined Star, Georgina and Indie, who were still eating their breakfasts. I noted a couple of madly butch female security guards sitting nearby at a discreet but obvious distance. I figured they were with Indie.

Star and Georgina had their hair identically corn braided like Indie's and were deep in conversation about the pet shed renovation next year and speculating on what that might mean for Brian, Hilda and Dorothy, the rabbit I co-owned with Georgina.

I was about to join in when Star asked Indie about the animals in the zoo in her palace in Scotland. I dunked a piece of croissant in my hot chocolate and tried to follow what she was saying. I was concentrating on not feeling jealous of Indie when Star nudged me so hard the croissant fell into my hot chocolate.

'By the way, that wasn't a real spliff that George was smoking with Honey last night, darling,' she whispered. 'It was just a trick.'

'What?' I enquired, as if I was wildly cool and not the least bit fazed by the spliff. I began scooping croissant out of my hot chocolate, trying not to let my mind dwell on why she hadn't bothered to tell me of the trick beforehand. It would have saved me from making a fool of myself.

'It was all Star's idea,' Georgina cut in. 'Remember how

we were making up ways to get back at her for all the fat remarks she makes about us?' she reminded me.

'Yes, but . . .'

'Star made a roll-up using these herbs her father's been using.'

'He's trying to wean himself off weed,' Star interjected.

'Oh, that's good,' I agreed, spooning some soggy croissant out of my hot chocolate.

'It's not been any help though,' she added. 'He just mixes the herbs with weed.'

'That's rock stars for you,' I sighed, as if rock stars and I were always in detox together.

'I thought I'd get her to smoke it as payback for the way she's always having a go at Star for her father's plebbie drug use.'

'And how fat we are,' Star added.

'I knew she'd share it if *I* offered it to her,' Georgina told me confidently. 'And you won't believe this! She's already approached me this morning for *more*.'

We all laughed, even though a part of me was still put out that they hadn't included me on the plan earlier.

'So it was just herbs?' I confirmed, still slightly unconvinced. 'But she had the munchies even! Honey never eats sweets; she just uses them to bribe Year Sevens to do her blues!'

'I know, wasn't that incredible? I've never seen anyone gobble down calories so fast,' agreed Indie, looking at me. She threw back her head and laughed long and loud, completely unembarrassed by all the looks she was receiving from other tables.

'We wanted to let you in, but we couldn't in case you started giggling,' Star explained sweetly, giving my hand a squeeze.

'I wouldn't have giggled!' I exclaimed indignantly.

'Yes, you would. You even giggled when you had your navel pierced. And that hurt.'

'The thing I loved the most was the way she even started talking like she was stoned,' Georgina marvelled. 'You know, in that slow, "Hey man, where's my brain" way.'

I brooded on how they'd voted not to share the joke with me beforehand as I fished out most of the croissant.

'Are you still going to do Latin this term, darling?' Star suddenly asked, changing the subject as Honey approached our table and nestled herself neatly beside Georgina.

I tried to get the rest of the sloppy croissant into my mouth. 'Yaah, we both are,' I reminded her, deciding to abandon the croissant as a lump fell on my tie.

We'd both signed up for Latin, Ancient Greek and French in Year Ten for our GCSE subjects because they'd all be quite easy As and we'd have more time to focus on our fencing. Star looked at me now as if I was mad. 'I *loathe* Latin with every fibre of my being, Calypso.'

'So do I,' I replied defensively.

'So Daddy told me I can chuck it. Besides, I need the extra time to concentrate on my music,' she said.

'Can you do that?' I asked, pretty certain that you

couldn't. I looked at the soggy flakes of croissant still floating in my hot chocolate.

'If your father built the music wing you can do pretty much anything, Calypso,' Star joked. Actually, it was probably true.

'Yes, why don't you get *your* father to build us something?' Honey asked me faux-kindly before quickly adding, 'Oh, that's right, I always forget. He's got no money, has he?'

'Shut up!' Star and Indie said in unison, only Star added the word 'bitch' at the end.

'Darling, that spliff gave me the best night's sleep since Mummy gave me that Valium,' Honey raptured.

Georgina almost burst into giggles as she leant over to tell me, 'I'm chucking Latin too.'

'What?' asked Clemmie, joining our table as I took a bite of my dry croissant.

'Calypso's still doing Latin,' Georgina explained, making it sound like I was electing to do voluntary lunch clearing.

'God, what for, darling?' Clemmie asked, looking at me as if I was barking.

'They said it would be quite an easy A for me. We were all doing Latin last year, remember?' Was I the only one who found this new turn of events perplexing, I wondered, as I looked at the girls munching their breakfasts around me. 'Have you dropped it too, Clemmie?' I asked, trying not to sound as confused as I was.

Star snorted as if we hadn't *always* chosen our subjects

together. 'Calypso, if you really find it that easy, why not chuck the lessons and sit the exam anyway?' she asked.

'Yaah, I guess I could.' I shrugged, feeling the colour rush to my face. 'When did you decide this, though?'

'It's not a big deal. Georgina and I spoke about it on the flight back and then I asked Daddy before Ray drove me back to school.'

'I didn't ask anyone,' Georgina added.

Clemmie shrugged. 'Nor did I.'

Georgina, Star and Clemmie all rolled their eyes at how seriously I was taking it all, but Star knew that Bob and Sarah would never allow me to drop subjects without a big brouhaha. 'I should have told you, but I didn't realise you cared.'

'I don't mind,' I lied.

'Maybe if you spoke to Bob,' Star suggested. 'You know, explain to him how useless GCSEs are. Eight subjects are plenty after all.'

'And besides, the best public schools are dropping them now, it's such a pointless diploma. Eades has dropped GCSEs altogether,' Clemmie added.

'As Daddy would say, "Structured exams are just a political subjugation of youth, man,"' Star added.

Everyone giggled. Tiger had become a bit of cult figure amongst the girls since his appearance last term at the launch of our satirical magazine, *Nun of Your Business*.

'Is that really how your father talks?' Indie asked, giggling at Star's mimicking of her perpetually stoned sounding father. Because even when he wasn't stoned he still sounded stoned.

'There's no way I'd let *my* parents choose *my* GCSEs,' Arabella added as she climbed onto the table with a bowl of cereal. 'It's my life. My parents wouldn't dare imagine they had the remotest right to ask what subjects I'd chosen. I'd cut them off, totally cut them off' – she imitated a pair of scissors cutting – 'if they tried to influence my life in any way whatsoever.'

'Off that table right now,' ordered one of Sandra's henchwomen walking by. 'Tables is for sitting at innit, not on. I don't know what your parents is teaching you, I don't.'

'Grammar mostly,' Honey sneered, and everyone laughed. Arabella still sat down on the bench, though. 'My parents couldn't care less what I study or what grades I get. They haven't ever read one of my reports.'

'Nor have mine,' Georgina agreed.

'Sophisticated people realise that life is for living, not working,' Honey remarked pointedly, knowing I didn't have a trust fund to rely on like everyone else in the school. 'Besides, I'm probably going to fail everything anyway, what with all the time I'll be taking off this term. Darcy Greggs wants me in his show at London Fashion Week,' she explained. 'Mummy says it's the opportunity of a lifetime.'

'More of an opportunity than Latin, that's for sure,' agreed Star, necking her juice.

I felt like I'd been slapped. After all our years of mutual

loathing of Honey, it was as if Star were siding with her against me – even if it was over something as dismal as Latin. I looked around the group of girls as they nodded their heads in agreement and spooned their cereal or dipped their croissants. I felt like I was in a play without a script.

'It's not as if I don't loathe Latin too,' I explained helplessly, 'but I do think that I'll be able to do quite well without putting in much work, as my main objective is to focus on my fencing.' I looked to Star for support on this as we'd been fencing from the first day we started at Saint Augustine's. We were sisters-in-arms, and over the summer we'd discussed at length how pleased we were that we'd chosen easy subjects that wouldn't be too demanding and cut in on our fencing.

Star avoided my gaze in a guilty-ish sort of way and began playing with her braids. I carried on gamely. 'Maybe you should reconsider, because we're going to need all the easy subjects we can get with the Nationals coming up, Star.'

Everyone blinked at me disinterestedly, as if I'd been talking about the variety of school jumpers on offer this season. Honey took this opportunity to inform Georgina that she had already secured front row seats at the show for her and her mother. But I barely heard her because suddenly Star, still playing with her braids, remarked casually, 'Actually, Calypso, I've decided to drop fencing.'

'No!' I blurted before I could stop myself. 'You can't drop fencing!'

Star and I had first bonded on the piste. Fencing was how we had distinguished ourselves from the ghastly Sloaney girls she'd always professed to hate. It was the cornerstone of our relationship. She couldn't drop fencing. It would be like dropping . . . well, it would be like dropping *me*. 'Why?'

She avoided my gaze by looking deeply into one of the corn braids in her hand. 'Yaah, see, Calypso, I'm going to focus on my music.'

I watched as Indie and Star smiled excitedly at one another. 'Indie and I have already spoken to Sister Constance and we're going to lay down some tracks for a demo CD,' she added.

'Isn't that cool?' Indie finished, her eyes brimming with enthusiasm.

I felt like I was hovering outside my body as I watched Star and Indie look at me as if I should be thrilled. As if I should be jumping up and down with glee that my best friend was walking away from our greatest bond. Instead, I looked at her like she was someone I didn't know anymore.

What had happened to Star and Calypso, the sabreurs, the girls who wore their pain like lip-gloss, the Star and Calypso who rinsed boys on the piste and kissed them off? Besides, Star had a massive crush on Mr Sullivan, so I didn't know how she was going to cope without a daily shot of him. And then I remembered we had a new fencing master this year.

Portia joined us then, sitting down in her quiet, long-legged, elegant way and touched my arm. 'Guess that leaves just you and me on the sabre team, darling.'

'I guess it does,' I agreed, only I was looking at Star as I said it. 'The thing is you need three people on a team in order to fence.'

And then suddenly, Indie turned to me and remarked, 'I'm doing Latin, actually. I'll come by your room after inspection. We can share the joy of verb declensions together.' She turned back to the others. 'I'm following Calypso's plan to go for the easy A-star. I'm doing French, Italian and Ancient Greek as well.'

'Ancient Greek!' Honey shrieked in her hyena squeal. 'No one does Ancient Greek, apart from miserable train wrecks like our American Freak here, of course. But no one who *matters* does Ancient Greek. It's a dead language.'

'I wish you were dead,' I almost said, and then I realised Star had said it for me. She looked at me and I saw she was miming lip-gloss application and looking at me as if wanting my forgiveness. Honey continued to laugh, though. Most girls look even lovelier when they smile and laugh, but because of all her cosmetic enhancements, Honey looked hideous. The Botox meant all the wrong parts of her face moved. When she finally stopped her giggles, the table was silent and we stared as Indie slowly and contemptuously raised one eyebrow to her.

'See, that's where you're wrong, Honey. I'm as far from being "no one" as you are ever likely to meet in your dismal little world of wind-ups, put-downs, bad piss-takes and designer nastiness.' With that, Indie stood up in the most composed way I've ever seen anyone other than Portia stand up. She gave Honey the most withering look I'd ever seen – and believe me, at Saint Augustine's I've seen plenty of withering looks.

Everyone's eyes flicked between Indie and Honey. Honey seemed to shrivel with each passing nanosecond of the look Indie gave her. I was right. Between Miss Bibsmore and Indie, Honey was going to have a rough term. I almost felt sorry for her.

Indie smiled gaily at the rest of us, reminded me she'd drop by my room before Latin and excused herself with a sweet little wave and walked out of the ref imperiously, trailed by her bodyguards. The effect was slightly spoilt when one of the guards, attempting to put Indie's tray in the tray trolley, was ticked off by Sandra and told to fetch 'the little madam' back to do it for herself.

Star and Georgina, their corn braids as stiff and hard as the lump forming in my throat, giggled at the poor bodyguard humiliated in front of a school of girls for being a lap dog. 'Perhaps Cheltenham ladies let body-guards fetch and carry?' Star joked.

'Imagine if they allowed that here! We'd all make our parents assign us bodyguards if that were the case!' Georgina laughed.

Honey didn't join in; she just stared evilly after the disappearing figure of Indie.

ELEVEN

Old Enemies, New Friends

'I'll see you in the salle before French, then? Mr Wellend is expecting us.'

'Mr Wellend?' I repeated, confused.

'The new fencing master?'

'Oh yaah,' I agreed, remembering that not even fencing was going to be the same this term.

Portia added, 'Think of it this way: now that Star's chucked it, he'll have more time to focus on us, darling. We can be his star pupils.'

I smiled, knowing she was reaching out to me, but the truth was I felt like the ground beneath my feet was shifting and that it was only a matter of time before I lost Star and Georgina to Indie for good.

After breakfast, we went to chapel and then back to our rooms to make our beds and clean our teeth before room inspection. Any fantasy I had briefly clung to that Honey's newfound enemy, Miss Bibsmore, would dilute Honey's horribleness evaporated as soon as the first bell went and Honey accidentally-on-purpose spilt a full glass of water on my bed, seriously drenching my mattress.

Portia was in the bathroom brushing her teeth at the time and without a witness it was pointless to dream Honey would ever apologise. All I could do was pull the covers off and hope the mattress would dry out before I had to sleep on it that night. But I wasn't counting on any miracles.

Out of misery more than anything I turned my mobile on to check for messages, and Honey's meanness was suddenly the furthest thing from my mind. I had two new txt messages.

See you in Windsor on Saturday? Freds. x

To which I faux-casually replied,

You read my mind! x C

The next one was from Billy, sent at the same time, early this morning.

Wots up? Billy xx
Honey's just wet my bed xx Calypso

He sent me a txt straight back.

Incontinent little bitch! See you in Windsor on Saturday.
B.

Honey was in the en suite so I showed Billy's txt to Portia. As she scrolled down through the txts she pointed out that my battery was low. Then her face broke into a smile, and as she read the last message she began to laugh.

She was still laughing when Honey came out of the bathroom.

'What's so interesting about the txt, then?' Honey asked in an I-couldn't-be-less-interested sort of way.

'Oh, nothing, darling,' Portia assured her, handing me back my mobile and quietly attending to the tidying of her area.

I was feeling so happy that I didn't even feel pissed off when Miss Bibsmore came in and asked who wet my mattress.

'Just an accident,' I told her, no longer bothered by the soggy mattress I'd have to sleep on that night. Boys are brilliantly distracting like that.

Miss Bibsmore didn't look convinced.

Honey laughed. 'Americans are so clumsy.'

'I've warned you, madam, I'm on to you,' was all Miss Bibsmore would say as she eyed Honey up and down. 'Now don't forget, girls, you've been asked to report to the infirmary after lunch for your flu jabs innit.'

After Miss Bibsmore was out of earshot, I went, 'Oh needles, just what I need to make this day *perfecto*!'

It was the sort of joke I would make for Star usually, but Portia laughed and, weirdly, so did Honey. Then she said, 'So are you going to share that txt with me, then?'

I was saved from replying though because the bell to class suddenly went off, and Indie stuck her head into our room. 'Coming?' she asked.

I hastily plugged my phone into its charger and left it on my bedside table before chasing after her, followed by Portia.

'Enjoy your Latin, girls,' Honey called out after us.

Latin was in one of the older buildings and consequently freezing cold. I was so regretting taking it, and not just because Star had dropped it. We filed into the empty class and I grabbed a table by the radiator, which gave off a sort of mild warmth. Portia sat beside me and Indie sat in front.

Even though Ms Mills was always threatening the physical manifestations of our souls, at least she knew her stuff. Now that we were in Year Eleven, we'd been lumped with a Mrs Obar, whose only qualification for the job as our Latin teacher, we soon realised, was 'I've been a teacher for thirty-seven years! Thirty-seven years, so there's nothing you can tell me!'

Indie turned around to me. 'As if there is the remotest chance she'll ever draw breath long enough to let anyone tell her anything.'

Mrs Obar threw some chalk at her as if it was the most

normal behaviour in the world; then she ordered us to open our books, sit up straight and pay attention. I noticed Indie bend down and retrieve the chalk from the floor a little later when Mrs Obar wasn't looking.

After Mrs Obar struggled for a while with pronunciation, Portia put her hand up to question Mrs Obar on her specific qualifications to teach us Latin. Her response was to throw a piece of chalk at her as well, which Portia deflected with her Cicero translation book. Like Indie, I retrieved the piece of chalk from the floor, and later when Mrs Obar's back was to us, I threw it at her, which set all of us off giggling. Of course at our exclusive school no class had more than five in it, and in this case there were only the three of us, so our laughter didn't create much of a noise, and to preserve her dignity perhaps, Mrs Obar pretended she hadn't felt the chalk and continued writing on the board.

Indie turned around and passed me a note in her neat handwriting.

Next time throw the book!!

Mrs Obar didn't pretend to ignore the note, though. She swooped down on us like a witch in her black serge gown and snatched it up.

'And what might this note mean, Miss Kelly?'

'We were sharing a translation,' Portia told her swiftly. 'See?' Relying on Mrs Obar's ignorance, Portia pointed to a passage in her book.

'Oh, I see,' Mrs Obar conceded. 'Very good, Lady

Herrington Briggs, but Miss Kelly will eventually have to come to grips with her translations herself if she's to distinguish herself to the examiners.'

I struggled to turn my barely suppressed smile into a look of humble acknowledgment but failed when Indie burst out laughing in her distinctive fulsome way, for which she was given a blue.

By Year Eleven you just stick your blues into your book and hand them over to a Year Seven to do for you in exchange for sweets or some other privilege. But as I was already starting to realise, Indie wasn't like most girls.

She refused the blue that Mrs Obar passed to her, and merely looked at it as if it was a pair of dirty knickers. 'I'm not accepting *that*, Mrs Obar!'

Mrs Obar raised her voice. 'Excuse me, madam, but you will accept this blue or you'll be getting another.'

Indie stood up. 'Hardly!' she exclaimed in a voice of shock, her hand over her heart in mortification. Then she continued calmly, 'With all due respect, Mrs Obar, how can I possibly excuse you for wasting my time when I'm sitting eleven GCSEs and I've learnt absolutely nothing in your class so far. I'm sorry, but if I were to accept your blue in all conscience I'd be obliged to make a complaint to my father about the inadequacy of my tuition.' And then she played her trump card as she held out a clenched fist and opened her hand to reveal the piece of chalk Mrs Obar had thrown at her earlier. 'Also, I doubt he'll be thrilled to hear that my teacher has been hurling chalk missiles at me.'

I was as awed as Mrs Obar, who was blatantly humiliated and stuck for words. She stood there for a full
minute clutching her blue importantly, but eventually
she gathered herself together, shoved the blue into her
desk drawer and returned to the board, where she pro-
ceeded to write down the pages in our workbooks that we
needed to cover in prep that evening.

Portia, Indie and I all exchanged looks. I mouthed the
words 'soooo cool,' but by the end of class Mrs Obar was
even letting us chat amongst ourselves. She'd been
rumbled and she knew it.

Next class was English literature with Ms Topler. I
want to be a writer, but Ms Topler would make the most
enthusiastic novelist stick pins in her eyes. We were doing
Shakespeare's *King Lear*, which is my favourite play of all.
You'd think given how much I love the play and how it
was Shakespeare it would be hard to ruin. But I trusted
that Ms Topler's capable hands would dissect and decon-
struct my beloved *King Lear* into something we could nod
off to. I love Cordelia's honesty. I love that she dares to
stick up for the truth even though she knows her father is a
total grown-up, and ipso facto an egotistical hypocrite on a
power trip. A bit like Ms Topler, I was thinking as she
droned on and on about *hubris*. There's nothing Ms Topler
loves more than a good drone.

After lunch, I trudged off to Ancient Greek. Portia was
already there, and I sat at the desk beside her. Our teacher,
Doctor Buffner, told us that we'd be doing *Oedipus Rex*,

and for a special treat we were going to Cambridge after half term to see it performed.

'I hope they have a good DVD on the coach ride there,' I whispered to Portia, because that's usually the only fun part about school trips.

'I know, can you imagine listening to an *entire* play in Ancient Greek?' she whispered back.

We both simultaneously slumped on our desks at the very thought of listening to a whole play's worth of incoherent piffle.

Indie arrived late, and while she had a quiet word with Doctor Buffner, Portia asked me about Billy and Freddie and who I liked the most.

'Well, that's what I don't know,' I confided. 'But I keep telling myself, as soon as I see them it will all work out.'

'I think Billy's seriously fit,' Portia said. 'I mean as a fencer, on the piste. You know, he *is* the captain, and well . . .'

I looked at her quizzically. 'Fitter than Freddie?' I asked, suddenly feeling an acute need to start getting some perspective on the decision awaiting me, because like I said, as much as having a txt romance with two boys at once was fun, it couldn't go on indefinitely.

Portia didn't get a chance to answer though, as Indie joined us and class resumed.

After lunch, I made a quick detour to the pet shed to check on Dorothy, but my head was full of what Portia had said about Billy being fit. Even though she'd qualified it by referring to his fencing ability, I felt a bit uneasy. Not jealous exactly; in fact, it sort of tipped my affections in favour of Freddie. Poor Freddie, I thought, feeling fiercely protective of his looks. The truth was, though, they were pretty evenly matched in the fit stakes. Billy was older, which gave him added kudos, but then Freddie was heir to the throne. It was like I had both boys on a set of scales and I couldn't bear to imagine the balance being tipped in one boy's favour.

I picked up Dorothy. She'd put on weight, I decided, as I carried her over to the pet run for a little hop. The only other girls there were Year Sevens and Eights, so when they offered to look after her for me, I agreed, as I had to rush to the infirmary for the hated flu shot.

The queue was already snaking down the corridor, and because everyone was waiting to be jabbed in the arm with a needle, conversation was sparse. It was going to be a long wait. The sadistic Sister Dumpster (real name, Dempster) – who is not a nun at all and quite possibly worked for the Inquisition, she's so old and nasty – liked to take her time torturing us. Flu jab day was her favourite day of the year.

I was waiting with Star and we fell back into our familiar line of chat – ripping it out of our teachers and the disgusting lunch we'd just consumed. We both studiously avoided conversations about her giving up fencing, Latin and Ancient Greek, although actually I didn't really mind about the Latin and Ancient Greek because Portia and Indie seemed really fun. The fencing was another matter entirely, though.

'Sister Constance said the food was going to be more imaginative this term too,' Star moaned.

'I think she meant more imaginatively evil,' I told her, thinking that it felt as if nothing had changed between us. So I tried to tell myself that perhaps it hadn't really.

'What I want to know is how they make all the meat look identical? How can you make beef, pork, chicken and lamb look exactly the same? It's scary.'

'Well, we do have a salad bar that includes rocket leaves,' I teased, knowing how much Star loathes green things.

Finally it was my turn to have my arm jabbed.

'It's just a prick,' Sister Dumpster told me menacingly, her eyes dancing with happiness as she shoved in the needle, hard and deep.

Star told her she'd do it herself, but Sister Dumpster was resolute. 'It's my special fun and you're not going to spoil it,' she insisted. Well, what she actually said was 'I'm fully trained,' but everyone who overheard knew what she *really* meant.

Afterwards I headed off to join Portia at the fencing salle. 'Say hi to Professor Sullivan for me,' Star called out.

'He's not our fencing master anymore,' I informed her, and there it was, back again: the gulf between us. I saw it in Star's guilty expression and I'd heard it in my tone. I almost blurted out something childish like 'What's happened to us?' but thankfully I stopped myself just in the nick of time. Perhaps Portia's aloof demeanour was starting to rub off on me. . . .

'Well, have a good one anyway, Calypso,' Star said as we parted company.

I was going to miss fencing practise with Star, although she did allow herself to be distracted a bit much. Mostly by her pet rat, Hilda, or her snake, Brian, who by the way are quite possibly the happiest, healthiest pets in the pet shed. In Star's mind however they are more sensitive than all the other pets. She's convinced the rabbits and hamsters say mean things to them when she's not around and give them beady-eyed looks, which really upsets me because Dorothy hasn't got a mean fibre in her soft little body.

And although I can't speak for Honey's rabbit, Absinthe, in my opinion if any of the pets give beady-eyed looks, it's Brian himself. I swear, Star's snake, given half the chance, would eat Dorothy and the others. I've seen him eyeing them up – he practically licks his nonexistent lips as we take the rabbits onto the run. Not that I'd say that to Star. I always say things like, 'Poor Brian,' or, 'Poor little darling Hilda.' I even cuddle Hilda as if cuddling a rat is what I live for. Indie no doubt genuinely adores both Brian and Hilda and doesn't even have to pretend.

But I had decided to stop thinking mean, jealous things like that. Just like I have decided to stop being annoyed with Star for dropping fencing. Over that morning, I had worked out that developing an aloof demeanour like Portia could easily be the answer to all my problems. It was sad that Star and I would no longer be the swashbuckling sabreurs of old, but as Portia had put it, now that Mr Wellend only had two senior sabreurs, he'd be able to give us more specialist attention. Yes, an aloof demeanour would be the making of me. I would pay more attention to what I said, drop the whole blurting thingamee and work on floating through life like Portia in a dignified way.

Perhaps this aloof demeanour, which by the way I could already feel creeping into my character, would even help me with my Freddie/Billy choice.

TWELVE

Mr Bell End

Portia and I were in the salle d'armes changing into the numerous items of fencing kit and armour when she said, 'Was it Honey who wet your bed?'

'What do you think?' I replied as I pulled on my new breeches. Like most girls in my year, I'd had another growth spurt over the summer and had to buy new fencing gear online from Leon Paul. I have just about reached the end of my tether with this growth spurt business. I am now five foot eight, and if I keep going like this I'll be taller than Freddie and Billy. I was madly taking back all the petitions I had made to Our Lady in Year Seven to make me tall and slim, explaining that when I said *tall* and *slim* I had actually meant stunning and leggy, not a stick-like freakish giant.

'Why didn't you say anything to her, darling?' Portia asked.

'It's pointless challenging her. You know what Honey's like,' I reminded Portia.

Star and I could have had a great deal of fun out of the

What Honey's Like? conversation, but Portia was as silent as a throne. She simply went back to changing into her fencing gear as if that were the end of the matter. The next time she spoke was as we were heading out to the piste. 'Oh, I forgot, I spoke to Mr Wellend.'

'What's he like?' I asked, whispering because I could already hear him out there and I didn't want him listening to our conversation.

Portia began rearranging her plastic breast guard, which is a horrible nasty piece of armour that is roughly shaped like breasts and is always impossible to get entirely comfortable. 'He was fine about the extra tuition thing and he said that Emille – you know, she does *épée*, long, straight blonde hair, year below . . . ?'

I shook my head. Almost all the girls at Saint Augustine's had long, straight blonde hair, and while Portia had once been captain of the *épée* team, I had barely noted the girls that fenced foil or *épée*.

'Well anyway, she's moving on to sabre, so she can make up our team, which is brilliant.'

'Not as brilliant as Star,' I pointed out.

'No, but at least we can put up a team at interschool matches now, and also he was totally fine about the extra tuition thing. I think he's as keen as us, really, just a bit . . .'

'What?' I asked, starting to worry.

'Well, put it this way, he's no Professor Sullivan,' she said.

'You mean he's not going to speak to us in French?'

She laughed as she shook her head.

'Is he really old and horrible and wrinkly and mean?'

'I can't swear to his meanness,' she replied enigmatically as she retied her breast guard, 'but he is sort of odd. I mean old,' she corrected herself quickly. 'Old for a fencing master, that is.'

Quite old is a euphemism for ancient, and in my experience most ancient men are pretty odd; but Portia obviously wanted to leave it at that and so I dropped it.

Mr Wellend was waiting for us on the piste, practicing his theatrical lunges. He looked to be pushing fifty or something woeful like that. And talk about odd, this fellow took the biscuit. He had a beard, and I've never understood beards. Even when I was seriously young I was terrified of them. I always think that men with beards smell like soup. And this was one of those really neatly clipped beards that pointed at the end, like one of the Three Musketeers'. Far worse than the beard thing, though, he was actually wearing a silver medal – an Olympic silver medal *outside* his fencing gear.

'Right, girlies, let's start with some warm-ups, shall we?' was his opening gambit. He had a South African accent and spoke to us in a sneering, creepy sort of way. As Portia and I looked at one another, I could tell we were thinking the same thing. We had a madman on our hands.

I shoved my mask over my head to smother my giggles. 'No masks for warm-ups, girlies, no one's going to get hurt.' His voice was so slimy I couldn't bear it, and then he rubbed his hands together. Talk about oily.

I'm sure I must have been mistaken but I was almost certain I heard Portia whisper the word 'creep' under her breath.

I soon decided it was going to be quite good having Portia as my sabre partner. Like me, she was totally focused even in practise sessions. You can always lose yourself in fencing because you have to forget everything else and concentrate on the game.

Professor Sullivan was always going on about how fencing is a physical game of chess, and incredibly enough for a teacher, he's actually right! You have to anticipate your opponent's moves as much as plan your own, all the while staying in the moment, attacking and counterat-tacking. Mr Wellend put it slightly differently . . .

'Think with your brain, girlies, move with your body, slam 'em with your blade.'

I don't know whether it was Portia or me who came up with the nickname Bell End, but it wasn't long into our session before we were whispering asides to one another, doing piss-takes of Bell End's accent. Which is an achieve-ment in itself because as you can imagine, it's not easy saying the words 'bell end' (which is the name for the tip of a boy's . . . well, you know what) while keeping a straight face.

After fencing, I told Portia I needed to go back to my room for a tampon, as I'd just discovered I'd started my period. I was relieved in a way because I decided that was why I'd been so emotional about everything over the past twenty-four hours.

'Actually, I think I'll come with you,' she told me. 'I have to sort something out myself.'

We hurried back, anxious not to be late for our next class, which was French. I dashed straight into the en suite. I heard a bit of stomping about going on in the bedroom but thought nothing of it until I came out and discovered Portia struggling with a mattress.

'Can you help me get this onto Honey's bed?' she panted.

'Sure, what happened?' I asked as I supported the other end of the heavy mattress and helped her manoeuvre it into Honey's bed.

'Just swapping mattresses,' she explained blithely as she smiled at me. 'You don't want to sleep on a wet mattress, do you?'

I laughed and then hesitated for a moment, imagining what Honey's retaliation might be. 'She'll murder me!'

'Well, we'll murder her back then,' Portia shrugged. 'Besides, she'll probably blame Miss Bibsmore.'

This was a very different Portia Herrington Briggs than the girl I thought I knew, that was for sure. She was as serene as ever, but there was a warmth about her as well.

'Good idea,' I agreed. 'Besides, I'm sure Miss Bibsmore wouldn't mind.'

'She might even give us a trophy,' Portia added.

'Oh my, Sarah and Bob would adore that. They've always wanted me to bring home a cup.'

After we finished our war with the wet mattress and remade the bed, I checked my phone for messages from Billy and Freddie.

'Oh *merde*!' I cried, as I saw I'd left my phone on.

'What?' asked Portia.

'I left my phone on.'

'Ten to one Honey snuck a look,' Portia said, echoing my own thoughts.

'Now we'll definitely have to murder her,' I told her in mock solemnity.

'No other option,' Portia said, shrugging, and we burst into peals of belly laughter.

There were no new messages from the boys, but I didn't mind. I was feeling a million times better about everything right up until we walked into the French classroom and I had a perfect view of Star, Georgina and Indie chatting and giggling together. Normally, Star would have saved me a seat.

Portia scribbled away, taking notes conscientiously, while I watched my friends enjoy the royal company of their New Best Friend. I gathered myself together and began taking notes because I was working madly at developing my aloof demeanour, and girls with aloof demeanours don't behave like green-eyed monsters.

The problem was, though, I was still only a novice at this aloof demeanour business, and I found my eyes and attention constantly drawn to the lineup of Star, Georgina and Indie. They appeared to be passing notes. I was vaguely aware of Miss Devante droning on and on and on about the importance of the article, and I was scribbling away furiously to keep up the pretence of attention, but that's all it was, really, a pretence. My page was covered in a scrawl of hearts and arrows.

'Mademoiselle Kelly?' she suddenly snapped.

'*Qu'est ce que c'est?*' I asked as I realised I was the focus of her beady-eyed French attention.

'Tell us about your vacation, *en Français.*'

'Oh bugger,' I blurted before my aloof demeanour could stop me, which earned me a blasted blue.

Portia sidled up to me after class and said, 'My cousin's in Year Seven, darling, and she's fluent in French. Give the blue to me and I'll take care of it.'

'Are you sure? I could speak to Sister Constance. She might be persuaded to transmute it into a chore like floor sweeping.'

'Sister doesn't transmute punishments for Year Elevens,' she reminded me. 'But my cousin's cool. For a bag of Hershey's Kisses she'll do anything.'

I remembered being in Year Seven fondly now. Apart from being teased about my stupid accent, I'd had hardly any work to occupy me, and that, coupled with an insatiable appetite for sweets and a worship of older, worldly-wise girls, made doing their blues an absolute joy. It was so lovely and innocent back then. We didn't even know boys existed.

On top of that, back in Year Seven, Star would always have saved me a seat.

THIRTEEN

The Night of the Soggy Boggies

A part from our daily fencing practise with Mr Bell End, I found myself slipping into what Ms Topler referred to as a *malaise*.

'Miss Kelly, you aren't yourself,' she announced to me – and the rest of the class – during English.

'Oh really, who am I?' I replied, and everyone laughed.

'Don't be droll, girl. You know what happens to droll girls!'

'Actually, not really,' I challenged.

'Blues!' she threatened, before softening slightly. 'No, dear, I fear you are slipping into a malaise, just like those poor Brontë girls.'

I hate the wretched Brontë girls, I wanted to tell her, but then I realised it would just prove her point, so instead I replied, 'Yes, Miss.'

Because she was right, I was slipping into a malaise. Brought on, I expect, by lack of txt messages from boys –

not one since Monday! I know four days isn't a long time, and there were loads of reasons they might not have had the time to txt me. But I had begun to panic and started a nasty habit of shaking my phone. Of course it didn't help that every time I so much as looked at my mobile, Honey would pipe up, 'New message from Freddie or Billy, is it?'

And then when I'd say, 'No, they must be busy,' Honey would smile her *Apis Regina* smile (that's Latin for Queen Bee) and say, 'Yes, that's a positive way to deal with rejection, darling.'

Even with Portia around I never felt comfortable in the dorm with Honey there; and so after these exchanges I'd usually wander off to Star's dorm, where she'd invariably be chatting to Indie and Georgina. Or laughing at some new joke of Tobias's, who's always got an amusing story up his sleeve.

Of course I pretended everything was as it always was, because after all, there's nothing wrong with discovering new friends. That's what I kept reminding myself. It's not as if Star was being mean to me or cutting me out even. It was just that she wasn't favouring me. Now that she had found someone to share her minor chord compositions with, she was as happy as her rat Hilda. And as much as I was enjoying my unexpected friendship with Portia, and as much as I couldn't help liking Indie, I still wanted my old spiky Star back – the one who made sarcastic remarks about all the other girls and their conformism. The one who got my odd sense of humour.

The one who didn't look at me like a freak when I went on one of my rambling blurts.

This new, happy, friendly Star was either wandering around the school laughing with everyone or closeted with Indie in the studio, recording their miserable songs about the sorrows of being Rich, Spoilt and Disillusioned. Also there was something even worse than Star's friendship with Indie playing on my mind. Something I couldn't admit to anyone (and no, I don't mean the fact that I'd taken out my navel piercing, because I'd told Star the whole horrible tale of Sarah and Bob marching me into the shop and humiliating me in front of the entire population of Los Angeles. She'd laughed so hard, she was almost sick).

No, the real problem was that neither Freddie nor Billy had txt-ed me recently, and I was beginning to wonder if I'd finally been rumbled for double txt-flirting. Or maybe they'd found a new girl to txt. Maybe Honey was right; maybe I'd been rejected.

Maybe they were txt-ing Indie?

Don't worry, even I knew I was being irrational. My aloof demeanour practise was definitely starting to pay off. I was feeling much less conflicted (as Bob and Sarah would say) over Star and Indie's friendship. In fact, one evening in our dorm room, when Honey started winding me up about Freddie and Billy, Indie turned to her and asked, 'What about you, Honey? We never seem to hear you talk about any particular boy. Have you ever pulled?' She said it in a pitying way that implied she already knew the answer was no.

Honey almost imploded with shock at the suggestion that she'd never pulled. Before she could respond though, Indie began admiring my wristband. It was just one of those plastic charity bands that cost less than a pound, like the yellow LIVESTRONG ones, only mine was a blue BEAT BULLYING one.

'They're the only jewellery she can afford,' Honey sighed heavily, as if this was of great sadness to her.

Indie went, 'That's probably because she spends all her money on patience putting up with you.'

Portia and Star, who were in the room at the time, laughed, so they didn't actually see what I saw. Honey's face twisted into a look of pure hatred, only it wasn't Indie she was looking at; it was Portia.

The big drama of our first week back came on Friday night – a night that would be known forevermore as *The Night of the Soggy Boggies*. We'd often lie on our beds and shoot soggy wads of paper up on the ceiling or onto the mirror using the plastic casing of our Bic pens. But on this particular Friday night, things got a little out of hand.

One minute we were practising our cool dance moves in front of the mirror – well, Honey was anyway, and I think I speak for the world at large when I say she looked absurd – doing a sort of slinky tango with herself. Portia was reading an American *Vogue* I'd brought back from LA. I was pretending to read txt messages from boys who weren't sending them, because there was absolutely no way I'd practise my dance moves with Honey. Of course I practised my dance moves, but I'd slip down to Star's dorm these days for that sort of thing. Everyone looks a bit mad practising dance moves in front of a mirror, but as sorry a business as it is, there's no escaping it.

It's like Star says, 'English boys can't dance for toast so we girls have an obligation to hold up their side as well as our own.' Naturally Indie was immediately voted the most phenomenal dancer in our school – after Tobias, who has been taking special lessons all his life.

(Aloof demeanour note to self: Stop focusing on how marvellous Indie is!)

Anyway, there we were, having a typical Friday night, when Clemmie, Arabella and Georgina came storming into our room, and Arabella propelled a sodden loo roll at us.

Splat!

The noise was enormous, like the sound of a wet bag of sand hitting a wall. It landed on the pin board above Honey's bed (the one where she keeps all the paparazzi shots of herself with famous people). We all watched in stunned silence as the loo roll virtually crawled – like it was alive – slowly down the wall, eventually flopping lifelessly in a soggy mass on Honey's pillow.

Predictably, this was enough to escalate the soggy boggy prank into a full-on dorm war, with sodden loo rolls being hurled through dorms by everyone at everyone. We were behaving 'proper mad,' as the shopkeepers in the village would say.

Miss Bibsmore hobbled up the stairs just in time to

catch Honey, who had filled our bin with water and loo rolls and was dragging it up the wet corridor for an apocalyptic onslaught on Clemmie's dorm.

Miss Bibsmore raised her walking stick and then raised her voice to a level that could shatter glass as she screamed, 'Stop right where you are, Miss O'Hare, you spawn of Satan, you.'

Everyone froze, apart from Honey, obviously.

'Don't. Move. A. Muscle,' Miss Bibsmore repeated.

We all giggled because she was speaking the way super-heroes speak when they are heavily armed with super-strength weapons and powers. All Miss Bibsmore had in the way of superpowers was a limited ability to distribute blues, a history of childhood illnesses and a walking stick.

It surprised no one that Honey totally ignored her. I can't think that even Miss Bibsmore, scary as she is, actually imagines that Satan's spawn are in the least bit receptive to obeying orders squawked by mad House Spinsters, but still she persisted. 'I'm warning you, Miss O'Hare, my temper is on a very short fuse.'

Honey flicked her gorgeously long, blonde, expensively streaked locks across her shoulder and replied calmly, 'Might I remind you who pays your wages, Miss Bibs-more?'

Miss Bibsmore had her bottom lip out. She raised her cane and waved it about menacingly to show she *really* meant business. 'No, Miss O'Hare, you may not remind me of any such thing. However, you might well find yourself gated, or worse, if you don't stand stock-still this minute.'

Honey turned, and for a moment I thought she was about to hurl a soggy boggy at Miss Bibsmore. Instead she mildly remarked, 'We're in the middle of a soggy boggy war here and the battle has reached a crucial stage, if you don't mind!' Which implied that soggy boggies were on par with hard sums or letters home to parents.

Portia, Star, Georgina and all the rest of the girls who were watching the spectacle from the doorways of their respective rooms giggled. Hate Honey though I do, I couldn't help admiring her total lack of fear. Even Georgina was awed. 'Bless,' she said as Honey turned and continued imperiously up the corridor to Clemmie's room and slightly less imperiously commenced propelling her wet missiles at the shrieking girls inside.

I think we were all secretly impressed by Honey's audacity at that moment. Even Indie was giggling at her mettle as the shrieks and laughter of the girls inside being splattered with soggy boggies filled the corridor.

Miss Bibsmore wasn't so in awe, though. Not even slightly. In fact, she used her stick to smash the fire alarm glass, setting off the sprinkler system, and we all ran shrieking into our rooms to rescue our bedding.

Although hitting the fire alarm and setting off the sprinkler system is an age-old favourite with House Spinsters, they usually only resort to it in times of imminent disaster. Because as effective as the deluge is, it means calling up the local fire brigade, waking up the whole dorm, and setting in motion the fire emergency procedures where we all storm off to the tennis courts for registration and a report is filed with Sister, who would be less than impressed.

But Miss Bibsmore is no ordinary House Spinster.

Portia sensibly ignored the procedure, as we knew there was no fire, and started rolling up her duvet, pillow and sheets. I followed suit. Then we helped one another to squeeze our duvets and mattresses out the window of our room onto the hedges below. We weren't the only ones, either. Everyone was on the same page as to what needed to be done. There were mattresses, pillows, duvets and clothing flying from all the bedrooms on the first floor. By the time we got to Honey's bed it was already pretty soggy and heavy, but after a hefty struggle we eventually managed to hurl it out the window as well.

Then we all charged off to the tennis courts for registration, where an explanation of the dud emergency was given to Sister. Our dorm was all totally drenched and freezing by the time we returned to our building, but that didn't stop Honey screaming her head off about Miss Bibsmore being an insane witch and how her father was going to shower her in litigation suits.

Everyone took their place back in the doorways to watch the spectacle. In the silence that followed Honey's rambling rant, Miss Bibsmore calmly and quietly informed Honey that she was officially gated, and then, turning the corridor lights off, she hobbled away. We listened to the *tap, tap, tap*ping of her stick on the stone stairs as we all stood in the soggy darkness, contemplating our behaviour and the possible repercussions to come.

Amazingly enough though, apart from Honey, we all got off scot-free. Well, free-ish. We spent most of the night mopping up the mess and struggling up the stairs with our duvets, mattresses and pillows. Honey's mattress was too wet to sleep on, though, so she went and slept with Georgina in her bed.

'Honey's having a rough ride with wet mattresses this term,' Portia remarked as we lay in the dark. Even though we were exhausted from all the excitement, it was hard to get sleep.

'Perhaps we won't have to murder her after all, darling,' I replied, referring to our joke when we'd swapped mattresses.

'Bob and Sarah will be disappointed,' Portia sighed.

'I know, they would have loved that silver cup.'

'Perhaps we'll have a cup made up anyway and award it to you for your work with mattresses in the dormitory community.'

'You deserve that cup more than me,' I teased.

'No, but you can keep it, darling. Eaglemere is choking on generations of trophies already.'

I fell asleep soon after that. It was the best night's sleep I'd had since coming back. I never would have imagined that sharing a room with a girl like Lady Portia Herrington Briggs could turn out to be the blessing of lifetime.

FOURTEEN

Just One of Those Annual Euro Royal Bash Thingamees

The next morning was Saturday, so after breakfast, cleaning our rooms, going down for registration, attending chapel and two long hours of study followed by lunch, we all decided to take taxis into Windsor for an afternoon of Eades boy spotting. All of us apart from Honey, that is, because she was gated.

This was the first year that we could actually go off on our own into Windsor, so we took quite a lot of time dressing in our most casually stunning outfits and applying and reapplying lip-glosses. I almost felt sorry for Honey when we left her sitting on her bed, her arms folded, a pouty expression on her face.

When Portia asked her if she wanted anything from town she replied archly, 'Why, are you offering to bring me back a fit boy?'

I didn't say anything apart from muttering goodbye.

Sister Constance and her agents (also known as the teachers and House Spinsters) were always reminding us of the school rule for trips into town – 'Go out in threes, stay in threes and return in threes' – so I can't say I was surprised when Star, Georgina and Indie came tumbling into our room and breathlessly announced that they'd meet us in town. I mean, they shared a dorm together, so it was natural that they'd all go into town in a group; and even though local taxis *can* take four passengers, no one wants to sit next to the driver. So it would be childish to take something like that personally, but I did.

This meant that Portia and I had to find some random horsey girl called Anastasia, whom we really didn't know that well, to go to Windsor with us. The whole two miles were spent listening to her endless tales of how many polo players she'd pulled that summer. 'I am such a slut, darlings,' she told us, as if being a slut was a talent. 'But honestly,' she sighed. 'I can't help myself, they are just so gorgeous in their tight jodhpurs. I think I like the Argentineans best, but some of the Australians were rather nice this year. I really am the most dreadful slut, aren't I, darlings?'

Portia and I muttered agreeably and as non-judgementally as we could. Star would have pressed her elbow into my rib to try and make me laugh, but Portia was too aloof for that sort of thing. And I was trying to be.

We had the taxi drop us off at the stone bridge that curves over the River Thames and leads to the castle walls. As Sod's Law would have it, as we walked over the bridge into Windsor, the first Eades boys we spotted were Billy and a bunch of his fit friends. I was determined to be aloof – as serene as a throne – but my face was going to betray me. I knew it was going to as we approached them and the blood started travelling up my feet towards my head. Then Billy's posse peeled off, and it was just Billy walking towards Portia, Anastasia and me, like in one of those cowboy showdowns.

Portia offered to leave too, but I begged her not to. I needed her aloof demeanour as backup, in case my own fell flat on its face. Also Anastasia was still with us. I think she was still babbling on about her polo pulling score over the summer and groaning about what a slut she was.

All thoughts as to why Billy hadn't sent me a txt since Monday flew right out of my head, replaced by the memory of all the steamy txts he *had* sent me. As my legs grew weak from lack of blood, I envisioned myself swooning into a faint like a Victorian heroine, and Billy sweeping me into his arms and snog-aging me into a blissful reality.

My heart was pounding and my pulse was racing as I introduced Anastasia, but once she'd established that Billy wasn't a polo player she strode off on her own to find her polo buddies.

Billy was as fit-looking as ever and wearing really cool

trousers and trainers. He was also wearing a charity band like mine in green. Maybe that was a sign?

'Haven't heard from you in a bit,' he muttered, shoving his hands in his pockets, seemingly unable to make eye contact with me. This was bad. The blood was rushing round my head but I kept my cool(-ish).

'Funny that,' I remarked idly, as if I didn't care in the slightest about his recent lack of txts. I wasn't going to give him the pleasure. Also, looking at him, as a light drizzle started to fall, I realised something else. Now that my initial nerves had subsided, I couldn't help noticing that while my blood may have been displaced from one part of my body to another, my tummy wasn't doing funny tumbly things and my palms weren't sweaty. Could it be possible that I had only *imagined* that I fancied him all this time?

I suppose when a boy saves you from the jaws of a girl-eating dog, it's more or less inevitable that you'll feel a certain amount of emotion, I told myself as he looked up at Portia and asked her about her sabre form. He and Portia knew one another through fencing, and also her brother Tarquin was in his year; so while they chatted away like old friends, I began to feel like a bit of spare leg. I bet Billy was just doing it out of his shame at not txt-ing me, but still, it wasn't very cordial of him. They were virtually cutting me out.

'Busy week?' I interjected in a tragic attempt to turn attention onto myself.

Billy stared at me like I'd interrupted an important board meeting. 'What?'

I looked to Portia for support, but she looked out across the Thames.

'Busy week?' I repeated, as my aloof demeanour deserted me and dived into the Thames – perhaps that was what had caught Portia's notice.

'Pretty much,' he replied in an almost irritated tone. 'You?'

'Seriously busy.' I rolled my eyes in what I hoped looked like a sexy way but I'm pretty sure just look looked freakish.

He still wasn't looking at me. He stuffed his hands in his pockets and rocked back and forth on his feet, which annoyed me. I know that Portia was there so he was probably not in a position to explain things, but still, he was really making me feel rotten.

Portia muttered something about heading off to find Tarkie, but I wasn't going to make it so easy for Billy.

'I've got something to do, actually,' I said importantly. 'Why don't you help Portia find Tarquin, Billy?' I suggested bossily, half expecting that he'd fall on his knees and beg me not to leave.

But he didn't. Instead he said, 'Absolutely,' with a bloody annoying degree of enthusiasm.

'Right, then,' I muttered, adding, 'off I go,' just to make my seriously cringing, embarrassing exit complete.

I wandered off sulkily on my own looking for the others. Star had suggested we all convene in a tea shop past the castle walls, so I made my way along the cobbled streets, weaving my way through the throngs of tourists and students. I regretted not bringing an umbrella as a light drizzle began to fall, but not as much as I regretted a lot of other things. Bloody boys.

And that was when it happened. I walked slap-bang into Freddie and Billy's younger brother, Kevin, as I was turning down a narrow cobbled lane. And not only was my face red but my tummy was doing back flips and tumbles as Freddie smiled at me and said . . .

Well, I don't know what he said actually, my heart was pounding so loudly I couldn't hear a thing. Also my palms were sweating and all I could think of was how fit he looked with his wet hair plastered on his forehead, and then all I could think of was how hideous I must look with my wet hair plastered down my forehead. So instead of saying 'Hi' or something sensible like that, I just stood there like an idiot, watching his lips move and only barely controlling an urge to kiss him.

Kevin asked where Star was, so I told him that I was on my way to meet her in a tea shop farther down the main road. I could tell he wanted more detailed directions, but Freddie took me by the elbow and led me around the corner, and Kevin peeled off, as if some secret signal had been exchanged.

I couldn't see Freddie's security men, but they must have

been about somewhere, probably disguised as tourists. I didn't get a chance to have a look around for them, because once we were out of the rain in the shelter of an awning, Freddie took my face in his hands and kissed me long and slowly.

It was so lovely, just like the last time we'd kissed, only without Honey taking a photograph of us with her mobile and selling it to the tabloids. As his hands wove their way through my hair, I closed my eyes and allowed myself to relax, when suddenly Kevin was back again and coughing awkwardly by my ear.

Freddie ignored him and carried on kissing me, but I opened my eyes.

'Sorry, Calypso, sorry, Freddie, but which tea shop did you say Star was in?'

Not only did Freddie not open his eyes or take his lips off mine, he made 'piss off' signals at his friend and kept on kissing me. Which is the most marvellously cool thing that has ever happened to me.

'Sorry,' repeated the now-sodden Kevin, who shuffled off back into the rain, which had picked up force during our kissing. The awning wasn't offering us much respite anymore.

'Let's make a dash for it,' Freddie suggested, and we ran into a pizza place nearby that was popular with both Eades and Saint Augustine's.

Freddie ordered a pizza, half pepperoni (him) and half Hawaiian (me), but the best thing was, even while choosing and ordering, he didn't take his hand away from mine.

'It's so great to see you,' he told me earnestly. 'Why haven't you been responding to my txt messages, Miss Calypso Kelly?' he asked, opening my palm and running his deeply tanned fingers along my life line and up to my wrist.

Mesmerised as I was by his touch, I couldn't help being a bit cross about his accusation that *I* was the one not txt-ing *him*! Boys are always doing that.

'Me?' I asked indignantly. 'You haven't sent me so much as one txt since Monday.' I didn't mention that Billy was guilty of the same crime.

'Rubbish, I've sent several. Dozens. Hundreds possibly.' He said it so confidently that I couldn't really argue. Probably he'd been really busy at school, I told myself and changed the subject. 'Anyway, Sarah and Bob have said I can go to La Fiesta. Star, Georgina and me all bought our outfits in LA. I'm wearing *the* most adorably short little . . .' I hesitated, hoping his imagination would take over. 'Well, anyway, I won't describe it completely and ruin the surprise, but let's just say that it's more on trend than the tragic dress I wore to the Eades social.'

'That's the best dress I've ever seen on a girl,' he teased, referring to the last dress he'd seen me in, which was several sizes too big and safety-pinned up the back by Sister Regina.

'But anyway, this particular dress is soooo seriously phenomenal.'

Instead of laughing or showing any curiosity, he didn't even look up. He just kept tracing his hand along my wrist and up my arm. I felt all tingly and excited because here I was, an ordinary regular American girl – a commoner – sitting in a pizza shop in Windsor having my hand stroked by Prince Freddie outside one of his very own family castles. It was just so madly cool I was blushing, and even though sometimes the best things are expressed without words, after a while I became desperate for him to say something like how excited he was that he was going to see me at the ball.

But he didn't.

So eventually I pushed the issue myself. 'You *are* going to La Fiesta, aren't you?' I asked, looking deeply into his ink-blue eyes.

He looked away as if wondering where the pizzas were and ran one of his long-fingered hands through his jet black locks.

'No, actually, I've got a prior engagement.'

'A prior engagement?' I repeated, just because, well just because I was floored and I say dumb things when I'm floored.

He started holding my hand again, which was nice, but then he said, 'The pizza's taking a while,' as if he wanted to change the subject or maybe he thought eating pizza was more interesting than my tiny skirt and cashmere top with jewels on it, or the ball.

'What sort of prior engagement?' I probed lightly, looking around as if I was really desperate to get to the bottom of the slow pizza mystery as well.

He looked distracted although still managing to look distressingly fit. When I'm distracted I look mildly insane and addled. 'Sorry, what do you mean?' he asked, smiling his easy I'm-the-heir-to-the-throne-and-nothing-bothers-me smile.

'You said you had a prior engagement on the night of the La Fiesta Ball?' I reminded him, but all he said was, 'Oh, at last, here comes our pizza.'

As they placed our pizza in the middle of our little table, I wondered how on earth he could even contemplate eating after dropping a bombshell like that on me. All my school life at Saint Augustine's I had longed to attend one of these balls, and now that I was actually going to one, my prince charming (I'm being sarcastic) was off on a 'prior engagement,' whatever that means.

He was already chewing on a piece of pizza but sort of grinning at me at the same time. So I took a slice of the Hawaiian side and pretended I was just as hungry and not churned up inside in the least.

As we ate, he spoke of his holiday and asked about mine. I fell into the trap of pretending nothing was wrong, and the afternoon slipped by in companionable fake conversations. All I really wanted to discuss was this wretched prior engagement.

So why didn't I press him?

Why were we acting like I wasn't gutted?

Was I actually becoming English?

After the pizza we ordered tea, and as I was squeezing the lemon into mine (I normally take milk but I was enjoying the symmetry of drinking my Earl Grey just like Freddie) he said, 'It's a sort of Annual Euro Royal Bash thing we hold every year. Hellish, but it goes with the job.'

Bloody royals, I thought to myself grumpily as I looked outside at the rain.

Freddie laughed.

'What's so funny?'

'Bloody royals,' he mimicked, and I suddenly realised I'd actually thought out loud. I soooo had to stop doing that.

'Sorry.'

'Don't be, I say it all the time,' he teased.

As much as I wanted to stay with him, I was beginning to get seriously worried about the time and about getting back to school. Our curfew was four-thirty, and if we were late we'd get a gating, which would mean no more kisses and pizzas with Freddie. I began to panic about where the others were and whether I should call them. It's amazing how quickly time flies when you're with a prince down-playing a topic that's practically burning an ulcer into your stomach.

I didn't get a chance to probe further because just then, Kevin, Star and Georgina burst in on us. 'Calypso, quick,' Star insisted crossly. 'We've ordered a taxi and it's picking us up at the tea shop where you were *meant* to be meeting us! Indie is waiting there on her own.'

Star didn't even look at Freddie. She's never really forgiven him for the way he treated me over the tabloid photograph Honey took. At the time he actually believed Honey's story that I was some sort of Mata Hari-type girl, just dying to get my fifteen minutes of fame.

'What about Portia?' I asked. The rain was bucketing down now.

'She's probably spending some time with her brother,' Georgina replied.

'I can call Tarkie and check,' Freddie offered, pulling his BlackBerry out.

'I think we should,' I pressed. So Freddie made a quick call on his mobile and confirmed that Tarkie and Portia were together and that Tarkie was dropping his sister off at school in a bit.

So that was that. I said an awkward goodbye to Freddie, no kiss, not even an air kiss. More importantly, he made no promise to txt or call. I know we were with a whole pile of friends, but still . . .

Georgina, Star and I flew out the door, into the rain, and legged it to the tea shop.

I understood that Freddie had a prior engagement and that as heir to the throne, that went with the job, but I couldn't help wondering how Billy would have behaved in the same situation. Maybe I'd been a bit too hasty in dismissing Billy? Maybe he'd been awkward with me on the bridge out of guilt? He *was* in the Lower Sixth studying for his As, so it was hardly surprising *he* was busy. Freddie, on the other hand, wasn't even doing GCSEs, because Eades was too grand to even pretend to follow government curriculum, so he had no excuse at all. Bloody boys.

Indie was already sitting in the back of the local taxi, and I ended up being the one in the seat beside the driver, so I had to keep turning around to speak to the others. Georgina pressed me for details about my afternoon with Freddie, so I told her how he wasn't going to La Fiesta due to a prior engagement.

I made the words 'prior engagement' sound like some sort of weird, sordid activity, when Indie piped up, 'He's going to the ball at Windsor Castle. It's a sort of Annual Euro Royal Bash Thingamee. Daddy *always* makes me go.' She groaned, as if it was the most taxing evening imaginable. Only I bet it wasn't.

I looked at her stunning face framed by the long corn-braided hair and wondered how long I could go on pretending that I wasn't sick with jealousy.

'Poor you,' I told her as if I really, really meant it, and then the taxi driver let out a little windy pop.

FIFTEEN

The Familiar Sound of My Dreams Crashing around My Feet

The light drizzle had become a heavy rain, but we had the taxi drop us off outside the school in the hope we could still sneak in unnoticed and avoid a gating. We crept through the gates and snuck along the edges of Pullers' Wood, which smelt woodsy and beautiful in the rain. Finally we filed past the library, bent low so we wouldn't be spotted. We were an hour past curfew, and it was starting to get dark. If we were sprung now, it would mean a definite gating.

Our adrenaline was pumping at the possible repercussions, so we were trying to keep utterly silent, muffling even our panting breaths as we raced into the main building. My clothes were clinging to me, and I had only one thing on my mind – a hot shower – so I was a bit irritated when Star slowed me down as we were entering the main building and started whispering to me. 'Why are you wasting your time on a royal snob like Freddie, Calypso? Billy is nicer, fitter and a better fencer.'

I didn't respond. Partly because I was too desperate to get indoors to get embroiled in an argument in a cold corridor and partly because I was starting to agree that Billy would be a lot less trouble. And then my txt-alert rang.

So how short is this little skirt precisely?
Freds

I showed the txt to Star. 'Don't you think that's weird that after not txt-ing me all week and accusing me of not txt-ing him, he suddenly sends this?' I asked, which was another way of saying my life wasn't worth living now that Freddie wasn't going to the ball.

'How pervy! Let me have that,' she demanded.

I waited impatiently as she turned her back and typed in a message, and then she held out the mobile to show me what she'd written.

Bugger off x C

Before I could stop her, she pressed SEND.

'Why did you do that?' I asked in horror.

She kissed me on my wet cheek. 'Because you're worth it,' she teased in a piss-take of a famous hair commercial.

I understood that she'd never forgiven Freddie for believing Honey over me during the whole tabloid debacle, but he *was* in a really difficult position, and he had apologised grovellingly. As far as I was concerned it was water under the bridge (along with my aloof demeanour), and to quote Star, he was worth it!

I quickly sent a counter txt.

That was Star, seriously short indeed x C

As soon as we got to the dorms, the other girls charged straight off to their room while I crept into mine, hoping against hope that Miss Bibsmore hadn't done her rounds. I was incredulous when Honey greeted me looking freakishly chirpy and pleased to see me. She was posing in front of the mirror as if Mario Testino was in the room with his camera.

I was surprised to see Portia's phone lying on her bed. I presumed I'd made it back before her, as Freddie had told me that Tarquin was bringing her back in a bit.

'Hello, darling, how was it?' Honey squeaked with overfriendliness. She was even smiling at me – well, smiling as best she could through her collagen-enhanced baubleshaped lips.

'Yaah, fine,' I lied as I started to peel off my wet clothes and dry my hair. 'How was your day?'

'Terrific, actually. I went down to the pet shed and gave Absinthe and Dorothy a run. I hope you don't mind; they just looked so sweet together. Here, look at this,' she insisted as she grabbed her mobile, the same one she'd used to take the fateful shot she'd sold to the tabloids. The screen showed me a picture of Absinthe and Dorothy in the pet run together, looking like the best of friends.

I had just pulled on a dry pair of jeans and a t-shirt when we heard the now-familiar *tap, tap, tap* of Miss Bibsmore's stick on the stone stairwell and gave one another one of those 'Aaaaghhh! Here she comes!' looks. As Miss Bibsmore surveyed our room from the doorway, Portia's message alarm went.

'And where might Miss Briggs be?' she asked, looking at the vibrating phone. 'Curfew was over an hour ago.'

'She's in the loo,' Honey told her without even turning around, brushing her hair nonchalantly. 'Slight case of the runs,' she added, elaborating unnecessarily as she wrinkled up her nose job.

Seemingly satisfied, Miss Bibsmore hobbled out and continued her rounds.

I flopped on my bed, still dazed and confused. On the one hand Freddie had seemed really pleased to see me, but on the other I hated the thought of going to my very first ball without him. And there was still the issue of Billy. So much for my gut feeling that I'd know which one I fancied the most after seeing them. If anything I was more in the dark than ever.

Portia's message alarm kept going off, but just as I was about to ask Honey how long she'd been in the loo, Honey spoke to me. Not in a piss-take of my accent or a spiteful way, just in a normal friendly voice. When I say 'friendly,' of course I mean friendly in that special menacing feline way that Honey has.

'So, darling, did you manage to catch up with your two paramours, Billy and Freddie?'

Before I could answer and explain that actually I didn't, strictly speaking, have *two* paramours (and who calls boys paramours anyway?), Portia came panting through the door, drenched to the skin. 'Has Miss Bibsmore done her rounds yet?' she asked anxiously.

'Ages ago; but don't worry, I covered for you. Said you were in the lav, darling – with the runs,' Honey smarm-ed.

'Oh, thanks,' Portia replied. Then she spotted her phone. 'Oh, thank goodness, my phone. I've been running around Windsor looking everywhere for it. I had Freddie ringing and ringing it for me.'

What? I screamed, although thankfully the word didn't actually make it out of my voice box, which had fallen to my stomach along with my heart. I watched her open the back of her mobile. 'Odd, I could have sworn I'd left it off.' She checked her SIM card.

Honey said, 'Perhaps your mind was on other things, darling.'

All I was thinking was, Why was Portia with Freddie? How did they meet up?

He'd given me the impression that he was heading back to Eades . . . well, maybe he didn't actually give me an impression, but I'd presumed that he'd leave Windsor when I did.

'I thought you were with your brother?' I said, trying to keep the jealousy I was starting to feel out of my tone.

She answered lightly, 'Oh I was, but he had to go off and so I had some pizza with Freddie. I was absolutely famished.' She smiled at me.

How much pizza can one boy eat? I thought to myself – only I must have said it out loud because Portia replied, 'An infinite amount, believe me. Tarquin frequently eats two large pizzas on his own in one sitting.'

'Oh, so Tarquin was there as well,' I said with relief.

'No, just Freddie and me,' she replied, turning to face the mirror as she rubbed at her long hair with a towel.

'Just you and Freddie!' Honey repeated, only she said it suggestively, looking at me pointedly while raising one perfectly sculptured eyebrow.

'That's right, Honey. Freddie and I, me and Freddie, we ate some pizza.'

Honey looked stung by Portia's tone, which, while not nasty, was definitely warning, especially for Portia, who was always so calm and regal in her demeanour.

'I was just saying . . .'

Portia turned around and faced Honey directly. 'I'd much rather you didn't trouble yourself in my affairs, Honey.'

'Whatever,' Honey replied sulkily.

'Oh, and by the way Freddie asked me to give you a message,' Portia said to me.

'What, are you his carrier pigeon now?' Honey said in a bad attempt at sarcasm.

Portia didn't deign to acknowledge her rudeness with a response.

I sat there mute, desperate to hear what message Freddie had sent me through Portia, but Honey added, 'She might be American but she does own a mobile, Portia. I'm sure Freddie is perfectly capable of sending her his own messages.'

My cheeks burned with embarrassment. Portia looked at me meaningfully, but then the dinner bell rang, and Star and the others came in on their way to the refectory. Star surprised me by throwing her arms around me and crying out melodramatically. 'My best friend, Calypso! Navel buddies forever!' Georgina and Indie giggled, but I didn't know what to think. Had she told Indie that I'd had to take mine out and made me sound tragically under the thumb of Sarah and Bob? Indie and Georgina joined the group hug. Oh, how I wished I was alone with Portia so she could give me Freddie's message.

'So did you get away with it, then?' Star asked as we walked arm in arm down the narrow stairs.

'Completely fine. Miss Bibsmore came in after I'd already changed. And you?'

'Same. The old dear hadn't a clue.'

'By the way, thanks for covering for me, Calypso,' Portia added.

'Thank Honey. I actually thought you were back,' I replied, still feeling mixed up about her chumming around with Freddie in Windsor, and more importantly wanting to know what my message was.

Star snorted. 'Saint Honey, covering for her dear room-mate. Who would have thought?'

Honey, who was walking behind her on the narrow stairs, gave Star a little shove. Not hard enough to make her fall or anything, just enough to take the wind out of her sails. Probably because she couldn't think of a cutting enough retort.

'You're not still upset about Freddie not going to the La Fiesta Ball, are you, darling?' Star asked me as we waited for our plates to be piled with grey slops.

Yes! Of course I'm upset; I've waited for this ball all my boarding school life, and now Freddie isn't even going to be there! And Billy doesn't seem to fancy me anymore and Freddie's sent me a message and I still don't know what it is and you've dropped fencing and have become inseparable from Indie and . . . well, the list of my vexations was endless.

'No, I'm totally fine,' I told her with faux insouciance.

When we sat down, Star sat beside me on one side and Georgina on the other. Star was even making sarcastic remarks to Honey again. All was just as it should be. Maybe I'd been reading too much into everything, I tried to tell myself. Princes have commitments, and he had sent me a txt and a message via Portia. I still had to find out what Freddie had said. I took a deep breath and attempted to tap back into my aloof demeanour, but it didn't work. It didn't feel normal at all, really. Things *had* changed between Star and me now that Indie was here, and I knew it wasn't Indie's fault. In fact, she was actually really, really nice.

I looked across at Portia, who was sitting too far away to talk to directly. Bugger.

Georgina reminded me kindly that Indie wasn't going to the La Fiesta Ball either, as if *that* might make me feel better, and then Star announced that perhaps none of us should go to the ball.

'Think about it,' Star enthused, swirling her slops. 'We could have a house party at my estate. My parents are always so stoned they'd probably think it was *their* party.'

'Oh my god, darling, you're a genius. That sounds soooo perfect!' Georgina gushed.

'Oh my god, a proper party with champagne and caviar, you mean?' Clemmie chimed. Clemmie had taken to reading *House and Garden* and other domestic design magazines. She'd decided she wanted to be an events coordinator, which is a fancy way of saying party planner.

'Vintage all the way at Chez Dirge, darling,' Star joked. 'Well, Jim Beam and Coke anyway,' she added. 'Actually, guess what! Daddy's installed a Jim Beam water feature in the chill room.'

'Oh my god, how cool! Is it actually a fountain that spurts out Jim Beam?' Georgina asked.

'Better. It's this amazing statue of the Black Angel of Death that pees out Jim Beam into this Japanese black rock pool. Soooo typically Daddy.' She shook her head at her mad father the way most fathers shake their heads over their mad daughters.

'Oh, I adore Jim Beam,' Georgina moaned rapturously. 'It's so rock and roll. Like caviar.'

'Jim Beam, caviar, and boys on ice,' Arabella sang in a sultry accent.

Star added, 'We could even invite some fit boys from the local village. It could be really wild, actually. Maybe Daddy will buy some more quad bikes – think how cool that would be! We could have an all-week-long mad party screaming about in the mud.'

Everyone looked so thrilled at the prospect of not going to the ball that I wanted to be sick. Then there was an almighty crash of pots and pans in the kitchen, and for minute I thought it was the sound of my dreams crashing around my feet.

'But what about our outfits?' I asked, trying not to sound hysterical. 'Our cashmere tops?' I reminded the girls. 'Our shoes!' My voice was beginning to screech.

Star threw a pea at me. 'What about them, silly? We can wear them at our house party. Actually I'm kind of bored by the whole ball thing anyway, it's soooo Year Nine – even the Year Eights go now.'

So Year Nine. Her words seemed to sum up my life. It was all right for Star and Georgina to be blasé about the ball; they'd been to squillions of them. And Indie had her own royal ball to go to so of course she wasn't fussed. But I'd been waiting all my school life for this.

As I looked around the table at the excited faces of my friends, the only person who looked as underwhelmed as me by the whole idea of Star's party was Honey, who definitely wouldn't be invited as Star unashamedly loathed her.

I never imagined the day would come when Honey and I would feel as one about anything, but then again she had covered for Portia. And, she had also taken Dorothy out for a little run. Maybe Honey had changed?

'Of course you're invited too, Portia,' Star called down to her end of the table.

'Thanks so much, Star, but unfortunately I have a prior engagement,' Portia called back.

'A prior engagement?' I repeated. She had used the exact same phrase as Freddie had used, in the exact same casual, it's-so-not-a-big-deal tone.

'You too?' Indie asked. 'The Annual Euro Royal Bash Thingamee?'

Portia groaned as she nodded. 'Don't you just loathe them?'

'What can you do, though?' Indie groaned. 'I've got to go too. Daddy said there's no way I can get out of it.'

'At least Freddie will be there,' Portia added, looking at me as she said it. And I decided then what his message must have been. He must be taking Portia to the ball, I told myself as I listened to these girls chat about the horrors of attending balls I would never in my wildest dreams get a chance to go to.

'What about your brother?' I asked.

'Of course Tarkie will be there, but he'll never dance with me.'

Then the image of Portia and Freddie dancing together royal cheek to royal cheek flashed into my head, and I couldn't even bring myself to look at her.

SIXTEEN

An Emotional Game of Chess

S aint Augustine's fencing salle was pretty impressive
for a girls' school – especially given that loads of the
girls only took fencing as a way to meet the boys at
Eades. We had three pistes, all with the latest electrical
point scoring systems, and a salle d'armes covered in old
photographs and fencing memorabilia along the walls. We
had once also been fortunate enough to have one of
Britain's top fencing masters, Professor Sullivan.

But those days were gone.

I was really going to miss Professor Sullivan. I liked to
think I was his favourite pupil, based mainly on the fact
that he gave Star and me a lift to Star's place in London
one exeat. That, and the fact that he said he thought I'd 'go
far.' I quite liked the idea that someone thought me
capable of going far, as opposed to 'going *too* far!' which
is what Bob is always telling me.

There were plenty of younger girls coming up in sabre,

but Portia and I were the only two actual sabreurs left in the school now that Star had dropped out. That meant we'd have to rely on Emille from the *épée* team to fence sabre in interschool matches. It wasn't ideal. We'd had a few practise bouts over the past weeks, and Mr Wellend warned us that he'd be stepping up the pressure in earnest this week. I was quite happy for him to step up the pressure. The BNFTs were coming up after half term, and if I wanted to be included on the Olympic team for 2008, I was going to have to make the Nationals.

I'd had to force myself to be civil to Portia ever since she'd told me she was going to the ball with Freddie. Okay, I know she hadn't actually said she was going *with* Freddie, but I was uneasy about the situation just the same. She'd passed on Freddie's message eventually, and while it wasn't the bombshell I'd imagined, it was a massive let-down. 'Tell Calypso I'll txt her.'

I'd had plenty of time to brood about everything, and my brooding, coupled with the fact that the only txt message I received from him since Windsor was the one in which I replied by telling him to bugger off (or rather Star had told him on my phone) made me desperately worried.

As I attached Portia's back to the electrical cord that ran up to the recording device, I was fully aware that I didn't have the cool head, the *sang-froid* that Professor Sullivan was always on about.

We have to check that all parts of our electric kit are

working before play begins, which you do by tapping your sabre on your sword guard, glove, the lame metal jacket and the mask before the salute. Even as Portia and I tapped our weapons, I felt the rawness of my emotions begin to take over, which manifested when I 'tapped' her blade clean out of her hand.

While sabre is a combat sport, it's also highly intellectual and requires a great deal of balance. Emotion has no place on the piste, and I was one big ball of emotion as Bell End called the words 'En garde! Ready! Play!'

The attacker in sabre is at an advantage because she can vary her footwork and her method of delivering an attack. Whereas defending at sabre is more difficult as right of way is initially given to the attacker. Although the arm starts moving first, it doesn't straighten quite as fast as with a thrusting weapon, so even with the electrical recording stuff, it is difficult for the referee/ president overseeing the bout to decide who has the right of way. Basically, he'll be looking for the first person to straighten her arm, which in a nutshell means that you *can* play dirty.

The object is to make cuts with a hit that registers on the recorder, but not hard enough to hurt your opponent. But if you deliver strong cuts from the elbow, say, you can inflict a lot of bruising. Most sabreurs deliver actual cuts from the wrist because it gives them more control and accuracy with their weapon.

I could feel my anger towards Portia taking total control

of me. I did try and get a grip as I advanced with crossovers down the piste towards Lady Herrington Briggs, with her aloof demeanour and her royal ball and possibly my Freddie. As much as I knew I needed to clear my head of these thoughts, my heart just wouldn't let me. What I couldn't say to her in words, I was going to explain with my blade.

I knew the way Portia thought on the piste. I knew her inclination for speed and accuracy, and she knew my skill for aggressive cuts and my well-known talent for elegant *prise de fer*. We had joked only last week in fact that we could play one another's game as actors to perfection because we knew each other's form so well.

I think she knew what was coming when our swords were in line and she first threatened my target area. I stepped forward rapidly without straightening my arm, engaged her blade and as I took it with a classic circular parry of tierce, we were so close it might have looked to an onlooker like a lovers' embrace. But all the wrong emotions were in that embrace – I was not paying attention to my footwork. As I made another attack, I lost my footing and fell.

Bell End went ballistic. 'I told you, think with your brain, move with your body, slam 'em with your blade, Kelly. That's slam your opponent, not the bloody floor, ya idiot.'

Bell End may not have been as grand as Professor Sullivan, but he was bang-on in his assessment. I acknowledged this and tried to regain my lost *sang-froid*, but my humiliation after the stumble had only served to rattle me further. My form didn't improve, and after the bout, Portia and I took off our masks and shook hands formally, but neither of us spoke to the other. She knew what I knew now. I had it in for her.

Bell End was furious. 'Never seen such a waste of electricity in me life. And you're meant to be the captain of the bloody team, Kelly. One more performance like that and you can wave goodbye to your captaincy.'

'Yes, Bell End, I mean Mr Wellend,' I agreed as the tears welled in my eyes. I knew I was out of line . . . and worse, so did Portia. While we were showering and changing back into our uniforms, she didn't so much as look at me. She wasn't the sort of girl to have an argument. She was too regal and well brought up for that, and I didn't have the mettle to engage with her *off* the piste.

So there it was. Thanks to my own jealousy, I was now living in a dorm with two girls who hated me. I suspect Bell End was starting to think along the same lines as Bob – I was going *too* far.

As I lay in bed that night I realised I had behaved badly and I wanted to apologise, but I couldn't in front of Honey. And later when Honey started snoring and Portia was turning her light out, my shame only served to render me mute.

She wished me goodnight, though.

'Goodnight, Portia,' I replied in a tone that suggested we were as close as we had been the first week of term.

With Honey's evil on one side of me and Portia's disdain on the other, a sense of isolation engulfed me.

SEVENTEEN

Nothing Changes, Everything Changes

I n our first week back, Portia and I had shared seditious asides about Mrs Obar and her lack of qualifications to teach Latin. We even told her we'd be complaining to our parents. But the truth was, Portia didn't want to trouble her grieving father, and I didn't want to trouble Bob and Sarah, who were always very busy trying to make the money to send me here. While they didn't really understand what GCSEs even were, they were always madly impressed by my teachers whenever they met them.

Of course the lay teachers behave wildly different with parents than they do with students – I call it the Hypocritical Oath. The female teachers are the worst. It's really sick the way they fawn over parents and flirt with fathers – even Sarah agrees, although she'd probably adore Mrs Obar because she's so old, not to mention married. Not that marriage would stop Mrs Obar from flirting with Bob. Portia and I once even caught her flirting with Bell

End! 'Oh, Mr Bell End, stop, you're making me laugh!'
she cried. Only she called him Mr Wellend, and while her
words said 'stop' as we peeped from behind the wall, she
was stroking his muscles, yuk!

'Slut,' I'd whispered in Portia's ear, which made her
giggle.

'Tart,' she'd agreed, which made me snort with laughter
– and then we got caught by Bell End, who'd chased us out
of the salle and called us all manner of horrible names.

But that was then.

Ever since that practise bout we were unofficially not on
speakers, as Nancy Mitford would say. That is to say, we
still spoke, but only to maintain the barest of civilities.

Now I sat alone in Latin, leaving Portia to sit next to
Indie.

'Thirty-seven long years teaching girls like you the why-
fors and whereabouts of this and that,' Mrs Obar rambled
on, 'well, it's taken its toll on me, it has,' she complained –
which isn't even proper English let alone Latin. All she
ever wrote on the board were things that were in our
textbook, but she never worked through any of the ex-
ercises we'd be questioned on in our exams at the end of
the year, or anything useful like that.

Just the same, because she was a teacher, we had to
pretend to be madly awed. Otherwise she'd shower us in
blues, and there are only so many times you can slack down
a teacher and trail on down to the Year Seven dorms –
which were in another building – and talk them into doing

your lines for you. Also this year's bunch of Year Sevens were incredibly mature and hardly worshiped us at all, bless them.

Portia, true to her word, had persuaded her young cousin to do my French lines for me, but I obviously couldn't count on her goodwill a second time.

At the end of each class, Mrs Obar would pile us with work from the exercise book, which we'd then have to struggle with unaided as well as do our basic course work that formed part of our overall GCSE mark. It was a no-win situation.

It was like being on a treadmill.

Wake up.

Get dressed.

Clean our rooms.

Registration (so the school could check that none of us had escaped in the night).

Go to chapel for prayers and school news.

Attend classes.

Fence.

Eat grey slops.

Attend more classes.

Feed our pets and take them for a run.

Clean out the pet shed.

Do prep.

Go to study.

Go to the ref for more inedible grey slops.

Do still more study.

Shower.

Go to bed.

Read until lights out.

Sleep – and in my case brood over my lack of txts from Freddie and Billy.

We were all exhausted by the time exeat weekend came along, and because things had been so different between us, I was delighted that Star still wanted me to stay at her place in Derbyshire.

In the limo on the way up I admitted that I was pleased she'd invited me. 'Don't be mad, of course you have to stay. You always have to stay. You're my best friend, idiot.'

'Well, we hardly spend any time together anymore, and . . .'

'We spend loads of time together; it's just that we don't spend all our time alone together anymore thanks to you,' she said, pinching me in the side to make me laugh.

'Thanks to me?' I exclaimed, fighting her off.

'Yes, you're the one who ruined our status as the school freaks, remember?'

I pinched her back and dropped the topic. I didn't want to mention Indie or her dropping fencing, because then I'd have to mention Portia, and I was too embarrassed to go there.

We were in the limo on the way up to Derbyshire when my txt alert sounded.

Is there life on Planet Girl? Freds x

This time I didn't show the txt to Star for fear that she might tell him to bugger off again. I waited to reply until we were at her estate and she'd gone off to the kitchen to steal some sweets.

Where r u? x C
Windsor. & u? Freds x

I imagined him in his castle with his parents, the king and queen, and thought carefully about how I should reply. In the end I opted for something more exotic than the total truth.

About to go quad bike riding. x C
Alright 4 some! Freds x

I was so pleased that he was impressed. Even though we didn't actually *go* quad bike riding, it wasn't a total lie. We did *talk* about riding the quads, and Star's father, Tiger, was quad bike riding with friends all weekend.

The truth was we were so tired from three weeks of hard work all we could do was laze about in Star's enormous, king-sized, black-patent four-poster bed, with its heavy maroon drapery, eating sweets and watching DVDs. Star is so laid back she even told me I could keep Dorothy in the room. Even though most rabbits aren't house trained,

Star was positive Dorothy would do her wee and poos in the en suite, but of course she didn't, so the whole room had to be sprayed with Febreze.

Star even tried to train her by rushing her off to the loo and rubbing her paws in the wood shavings like you do when you train a cat, but it wasn't wildly effective. Hilda and Brian stayed with us too, and all three seemed to get on surprisingly well, apart from when Brian slithered over me in the night and I woke up screaming and had to pretend I'd had a nightmare. Star would be mortified if she thought I'd screamed because of Brian.

We kept talking about doing stuff, but neither of us pressed the issue. Even on Saturday night when a few bands and their flunkies turned up for a party, neither of us felt like going down or even playing our traditional pranks.

I was just happy to be alone with Star, hanging out just like we used to. Neither of us touched on any subject other than sweets, movies and our pets. We had a pet trick competition, but as we were the only two judges, it always ended up in a tie. But we liked that.

Star was trying to give up fags, and I was helping her by remembering to slap the nicotine patches on her.

'Oh, Sister Nicotine, you're such a good nurse,' she said as I stuck a patch on her one evening.

I had developed a special make-believe voice and old-dear walk for my part. 'Come on, luvvie take your medicine like a good little dear.' Then, out of the blue, Star confronted me about Portia.

'So what's up with you and Portia?' she said as I smoothed the patch on her shoulder.

'What do you mean, what's up? We share a dorm; we're perfectly civil.'

'Aaah yes, civil. Civility can cover a multitude of sins, darling, we both know that.'

'Well, she started it.'

'Started what?'

'I don't know what.'

'Well then why don't *you* stop it. Talk to her.'

'But that's just it. You can't talk to *her*. She's seriously . . .' I struggled to find the phrase I needed – something other than stuck-up.

Star helped me out by suggesting words like 'nice,' 'decent,' 'respectful' and 'loyal.' 'Look, Calypso, I saw you fencing with Portia the other day, going for her like you were Zorro or something. What were you thinking?'

'You were there! In the salle? Why didn't you tell me?' I shouted angrily.

'Calm down. Look, I came to see you, okay? If you want to know the truth I felt bad about everything. Dropping fencing, not spending enough time with you, everything. And then when I saw you going at Portia like that, I couldn't believe it was you!'

I dropped my head. 'I know,' I replied quietly.

'Why, then?'

'Everything's changed, Star,' I told her, and as I heard the words came out of my mouth I felt like Pandora opening up the box that would change the world forever.

Star ignored me for a bit, so I pushed the point. 'Come on, Star, you know it has. You're always with Indie now.'

She looked annoyed, and Star can look wildly scary when she's cross. 'Nothing's changed, Calypso,' she insisted in a voice that brooked no argument. 'Nothing, apart from your attitude.'

I made a decision not to push the point, but the gulf between us was palpable in that moment. I knew both of us could feel it, just as much as we could feel our own hearts beating. And then Star said, 'Shall we have another pet trick competition, then?'

And the gulf closed as quickly as it had opened. At least for the time being.

'You do realise,' she said on Sunday as we prepared to head back to school, 'that we haven't left this room, other than to go to the kitchen to steal food, all weekend?'

Our small weekend bags were already packed, Brian was wrapped around Star's neck and Hilda was peeping out of her blazer pocket. I was cuddling Dorothy as I looked around the bomb site of the room. It wasn't pretty with all our sweet wrappers and pizza boxes and DVD cases strewn about the bed and floor, not to mention the animal droppings.

'I think it's called growing old,' I said, cuddling Dorothy into my chest and kissing her wriggly little nose.

'No wonder my parents take drugs! Look at what we've become, Calypso!' She marched over to her bed and left a fifty-pound note on the pillow for the cleaner.

'We are disgustingly lazy,' I agreed.

'Even Daddy's been quad bike riding most the weekend,' she pointed out.

'True,' I agreed. 'Also your mother's been having her charity meetings.'

'So, basically at the tender age of fifteen we're already worse than drug-taking rock and rollers! We didn't even drink any Jim Beam from the Jim Beam feature in the chill room! We're boring slobs, and now I don't even smoke anymore,' she said as we clambered into one of her father's Range Rovers, where Ray was waiting to drive us back.

Just then, Tiger and one of his friends pulled up beside us on their quad bikes.

'Coming for a quick rage round the ranch, babes?' Tiger called out to us over the roar of the engines.

We looked at one another, left our bags with Ray and jumped on the back of the bikes. I got on with Tiger and held on to his leather jacket tightly as we pelted at breathtaking speed out into the fields across the streams and trout-filled river, through the woods and rocky crags. The wheels churned up mud, splattering our clothes, our faces and our hair. Tiger's friend rode beside us with Star. Even though we'd ridden the quad bikes on our own at the same breathtaking speed, we screamed and screamed and screamed like terrified children.

An hour later, caked in wet mud, we climbed into the Range Rover. I felt soooo deliriously happy, like a child coming off a fairground ride. I looked at Star, but instead of saying something relatable like 'Wow!' she said, 'Why don't you like Indie?' in the tone of voice you might use if you were asking why someone didn't like Brussels sprouts. Ray shut our door, and Star fumbled around to find the seat belt.

'I don't *hate* Indie,' I said with a little too much force. After all, I didn't hate Indie. How could anyone hate Indie? It was just that unlike me, she was so much like Star. They both loved their minor chord compositions, they were both brave and fearless, they were both self-possessed and cool.

'Good,' she agreed with an edge of warning to her voice. 'It would really piss me off if you did.' Then she gave my hand a squeeze as if everything was okay.

EIGHTEEN

A New Kind of Enemy

Back at school, the teachers ratcheted up the pressure another notch. But that was cool because with all the GSCE course work I didn't even have the time to monitor my lack of txt messages. My parents relied on e-mails to communicate, and the rest of my friends were here with me at school, so apart from Billy and Freddie there was no one left to txt me. Still it was dispiriting, especially when Portia's message alert was going off incessantly.

The longer I left it to patch things up with her the worse it became. I knew that, but I avoided the issue by hanging out in Star, Georgina and Indie's room.

I didn't want to make an enemy out of Portia, I really didn't. I'd never had an enemy like Portia before. Honey, now, *she* was my idea of an enemy. Lady Portia Herrington Briggs, though, was far too magisterial to express her feelings about someone as lowly as me.

The most powerful weapon Portia had in her arsenal was my own guilt, and that included how I felt about the photo of her family by her bed. Every time I looked at that photograph I wanted to make up. Even without the reminder of her loss, I actually liked Portia and I desperately wanted to sort things out with her. Before finding out that she was going to the ball with Freddie, we'd become close friends. But like I said, that was then.

Her wariness hovered over me like a cloud, darkening my every waking hour. The worst thing about it was that she wasn't even a bitch towards me. She remained civil and decent to a fault, which was much harder to bear than Honey's open nastiness. I'd never done anything mean to Honey, but I was totally responsible for Portia's wariness of me. I could have sorted it all out with a simple apology, but I was too jealous and bent out of shape over Freddie to do even that. Especially as day after day, my mobile remained silent and hers merrily rang and beeped with messages.

Indie and Portia barely mentioned the ball again – only insomuch as it meant they couldn't attend Star's house party and what a bore it all was, but how at least they'd have each other. But as far as I was concerned, the Annual Euro Royal Bash Thingamee was still there, just like Portia's title, just like her dislike of me, a constant niggling reminder that I would and could never be like her or part of her world, which, when it came down to it, was Freddie's world too.

Freddie might like me, and I really think he did, but he

was a prince, and I was an American nobody. Unlike Indie, I was as close to being a nobody as he was ever likely to meet. I was like a random stranger trying on the glass slipper. 'Close, but not close enough,' the Prince's enquiries would say.

As I lay in my bed night after night with Honey smoking herself stupid with the fake weed on one side of me, and Portia serenely reading on the other, I waited for my txt alert to sound. Checking I had a signal every few minutes, I finally convinced myself that Freddie probably only liked me for my wild-child Hollywood credentials – and even they were fake. I was about as wild as my pet rabbit, Dorothy, whose most reckless act to date was dropping her lettuce in her water.

'Many txts from Freddie and Billy today, darling?' Honey kept asking, sometimes even adding, 'It must be hard for Billy.'

'What?'

'Well, I expect you are going to the Royal Bore with Freddie, darling,' she said breezily, even though she knew as well as anyone else that I wasn't.

'Oh, that's right, I keep forgetting, he's going with *Portia* isn't he,' she'd add. 'Silly Honey.'

Then one evening when Honey and I were alone and Portia was having a shower, Honey remarked, 'Portia and Freddie seem pretty tight now.'

I flicked a page of *Nun of Your Business* as if I was actually reading it and replied nonchalantly, 'Really? Why do you say that?' Then I flicked another page just to punctuate the point that I wasn't the least bit interested in Freddie and Portia. The magazine, now run by the Year Tens, had gone downhill, and I was considering speaking to Sister Constance about it. It was meant to be a satirical look at Saint Augustine's school life but had become a boring gossip rag. Oh my god, was I turning into Ms Topler, our English teacher, complaining about the state of modern-day writing?

Honey turned to face me, blew a billowing stream of smoke rings and smiled. 'Well, they're txt-ing one another like mad. I imagined you would have noticed?'

Then, as if set off by satanic forces, Portia's txt message alert went off. She was still in the en suite, and Honey wasted no time in grabbing the mobile. I didn't even bother to stop her. For one, Honey isn't the sort of girl you rein in, and secondly, I was madly curious as she opened the message and shrieked, 'Oh, look, Calypso, it's from Freddie.'

She passed it over to me to read for myself in case I didn't believe her. I didn't want to believe her, and there were a thousand reasons why I shouldn't. It's not as if Honey has a close relationship with the truth, after all. So I ignored her offer and turned another page of the *Nun*. I began scanning an article I had written about fencing in a transparent attempt to suck up to Bell End, forcing myself to ignore the prickling sensation in my hand, which was itching to grab the phone and read the txt for myself.

'Oh my god, darling, you have to read it now, it mentions *you!*' she urged.

I looked her in the eye as she sucked hard on the last of her faux weed fag. She must have sensed my weakening conscience because the next thing I knew, the phone was thrust in my hand and my magazine was cast to the floor. Honey was right; if it was about me, I had every right to read it!

Can you tell Calypso . . .

But before I could scroll down further to read the rest of it, the phone was snatched from my hand.

I looked up and saw the look of hatred on Portia's face.

She didn't say anything. She wouldn't. She merely placed her mobile on the bedside table next to the photograph of her family, plugged in her hair dryer, and started drying the wet tentacles of her long black hair.

My face was burning. No, not with shame, not with guilt at reading another girl's txt message, but with fury, because all the half-formed suspicions I'd been harbouring about Portia and Freddie now seemed fully warranted.

'I believe you have a message for me from Freddie,' I told her, raising my voice above her turbo dryer.

Portia carried on drying her hair in front of the mirror as she replied quietly, 'As you appeared to have read it yourself, I deleted it.'

Honey was lying on the bed, flicking through the social

pages of the latest *Tatler*, looking for photographs of herself.

I winced. 'I didn't actually get a chance to read the whole thing,' I admitted as I began to acknowledge how wrong my behaviour actually was. *Say sorry, say sorry, say sorry*, my better self pleaded with my wicked self. But I couldn't apologise. I folded my arms and gave her a filthy look.

Portia eventually turned to me and, smiling serenely, said, 'Perhaps it would be better if you spoke to Freddie yourself, Calypso?'

I flopped on my bed. That was the whole point. I couldn't call Freddie to whine about only half reading a txt he hadn't sent to me. Portia knew that. I guess it was the toff equivalent of telling me to lock myself up in the Tower of London and throw away the key.

NINETEEN

When Your Obsessions Become Obsessive, a Nemesis Can Prove Very Handy

I didn't tell Star I'd peeped at Portia's message when she dumped her books in the booth beside mine during study period later the next evening. Star's jaundiced feelings about Freddie were one thing; her feelings about me sneaking a look at Portia's private messages from him would be another matter entirely.

At boarding school, you might share makeup, sweets, fags, phone listens and messages, but you didn't just help yourself to other people's phones without asking. I was in the wrong and I knew it and I didn't need anyone else to point it out to me – especially my best friend. So I sat in my study booth, poring over my Latin books as if I cared deeply about conjugations of verbs.

Honey felt differently about sharing my shame. I reddened as I heard her telling Georgina, 'Did Calypso tell you, she stole Portia's phone and read a message from Freddie telling Portia to tell her . . .'

That was the end of my focus. The examiners may as well fail me now, I decided, as my face went through every shade of red before finally settling on a nasty shade of heliotrope.

'It wasn't like that,' I protested.

Star looked disgusted. 'Calypso?'

'Look, Honey showed me a message which was about me, and then Portia walked in and . . .' That was as far as I got because Portia actually did walk in then and heard herself being discussed.

I fled the scene and went into the computer room because I was about to burst into tears. I was struggling with my course work, at war with my closest fencing partner, and had no idea if I had a boyfriend or not. I decided a bit of self-pity was in order, but the teacher in the computer room didn't agree. She told me to get back and do my study, so I did, only this time I sat amongst another group of girls from my year and logged on to my laptop to see if I had any e-mails from my parents.

Unlike the other parents, who send postcards and letters, Bob and Sarah don't *believe* in snail mail, so I have to settle for e-mails. Essentially this means I have nothing from my family to pin on my pin board, which makes me look like an unloved child.

I was feeling very unloved at that moment.

But there wasn't an e-mail from Bob or Sarah – well there was, but I didn't look at it, because right underneath there was one from Freddie.

Dear Calypso, given your resolute refusal to respond to my txt messages, voice mails and phone calls this week, I am giving you the opportunity to communicate with me by e-mail. F.

This set my mind racing. Freddie was trying to contact me. Maybe the problem wasn't him? Maybe it wasn't even me? Maybe it was my bloody ancient brick of a phone? I started typing rapidly.

I'm sorry but I didn't get any messages, I began to type, before immediately deleting it, deeming the message too seriously tragic. I tried again, but Soz darling . . . was also deleted. It sounded soooo Honey. In the end I settled on:

Sorry, I am a wicked girl also I think my phone might be fruuped. x C

He e-mailed me back immediately. He was online, I was online. If this wasn't fate, I didn't know what it was.

Sorry about my previous engagement, I really would have rather gone to the La Fiesta Ball with you but

there is no way I can get out of this. I promise, I would if I could.
Best,
Freds

And I knew it was cheeky, but I immediately e-mailed back:

In that case, any chance you can take a date to this Euro Royal Bash Thingamee? xx C

I pressed ENTER before I could reconsider and an answer came straight back.

Can I come back to you on that? It's not that simple. I'll see you at fencing Monday anyway, we can talk then, Freds.

Two things stood out.

1) He hadn't sent me a kiss in either e-mail (note: I had sent him two!).
2) He *had* used the special nickname I had given him.

There was no way I was going to be able to concentrate on my course work now. I logged off without even reading Sarah and Bob's e-mail.

I was half expecting what happened next. After lights out, when Portia and Honey were both asleep – actually even I was fast asleep – Star snuck into my room and woke me up.

'I'm really worried about you, Calypso,' she said as I made room for her under the covers. 'Don't you think this problem you've got with Portia is becoming, well . . . a bit insane?'

Even though I thought she was right, I replied, 'Not at all.' And then to change the subject, I added. 'Freddie e-mailed me tonight.'

'Look, Calypso, maybe he does like you, maybe he doesn't, the point is you do have other things in your life.'

'I don't understand what happened that day in Windsor. Freddie and I were really getting on well,' I told her.

'You mean because you shared a pizza with him?' Star reasoned, her tone dripping with cynicism. I hadn't told her about our kiss nor the txts I'd received when we were on exeat in Derbyshire.

'The point is, as soon as I left, he met up with Portia and shared a pizza with *her.*'

'*Quelle horreur!*' she cried out silently, throwing her hands to her cheeks in mock shock. 'That a boy might share two pizzas in one day!'

'Seriously, Star! Is he just mucking about with me or does he think of me as a mate? And this sending messages to Portia about me – it's all so demeaning. If he wants to give me a message why doesn't he give it to me himself?'

'You just told me that he e-mailed you.'

'Yaah, but there were no kisses on the end.'

'Mmmm. It's a tough one. The only person who can help you though is Freddie, so unless you're prepared to confront him personally you've got to drop this thing with Portia. It's not her fault and she's got enough to deal with, don't you think?'

'I know, I want to, but I just keep . . .'

'Blurting?'

'Yaah.'

'Why don't you do this to start with? Forget Freddie and his pathetic Royal Bore because that's what it is, darling, a lot of old royals showing off their jewels and titles to each other. Forget the La Fiesta Ball. If I'm not in London you can't stay in our London house alone, which means you don't have anywhere to stay because everyone's coming to Derbyshire. So here's the plan. Come up to my house party.' She nudged me. 'Come on darling, it'll be a laugh. And without you I'll only pine.'

I smiled in the darkness at my friend's concern. The gulf didn't seem so huge now – and then I remembered. 'I've already bought my ticket, though . . . we all did.' She didn't reply, but we had a cuddle, and she scuttled back to her own room, leaving me in the dark as it slowly began to dawn on me that she was right. Without Star's London house, I had nowhere to stay during the half-term break. I was going to have to let go of my long-held dream of attending a Capital VIP ball. Like so many of my dreams.

'You can always stay at my house,' Honey's voice piped up out of the darkness, and for a bit I thought she must be talking in her sleep. 'It'll only be you, me and the servants. Poppy and Mummy are going to LA for the Dulson premier,' she whispered.

The Dulson film was *the* most hotly awaited film in the world.

I told her I'd think about it in an out-of-body-ish sort of way, still wondering if I'd really heard properly. I could see the flame of her lighter as she lit a cigarette. She opened the window up an inch and blew out a puff of smoke.

Could it be true that Honey, my nemesis, the girl who had made my life hell all these years, was offering to have me as a house guest in her famous Chelsea mansion?

I didn't get time to dwell on this as we heard the *tap, tap, tap* of Miss Bibsmore coming up the steps. Any sensible girl would have put out her cigarette and sprayed the air liberally with Febreze. Honey continued to lay there in the dark though and smoke.

The fluorescent lights flickered on.

'I thought I smelled smoke, Miss O'Hare.'

'Oh, bugger off. I can't sleep without a cigarette. It's not my fault they make cigarettes addictive. Speak to the tobacco giants, Miss Bibsmore. I'm just a victim of their corporate might.'

'Hah. You're about to become a victim of my might, Miss O'Hare an' all. Twenty pounds please.' She stuck her hand out for the cash.

Honey pulled her duvet up around her chin and looked at Miss Bibsmore like she was a crazed lunatic. 'Leave me alone.'

'Come on, open up your tight little fist and hand over the readies. Twenty pounds on the spot fine, that's school rules an' all. You knows it, I knows it, so if you have a problem with it, you can speak to your corporate giants innit!'

Honey put her cigarette out ostentatiously and pulled twenty quid out of her top drawer. 'There, you miserable old witch. Take the money I was saving up for my cancer treatment.' She threw the note at Miss Bibsmore and watched as it fluttered to the floor.

Miss Bibsmore creaked and groaned as she bent to pick it up.

'You really need to exercise more, Miss B. Your joints are creaking,' Honey told her in a voice of faux concern.

'Well I 'ope your joints hold up over the next week an' all. You're on litter duty, starting tomorrow. Nightie night, girls.'

TWENTY

If You Can't Pull the Boy You Want . . . Pull the Boy You're With

S aturday was one of those beautifully sunny days you occasionally get in England in autumn. I couldn't wait to feel the sun on my face, but Star and Indie decided to spend the day in one of the music rooms working on their latest track about a girl who feels burdened by the enormity of her privilege. Apparently it was *seriously* coming along, and for the first time I didn't really mind that it was Indie having to share that experience rather than me.

Georgina elected to stay and listen, but I'd already heard most of what they were working on and it sounded like a bag of cats being murdered, so I jumped at Honey's suggestion to share a taxi to Windsor with her and Portia. At the back of my mind, I guess I thought this might be my chance to make peace with Portia.

'What about your litter duty?' I asked Honey.

'Oh, I paid a Year Seven to do it for me.'

'Frightened one to death to do it, more like it,' I thought I heard Portia mutter, but I didn't see her lips move, so I decided I must have imagined it.

I was feeling a bit quiet and self-contained myself as I ran through the apology and make-up speech I needed to make.

Honey, sitting between the two of us, chatted away merrily. 'Even though I've decided it is too, too tragic to pull school boys at my age, I think, as I'll be sixteen next term, realistically I'm going to have to settle for them during term time darlings. Such a drag, but there it is.'

Neither Portia nor I responded. Apart from anything else, we'd both heard the speech several times already that term. The taxi driver responded, though. 'On the pull, are we girls?' he asked jovially.

'Oh, shut up, you village-dwelling peasant,' Honey snapped – and he duly did. 'Which is why I thought we may as well go to the Three Swans,' she added to Portia and me.

Portia was as silent as the Sphinx.

'But that's a pub, isn't it?' I blurted.

'We *are* allowed to go into pubs, darling,' she reminded me. 'Just not allowed to order alcohol.'

'Oh,' I said, feeling like the fourteen-year-old know-nothing baby I was. 'Don't you have to be accompanied by an adult?'

'Oh, Calypso, Calypso, Calypso. That is why, darling airheaded creature that you are, I did you the massive favour of calling Billy. He's going to be there with some of his friends. You know he used to go out with my sister. She dumped him for someone less plebbie, of course, but he utterly adores *moi*.'

I thought Billy dumped Poppy, I was thinking to myself, but typically I must have said it out loud.

But as it turned out, it can't have been me who said it, as the next words that came from Honey's lips proved. 'How would you know anything, Portia? Shouldn't you be busy mourning the death of your mother instead of listening to malicious gossip?'

'Honey!' I snapped, leaning over to Portia to show my solidarity, but she had turned her face towards the window.

I tried to reach out my hand to her but we were pulling into Windsor; and before the car even drew to a standstill, Portia had already unbuckled her seat belt, jumped out of the moving car and run off through the streets. The driver went mental.

'I think we'd better run after her,' I told Honey. 'That was really poisonous, even for you, Honey.'

Honey fluttered her implausibly long fake lashes and arched one professionally plucked brow. 'Don't be so wet, Calypso. Forget about old Misery Briggs, darling. She's *such* a drama queen.'

Even with all my resentments against Portia, one thing

she was not was a drama queen. Honey had no competition for that particular crown.

'Honey, we've got to chase after her. We can't just leave her when she's so blatantly upset. That was really horrible of you,' I repeated.

Honey paid for the taxi and then, taking my hand in hers and swinging it like we were the best of friends, led me through the sunlit cobbled streets towards the pub. 'She's probably run off to cry on her brother's or Freddie's shoulder, darling.'

I winced, but knew it was pointless to react.

'Let's meet up with the others at the pub. If she wants to find us at least she knows where to look.'

'I suppose that's true,' I agreed, conceding defeat despite my disappointment that Honey had now blown my chances of sorting things out with Portia probably forever.

'Besides, I don't know why you care; she stole Freddie.'

'What do you mean?'

'Look, it's all over Eades that they are an item.'

Honey checked my reaction as we were entering the Three Swans.

'But not to worry, darling. I couldn't tell you in the taxi with Misery Briggs, but Billy wants to get back with you.'

'Back with me where?' I said as the smell and noise of the pub arrested my senses. I'd never been in a pub before, so I didn't know what to expect as we pushed the door open on the low-ceilinged, smoke-choked room. I looked around but I couldn't see Billy anywhere. I saw Poppy, though. She was sitting in a red velvet upholstered corner booth smoking with two other Upper Sixth girls. I remembered the Post-it Notes they slapped on my back last July when Honey was running her Post-it Note campaign against me. We made our way towards them. They were all smiling at me as if I was the only girl in the world they wanted to be with, asking me what I wanted to drink and telling me how much they adored my outfit.

'You look stunning, Calypso,' Poppy said, making room for me in the booth. My instinct was to run but everyone seemed so friendly, and I didn't really have anywhere to run to.

'I know! Doesn't she do wonders for an American?' Honey boasted. 'She's practically got style, almost.'

I scrutinised Honey's face, but she looked genuinely proud of me, and so I relaxed and sat down. Poppy and company were accompanied by about half a dozen madly fit Upper Sixth Eades boys. Poppy introduced me, and they all stood and air-kissed me before falling back into a conversation about some arcane game of football they play at Eades.

A boy named Charles Von Archmontberg asked me if I wanted a drink, but before I could answer, Poppy dived in. 'Just get her a vod and Diet Coke, darling, and another for me.' She blew him a kiss, but he looked to me for confirmation. I smiled and nodded nervously. I wasn't about to disagree with Poppy O'Hare.

'Here's yours, darling,' Poppy told Honey, pushing a

glass across to her half-sister. 'Vod and Diet Coke, but pretend this straight Coke is yours if anyone asks,' she warned, pushing another glass across to her. Then she turned away and rejoined the conversation she was having with the boys.

'So when is Billy coming, then?' I asked, looking about the heavy low-beamed pub full of Eades boys and Saint Augustine's girls. I scanned the room, with its dark oak furniture, plush patterned carpet and walls covered in etchings of Windsor Castle, in the hope of spotting him.

Poppy turned to me. 'God, I hope not,' she groaned, blowing a plume of smoke right in my face. 'That hideous little pleb. Ugh!' she shivered at the memory. 'Goodness knows what I ever saw in him.' She took a long deep drag on her impossibly long, thin pink cocktail cigarette and blew some more smoke in my face.

I turned to Honey and tried not to cough. 'But you said . . .'

Charles returned with my drink and plonked it in front of me. 'One vodka and Diet Coke,' he declared, smiling in a flirty way at me.

Honey laughed her hyena laugh. 'Oh, I just told you Billy would be here to make sure you came, darling. I had to save you from Misery Briggs, and I knew you'd come if you thought Billy was going to be here.' She nudged me. 'He really did call me though to tell me he fancies you. Whoops! I wasn't meant to tell you that,' she said, putting her hand over her mouth as if she was ashamed.

'Got the hots for the Gypo, have you?' one of the boys asked nastily, and all the others laughed loudly.

One of them, I think his name was Peregrine or something stupid like that, leaned in so closely I could smell the Guinness on his breath. 'You *do* know his father rents limos?'

'Well, your father sells mineral water, Grins,' declared another boy, who'd been introduced to me as Sebastian.

The rest of the group, including the girls, found this so hilarious the table rang with guffaws and shrill laughter.

Peregrine defended himself above the noise. '*Owns* Britain's major spring water company, I'll thank you,' he said, taking a gulp of Guinness. 'Been in the family for generations.' With that, he poured what was left of his Guinness onto Sebastian's lap. After that, one thing led to another. The crowning moment came when Cameron and Archer poured their drinks on top of Peregrine's head with the chant, 'Chav, chav, chav.'

I was in Hoorah Henry Hell, and as I looked around me, I couldn't really see a polite way of getting out of this aristocratic pub brawl. So I just stood up and legged it like a mugger down Oxford Street.

Sometimes escape is the better part of valour, I think.

I charged through the cobbled streets, heading towards the tea shop I'd caught the taxi from last time I was in Windsor. Everything had been so clear that weekend, before Freddie mentioned the ball. I was so relieved to see Billy chatting to another boy that I threw my arms around him like in a damsel in distress. 'Save me, Billy!' I cried.

He laughed as he untangled my arms from around his neck. 'Slow down,' he said, grinning kindly. 'What do I have to save you from this time? Another dog?'

'Hardly, this was far more hideous. I was in the Three Swans with Honey and Poppy.'

'Nice company you're keeping,' he added ruefully.

'And loads of Eades boys. It was hideous, Billy. They were all pouring Guinness over one another, and I was just sitting there with Poppy and her friends, and Honey of course. They seemed to find it the most natural thing in the world.'

'Waste of good Guinness,' Billy remarked, and in that smile, I saw again all the things that had attracted me to him in the first place. I needed to know if what Honey had said about the way he felt were true. He was squinting into the sun, and as he ran his hand through his blonde mussy hair, my tummy did what can only be described as a massive back flip.

'By the way, this is Tarquin – you know, Portia's brother? Tarquin, this is Calypso, the one you've heard so much about.'

I went bright red as Tarquin put his hand out to shake mine.

'How do you do?' I said awkwardly as I saw Portia heading towards us.

Billy suddenly looked nervous. 'You *did* get my txt?' he muttered to me so that Tarquin couldn't hear.

Tarquin looked uncomfortable.

'Which txt would that be?' I asked flirtily as I watched Billy's face redden. I couldn't believe he was still ashamed about not txt-ing me. 'Honey said something to me, though.'

'Only, I didn't mean to give you the wrong idea. Honey?'

Guilt was written all over his face. He'd obviously been too busy to txt but he didn't want me to think he'd forgotten me. And now he knew Honey had blown his cover. Bless.

'Forget about txts, forget about Honey anyway. I've got the same ideas I've always had,' I assured him, flirtily grabbing his hands in mine. Before he could respond, my witty repartee was interrupted by Portia's arrival.

I waited for her to say something to me. Something like 'Hello,' or, 'Oh, I see you've met my brother.' Or even better, 'Why don't we put the past behind us and just be friends like we were at the start of term?'

But she didn't say any of those things. What she actually said was, 'So, should we head off, then?' She was looking at Billy and her brother as she said this, not at me.

'Yes,' agreed Tarquin. 'Best be off.'

Billy looked at his watch. 'Yaah, we'd better push off,' he agreed, adding, 'Thanks again, Calypso, about, you know, understanding.'

'Oh, that's okay, I love understanding,' I blurted and

then I thought, what am I supposed to have understood, actually?

'So will we see you later, then?' he asked after the others had already headed off.

That was all the encouragement I needed to go blurtatious, and a stream of madness came pouring forth as it does when I'm faced with the eyes of a fit boy boring into my soul. 'Yaah, that is, I hope so, Billy. It's just that, well, I'll see what I can do but I'm very busy today and I have to meet my . . . friends.'

'Not Poppy, Honey and the Guinness wasters?' he asked, beginning to move away himself. 'Laters,' was all he said as he turned and joined Portia and Tarquin.

I put the icing on the cake of my rambling blurt and called back, 'Yaah, laters,' only I didn't move because, well, it was just a blurt. The fact was, I wasn't in the least bit busy, and all my friends were back at school in the music room.

It didn't really matter, because none of them turned around. I felt like a crime scene as I stood there in the bright autumn sun for all of a minute before deciding that with Star, Indie and Georgina back at school, I had little choice. I was meant to stay in a group of three at all times. Also I didn't want to take a taxi back to school on my own with a potentially grumpy driver who expected enormous tips from posh school girls, so I wandered back to the pub as if I hadn't ever left it.

I opened the door of the smoke-choked pub, remorseful

at having to return to a group of people I really didn't like. Also I was nervous about being carded. Even though I was tall, I was only fourteen and nine and a half months, and the only ID I possessed was my school library card, and it wasn't even forged! I looked guiltily around the packed room full to the rafters with older Eades boys and Saint Augustine's girls. No one appeared to notice me as I made my way over to the guffaws and shrieks of Honey et al.

'Sorry about that,' I told Poppy, Honey, the other two girls and the Hoorah Henrys as I sat back down in the booth. 'I just remembered I had to get some money out of the cash point.'

Yaah, that would be the day. I didn't even have an ATM card.

TWENTY-ONE

Think with Your Brain, Move with Your Body, Slam 'Em with Your Blade!

On Monday, the Eades fencing team loped into our salle with their special we-own-the-world walks, followed by their security men with their we-might-look-like-idiots-but-we-spend-a-lot-of-time-following-these-boys-who-own-the-world-about-so-don't-mess-with-us-alright swaggers.

I felt very alone and strange without Star to back me up and Portia hating me. Bell End was chatting to the Eades fencing master, Professor Eichstiech. If Star had been here we would have debated whether the two of them were going to hate each other or get on like a couple of weird men with beards.

Professor Sullivan, our old master, had always eschewed

the company of other fencing instructors. He was a man apart and we liked him like that. Bell End was a different sort of fish – he was much keener to jostle for the top dog spot. The first with the chalk in his hand, the first of the two to slap the other on the back, you know the sort of chap.

Eichstiech had an Olympic gold, which rumour had he hadn't taken off since he'd won the wretched thing sixty years ago. Although at least he didn't wear it outside his clothes the way Bell End did.

Both Billy and Freddie hung back with their team before play. It was just a 'friendly,' but we still had to rustle up one of the younger, more promising épéeists to make up our sabre numbers. Her name was Emille and she was seeded out before I'd finished my stretches. This meant that between Portia and me, we could only afford to lose one bout if we weren't to lose the match. Good one, Star.

When Freddie and Billy saw Portia, they waved at her like a two-boy fan club. Looking at Billy, I caught his eye, and he smiled. I wondered if perhaps I hadn't been a bit hasty in deciding I didn't fancy him. I mean, he was *soooo* blond and fit and not to mention about four inches taller than Freddie and two years older. Looking at Freddie, I still wanted to fall into a heap of desire, but Star's reasoning wasn't to be so easily dismissed. She was right – Billy *was* far less complicated. Maybe he deserved another chance.

With Portia as my unspoken enemy, I was lurking with the year below, doing my Supermans, which I suppose made me stand out, only not in the fantastically cool way I wanted to stand out.

I spotted Billy out of the corner of my eye, loping over to Portia and saying something to her, probably 'Where's Calypso?' to which she probably replied, 'I don't know, but I hope she has that flesh-eating germ, don't you?' Only Portia wouldn't have actually put it like that. She would have just implied it with an enigmatic shrug. Just the same, whatever she said made Billy laugh.

Billy's name was called with mine for next bout by Professor Eichstiech. Normally, Portia would have hooked me up at the back to the electrical apparatus. But given she was now my enemy, I figured I'd have to rely on Emille, or worse, fumble pathetically on my own in front of everyone. But unlike a normal enemy, Portia was too much of a toff to be petty. I realised her aloof demeanour wasn't going to wobble over someone as insignificant as me as she hooked me up in a more or less friendly fashion. She even wished me luck. This made me cross because I wished she *was* petty so that I could tell Star and everyone else how petty she was.

I could feel Bell End's eyes on me as Billy and I touched our gear to make sure it was wired up to record hits properly. In consideration of my reckless emotional game with Portia, I emptied my head of all thoughts. I didn't want to end up in a humiliated puddle at *Billy's* feet. I could feel Billy's eyes on me even though I couldn't see them behind his mesh mask after our salute.

Professor Eichstiech called, 'En garde! Ready! Play!'

I made a compound attack from the start, a feint to provoke Billy into a parry and then a *trompement* to deceive the parry. But I lost my right of way with a crossover, which is illegal, as you can't cross your legs in play.

After a yellow card (penalty), I was starting to wish I really was in the infirmary with that flesh-eating disease. Billy anticipated every move I made and successfully riposted. I knew things were going badly, but later I came forward fast, picked his blade up and made a cut across his chest, after which I began to gather my nerves and concentrate. Just the same, my comeback, such as it was, came too late to win the bout.

Bell End took me aside after I had shaken Billy's hand and congratulated him for rinsing me. 'Bloody, bloody idiot,' Bell End said. He also used another word which, if a pupil used it, would mean a gating. He was shaking with anger he was so rattled, and I suspected it was because this was his first outing to Eades as the new fencing master, and he probably thought he had something to prove. 'Stop being such a bloody girl, Kelly. Now get a grip, think with your brain, move with your body, slam 'em with your blade.'

I went over to the refreshment table and drank a juice so I wouldn't have to watch Portia fencing Freddie. I even chatted to a group of Year Sevens just so I could keep my back to the piste.

Billy came over and said 'Hi,' which startled me so much I spilt the juice down my white jacket. Thank goodness I'd taken my metal lamé off, otherwise it would have been ruined and I'd have had to borrow Portia's.

'How's things?' Billy asked, looking at the spillage.

'You were with me on the piste,' I snapped, imagining he was having a dig at my form as I dabbed away hopelessly at the orange stain, lest it spread over my breast.

'Good bout, I thought,' he said.

'Well, you would, wouldn't you. You weren't rubbish.' I was quite glad I had the spillage as it meant I didn't have to look at him and show him my blush.

'Here, let me,' he offered, dipping a paper napkin into his plastic cup of sparkling mineral water and dabbing at the spot on my chest.

Even though I was wearing my breast armour it still seemed incredibly intimate. I looked down at his long fingers as the stain disappeared, and then I looked up into his eyes and there it was, that look of adorable protectiveness, just like the time he saved me from the girl-eating dog.

'I wondered if you were going into Windsor this weekend again?' I blurted idiotically.

He nodded. 'I think that's it, don't you?'

I looked around confused.

'The stain,' he explained, pointing to my chest. 'I mean, I think it was a successful operation.'

'Oh yes, the stain. You've done the most incredible job. I mean, you could do it professionally if you wanted. Not that you would,' I added, realising what a hole I was digging. 'I mean, you're madly bright and, well, you probably wouldn't dream of becoming a stain spotter, would you? That would be ridiculous.'

He laughed. 'You always make me laugh, Calypso,' he said.

'You make me laugh too,' I told him flirtily.

He looked awkward then, as if he had to run to the loo. 'Anyway, thanks for being understanding about the txt and, well, everything.'

'You mean lack of txt,' I teased. Only Billy didn't smile back. He looked confused. 'Not that I mind,' I hastened to add. 'I mean, you've been busy with the fever of exams building up. And it's not as if I've been staring at my mobile waiting for it to ring or anything blatantly tragic like that. No, I've been wildly busy myself,' I rambled on. 'Hardly even know I own a mobile sometimes.'

That was when I saw Freddie looking at me. Only he wasn't looking at me in a nice way. He was shaking hands with Portia and looking at me like I was the biggest bitch in the world. In that paranoid second, I decided she must have said something nasty about me to him.

While I was looking at Freddie, Billy shuffled off, muttering something about Portia winning again. Bloody Portia, I thought before remembering she was on my team.

'Lucky none of the teachers saw you,' one of the girls from a lower year whispered to me.

I turned to her distractedly, having no idea what she was talking about.

'You and the Eades captain, Billy, isn't it?'

'You were all over each other,' added another. 'We'd never get away with that. It must be so cool being in Year Eleven,' she said dreamily.

I wish.

I didn't get a chance to speak to Freddie before our names were called because after his bout with Portia he was surrounded by all the fawning girls in lower years. And then when our names were called together I was in an unfit state to fence again. As we touched each part of one another's bodies and blades to make sure the electrics were working, I felt the blush creeping up. Emille had already lost two of her bouts. I had lost one. Portia had won two. If I lost this bout, we'd be counting on Emille, which meant we may as well surrender. I had to beat the prince's arse.

Wired up, standing on the en garde line, attached to the electrical point recording device, I saluted him casually. Then, placing my mask over my face, I concentrated my mind as best a girl can when she's an emotional whirlpool of confusion over which fit boy she fancies the most or, more to the point, which fit boy fancies *her* the most.

Then the president called 'Play,' and I advanced swiftly down the piste, preparing for a focused attack. I knew

Freddie's form well. I just hoped he hadn't shifted it since we last fenced.

What I really wanted to do was break distance (a fancy way of saying run away back down to the other end of the piste) to stop from impaling myself on his sword and throwing my arms about him and pulling him then and there in front of the world. I'd seriously be disqualified for that, though.

I was *sang-froid* personified as I advanced towards HRH, though. Billy may have rinsed me, but that only made me more determined to see that it didn't happen a second time. I won my first point, and after that I made damn sure Freddie's target area was continually threatened for the rest of the bout.

I was unbelievable, in fact – shocked by my own ice-cold nerves and amazed by my ability as each lunge set the electrical recorder lights flashing and buzzing like a techno nightclub show. I was a veritable Olympian. I'd never played so well, although every move I made felt familiar and right – in fact there was an eerie sense of *déjà vu* about the whole bout. I was indestructible, and what's more I didn't even feel the few cuts Freddie *did* manage, and in sabre that's something. After a bout my torso and arms were always covered in bruises and welts.

I made an offensive action so as to draw his counter-attack, parry and riposte. When the distance between us was so close that I wanted to rip my mask off and snog-age him senseless, I remained the consummate professional. I was going to fence in the 2008 Olympics, and no boy, however fit or royal, was going to hinder my play. I delivered my cut as Bell End's words rang in my ears, 'Slam 'em with your blade!' And slam him I did, good and hard, setting the buzzers off.

At the end of the bout, I triumphantly tore off my mask and walked toward Freddie to shake hands. I could hear Bell End clapping and yelling like a football hooligan through cupped hands, 'That's my girl! Well done, Kelly. Cut the little prince down to size.'

'Good game,' I said as Freddie shook my hand formally.

I knew that my head was a sweaty pulp, but for once I didn't care. The clear head I'd maintained during play became a muddle of confused feelings as I looked into Freddie's ink-blue eyes.

Portia was detaching me from behind, but the electricity of what I felt for Freddie was still coursing through my system. He was still distressingly fit, even with his hair all plastered to his head, and suddenly I wondered what would happen if I did just kiss him there and then on the piste? I reached my hand out to brush away a lock of hair from his damp forehead.

He didn't move to stop me, but he said, 'You and Billy looked like you were getting on well?'

It was a question I didn't know how to answer immediately, and as it happened it was one I didn't get a chance to because Star came bursting into the salle and started calling my name. I wished she hadn't made her entrance just at that moment, because I knew now that I needed to talk to Freddie properly – to see where things really lay between us.

'Darling!' she called out in an OTT drama queen-ish way as she threw her arms around me. At first I thought she was just messing around, and Freddie laughed, but he still left without having said anything really meaningful, like, 'I won't go to the Euro Royal Bash Thingamee if I can't take you with me, Calypso.'

I didn't even get time to finish my fantasy before Star pulled me away. It was only when we got into the changing rooms that I realised she was really crying.

'It's Brian – he's gone missing!'

TWENTY-TWO

Mayhem in the Pet Shed

'I'm sure he'll be okay, darling,' I reassured her after I'd changed out of my gear. 'Snakes are quite good at looking after themselves, remember?'

Star looked at me pointedly as she replied, 'They also eat rabbits and hamsters, remember!'

'Dorothy!' I cried, charging off towards the pet shed, envisioning my poor little rabbit as a bulge halfway down Brian, the reticulated python.

Star grabbed me by the arm, though. 'Dorothy is *absolutely* fine,' she insisted crossly. 'Georgina's waiting at the pet shed in case Brian comes back.'

'Phew.'

'And for the vet.'

'Oh, thank God. For a minute there . . .'

'See how you reacted when you thought Dorothy was in danger,' she pointed out, a little self-righteously.

But then something hidden in her sentence suddenly hit me. 'What do you mean, waiting for the vet?'

'Well, unfortunately, Absinthe's got a bit missing off

her,' she explained as she continued her trot towards the main building.

My voice was weak with horror as I chased after her. 'A bit missing off *what?*'

Star was running along purposefully, pausing to peer into hedges and shrubs as she replied casually, 'Only her ear. I suppose it's mostly blood, but can we stop discussing Absinthe? The main thing is finding Brian.'

We dashed a little farther along the net ball court, checking along the longer grass that ran along the fencing for Brian. Coming out of the chapel, we were stopped by a group of seven elderly nuns who were holding hands. They were all really small and old but ever so friendly.

'Hello, girls!' they called out in their thin little nun voices. 'Isn't it a lovely day for a stroll?'

'Yes, sisters,' I agreed, joining Star as she fell to the ground to run her hands through a patch of long grass.

'Enjoying the fresh air, are we?' one of them enquired sweetly.

'No, I've lost my snake,' Star explained, desperately.

'Oh heavens, I do hope he's not lost,' one of them said. The others all agreed fervently. Some of the elderly nuns are a bit potty.

'I just told you he *is* lost,' Star insisted, trying not to get cross with them. Looking up at their little soft faces creased with years of prayer and concern, it was hard to be cross.

'Heavens, Star, not dear little Brian!' they exclaimed in

one voice. They looked as stricken by her loss as she was as they clutched their rosary beads.

'In that case we must all go back into the chapel immediately and say a prayer to Saint Anthony for your snake,' said Sister Joseph firmly.

'What a good idea, Sister,' another nun said.

The others all nodded.

'Yes, Sister Michael, remember he found your glasses this morning before we'd even got down on our knees, didn't he?'

'Did he?' Sister Michael looked a little vacant.

'Yes, Sister, he always does the trick, does Saint Anthony.'

We left them chatting about the marvels of Saint Anthony as we legged it to the next patch of shrubbery.

'Poor Absinthe,' I muttered. 'You don't think it could have been Brian that . . . ?' I asked, because she hadn't made that bit clear.

She was scouring a large shrub outside the main building as she replied, 'Don't be absurd, Brian wouldn't hurt a fly. Not that I'd blame him – if he did eat the ear, that is. Absinthe makes the most hateful faces at him when there's no one around to supervise.'

Now she was going too far. As much as I'd love to hate Honey's rabbit, she was a sweet little thing, much nicer than last season's rabbit, Claudine, who was always biting. Absinthe might be ridiculously mauve, but she didn't have a mean bone in her body as far as I knew. 'That's not true,

Star, she's just a little rabbit, and how's Honey going to feel when she finds out?'

'Honey?' She coughed and pretended to fall over. 'Honey, *feel*? Ha! You of all people know what she's like.'

There was nothing I could say to that, so after helping her scour all the shrubbery around the main building, we legged it up the narrow stairwell towards our dorm rooms.

'He's so incredibly intelligent, Calypso; you're always saying so yourself.'

It's true. I do always agree with Star that her snake is intelligent, sensitive and even cuddly, but I only say those things because I love Star so much. Truth is, I'm a bit afraid of Brian and his beady eyes and flicking tongue. I know he's not poisonous or anything, but if looks could kill, all the pets in the shed would be dead.

'So that's why I've been teaching him this special skill,' she announced.

'What sort of skill?'

'Well, I wanted to be sure that he knows his way around the school so he can come and find me if he's upset or something.'

'Brian's a snake, Star, not a homing pigeon.'

'He's always showing Daddy around our manor when he gets lost.'

Given that Star's father is perpetually stoned and spends most of his time lying unconscious on the floor, I wasn't madly impressed by this skill, but I kept my doubts to myself.

'That's why I leave his cage open. So he'll come and find me if something's wrong. Hilda's taken Brian's disappearance very badly, by the way.'

'Hilda?' I repeated, before I could stop myself. I swear, Star's rat, Hilda, thinks of nothing but escaping Brian. She's always running dementedly around in her little rat wheel. I couldn't accept that she wouldn't be throwing her little rat paws in the air at Brian's disappearance.

But as I trotted along the corridor after my friend, I made what sympathetic noises I could. I know it sounds bad, but a part of me was actually pleased that I was the one Star had come to find in her hour of need. It was just like old times.

'This is the main route I've been teaching him, see. I wanted him to know how to find me in the night. He's nocturnal and pines for me. You know at home he always sleeps with me.'

'Yes,' I agreed, remembering our exeat weekend. Whenever I stay with Star I'm always afraid that I'll wake up with Brian around my neck.

As we dashed into Star's room she began to cry hopelessly. 'I can't bear thinking about him being lost, frightened, dazed and confused. What if he gets run over?'

I put my arms around her. 'He's got a good head on his shoulders,' I told her, as if Brian was some madly sensible being (with shoulders), which I promise you he's not. I mean, for a snake he's bright enough I guess, but . . .

We started to strip-search the room. I helped her check in all the cupboards and drawers, tearing all her bedding apart because Star was convinced he liked to cuddle up to her *smell*.

We'd already missed lunch, which was bad enough because we would have to have a talk from Sister Dumpster about the dangers of anorexia. If we didn't find Brian in the next few minutes we were going to have to tell Sister Constance that she had a six-foot reticulated python on the loose.

I repeated this realisation to Star, who started to cry even harder. 'We *can't* do that, Calypso. Sister will totally overreact and ban him from the pet shed.'

'We'll have to, Star, otherwise, well, he could . . .' I trailed off, not wanting to accuse Brian of anything – especially as Star wasn't even convinced that he was actually responsible for nibbling Absinthe's ear.

I was opening Indie's bed drawer when Star cried out, 'Brian!' and her tears of despair turned to tears of joy. But as I went over to cuddle her – Star that is, not Brian – all was not as well as I'd hoped. Brian was coiled around another rabbit, which he was in the process of swallowing.

I screamed in horror, and at that moment Honey came running in, followed by Miss Bibsmore. We grappled with Brian and what turned out to be Tobias, Georgina's teddy bear and lifelong companion. And before you think to yourself 'Oh well, he's just a *toy*,' remember, as far as

Georgina's concerned, he's her soul mate, with opinions on a wide variety of subjects. Oh, and let's also not forget that Georgina's father pays twenty-four thousand pounds a year in school fees so that Tobias can attend classes.

As we struggled to free Georgina's beloved bear from the jaws of death, Tobias's insides burst, and there, concealed in a muddle of fluff, was Georgina's Tiffany flask. Or rather her mother's Tiffany flask, which I suspected contained a stash of vodka.

TWENTY-THREE

One Teddy Bear, Caught Red-Handed . . .

Miss Bibsmore grabbed the flask, opened it up and sniffed the contents. Star was totally oblivious to anything as she rapturously cuddled and stroked her snake. Honey stood behind her nemesis, giggling.

Miss Bibsmore turned to her. 'You think this is funny, do you, madam?'

Honey didn't stop laughing as Miss Bibsmore waved the flask in her face. 'I presume by your inappropriate laughter that this item is yours then, madam!'

Honey sneered so hard the uneven bubble of collagen in her upper lip looked like a giant blister about to burst. 'Don't be insane. Why would it be mine? This isn't even my room!'

'I may not have all the whys and wherefores yet, missy, but mark my words, I'm on to you, Miss O'Hare.'

'And my daddy's lawyers are on to you, so I'd be very

careful about defaming my reputation if I were *you*, Miss Bibsmore.'

'If you were *me*? If you were *me*?' Miss Bibsmore squealed and then cackled mirthlessly in a mad-ish sort of way. 'If you were me, you'd know what it is like looking after ungrateful, spoilt girls like yourself, Miss O'Hare. You wouldn't last a day on my legs.'

Honey, her hands on her hips, rolled her yes and replied, 'Oh, go back to your squalid nineteen-fifties-decorated flat, you mad old witch.'

Miss Bibsmore ignored her as she took another sniff of the flask and then stuck one of her stumpy fingers inside, tipped it up and licked her finger loudly. She looked around at us, taking in each girl in turn with a piercing look that seemed to reach right down to our very souls – well, that's how it felt to me. Honey merely flopped idly on Indie's bed and started shuffling through the stuff in her bedside drawer. Star ignored her too, as she was still stroking Brian. And as for Tobias, well, he was lying lifelessly on the floor with his inside fluff spewing out, so his soul was bared for all to see anyway.

'Well, is anyone going to own up to this?' Miss Bibsmore demanded, holding the flask in the air. 'Because it didn't get 'ere by magic!'

Honey looked up innocently. 'How do we know it's not yours, Miss Bibsmore?'

'Don't you cheek me, Missy; I'll have your guts for garters, I will an' all.'

Honey looked the picture of blonde-haired blue-eyed innocence. 'I'm not cheeking you, Miss Bibsmore. I'm being deadly serious. How do we know you're not a secret drunk? Or perhaps you planted it? People like you are always planting things because you're bored and envious. I know it must be hard for you, being surrounded by beautiful teenage girls day and night, but really, Miss Bibsmore, turning to drink is *never* a solution.' Honey said all this casually, without even looking up as she searched more deeply in Indie's bedside cabinet.

Miss Bibsmore shuffled over towards her. 'The only thing I'll be planting, Miss O'Hare, is a mountain of blues on top of you.'

Honey remained unfazed. 'Well, given that the flask was found on Tobias, common sense would seem to dictate it is his. After all, he's always been a bit out there, hasn't he, darling?' She directed this comment to Star, who predictably enough ignored her.

'I suppose you think that's funny, Miss O'Hare?'

Honey ignored her. 'Oh, look, Indie uses a vibrator,' she declared as she pulled a pair of hair-straightening tongs out of Indie's drawer.

Miss Bibsmore raised her voice. 'I'll ask again. Who is responsible for *this*,' she yelled menacingly, holding out the flask.

'Sorry, are you offering us a drink, Miss?' Honey asked blinking innocently. 'Because I wouldn't want to have to report you, Miss Bibsmore.'

Star and I said nothing. I was hoping that if we stayed quiet for long enough, Miss Bibsmore would grow tired of standing there holding up the flask and shuffle off. Deep down I knew that wasn't likely, but Honey had turned on the straightening tongs and was using them on her hair, which created this weird sense that everything was actually completely normal. Just another day in dorm-hell with Honey that would eventually pass just like all the others had.

'Lost the power of speech 'ave we, girls? Well perhaps you can tell me who owns the bear, then?'

I looked at poor Tobias and wondered how Georgina was going to take it, seeing him splattered on the floor like roadkill. But I reminded myself that she must have opened him up and concealed the flask inside him in the first place, and then Star announced, 'It's my bear, Miss Bibsmore.'

'Yours?' Miss Bibsmore repeated, as if not quite accepting the fact.

'Yes. Mine, Miss.'

'Pass me the bear,' Miss Bibsmore insisted.

Honey bent down, grabbed the ripped Tobias with all his insides coming out and flung him at her. Miss Bibsmore caught him adroitly and examined him carefully. 'Well, I can't see a name tag so at the very least whoever owns the item'll be receiving two blue tickets, one for 'aving a personal item untagged and another for having a pet in the dorm,' she said, pointing to Brian. 'As for this' –

she held up the flask again – 'we'll have to see what Sister Constance has to say. You can come with me,' she said, pointing to Star. 'As can you, madam,' she added, pointing a gnarled finger at Honey.

'Me?'

'Yes, you, Miss O'Hare. Now hurry along; you can carry the bear and the flask, and no funny business neither.'

'Why me? This isn't even my room, that's not my bear and I haven't got a pet in the dorm.'

Miss Bibsmore pressed her face close to Honey's. 'Because, Miss O'Hare, I don't like the cut of your jib.'

'I'll come too,' I blurted.

Miss Bibsmore looked at me beadily. 'If you wish. But I don't advise it, Miss Kelly.'

Star shook her head at me, a gesture that caught Miss Bibsmore's eye.

'I don't know what's going on here, but I smell a rat.'

For a moment I thought she meant Hilda, but then I realised the seriousness of the matter and began to contemplate the consequences of what could happen. A sinking feeling fell upon me as I followed Star and Brian, who were following Honey with Tobias and the flask. Behind us was the sinister *tap, tap, tap*ping of Miss Bibsmore's stick as we made our way to Sister Constance's office.

As we filed down the corridors lined with a century's worth of photographs of illustrious old girls, shelves of trophies, plaques and other evidence of their achievements,

I felt humbled and unworthy. I'd never really imagined a plaque to Calypso Kelly, but the realisation that I might *never* have one made me feel like I was squandering my life.

I know that probably sounds quite melodramatic for a fourteen- (and nine-and-a-half-months) year-old, but then Sarah doesn't call me Queen of the Doomsday Prophesies for nothing.

TWENTY-FOUR

If You Ask Me, It Was Her Brain That Needed Botox!

Sister Constance sat at her desk serenely as Miss Bibsmore explained the events of the last ten minutes. Sister didn't interrupt or ask any questions; she merely made a sort of steeple with her fingers and nodded as each of the items – Tobias, the Tiffany flask, and the issue of Brian – were laid one by one on her desk.

Sister Constance's ominous silence, combined with the sombre and detailed way in which Miss Bibsmore explained the case, lent a courtroom-like atmosphere to Sister's office.

Eventually Sister said, 'Thank you, Miss Bibsmore, you can leave this with me. I know how busy your schedule is.'

'Right you are, Sister,' Miss Bibsmore agreed. Clearly she would have preferred to stay. Nonetheless, she backed out the door reverentially but stopped short of leaving. 'With all due respect, if you want my opinion, Sister, Miss O'Hare is the most likely culprit. I've had my suspicions about her since I first laid eyes on her, I have.'

Sister Constance nodded as if taking this on board. 'Thank you, Miss Bibsmore. I'll take it from here.'

So for the next hour (probably around five minutes but it felt like an hour) we all sat gathered around the desk, gazing and contemplating the evidence in total silence. Sister Constance appeared to be thinking, or at least praying very hard. I looked up at the giant crucifix on the wall above her and began to wonder about Absinthe and whether I should interrupt Sister's thought/prayer process and tell Honey that her rabbit had been attacked by Star's snake. But just at that moment, Honey pulled a Chanel compact from her pocket and started looking at herself.

'Miss O'Hare,' Sister Constance spoke in a warning tone.

Star and I simultaneously took our lip-gloss from our pockets and began to apply.

'Do you think I need more Botox, Sister? I mean, obviously I don't have any lines like you, but it does give your eyes a bit of a lift,' she enquired chattily, demonstrating how she'd look with higher brows by stretching the skin on her forehead.

Sister Constance sighed wearily. 'You are a very silly girl, Miss O'Hare, and rather than looking to a mirror for guidance, you should pray to our Blessed Virgin Mother.'

Honey rolled her eyes at me. I pretended not to notice.

'Let's discuss the evidence here, shall we?' Sister continued. 'A snake.' She gestured to Brian, whom Star was still stroking. 'And a flask of what appears to be vodka, according to Miss Bibsmore.'

'Can I just interrupt for a moment, Sister?' asked Honey, continuing without waiting for an answer. 'I frequently smell alcohol on Miss Bibsmore's breath.'

'No, Honey, you may not utter a word unless I ask you a specific question. Then of course there is Georgina's bear, Tobias,' she added as she gently patted the remains, which were strewn forlornly across her desk.

'No, Sister, like I told Miss Bibsmore, the bear is mine,' Star cut in.

'Yes, I've grasped the ludicrousness of your claim, thank you, Star,' she said gently. 'But Tobias has been a fee-paying student of this school as long as Miss Castle Orpington has, and I place my reputation on recognising *all* my pupils and their family associations.'

Star blushed and looked strangely stuck for words.

'Perhaps the first thing we need to do is place Brian back in the pet shed so that you can focus on the seriousness of the matter at hand. You might also ask Georgina to come and see me.'

'Yes, Sister,' Star agreed, and backed out of the room with Brian, leaving just Honey and me.

Honey snapped her compact shut and stood up angrily. 'Well, as it wasn't even my room the flask was found in, I don't see why I should be kept from my next class,' she complained. 'Daddy would be furious!' She looked like she was about to explode with exasperation, and even though she's the nastiest girl that god ever breathed life into, I felt it was time to step in.

'Actually, Sister, Honey's rabbit's been injured and the vet's been called. Georgina's at the pet shed now waiting for him to arrive.'

'What?' cried Honey with a look of genuine despair on her face. I felt really, really terrible for a moment, before realising the fallout that would ensue when she discovered that her rabbit's attacker was probably Star's snake.

'How did this happen?' Sister Constance asked calmly, looking directly at me.

I did a little cough. 'Well, see, the thing is, Sister. Well. That is, we can't be sure but we think, maybe, only maybe though, when Brian escaped he might have taken a bit of a nibble . . .' I trailed off, unable to bring myself to directly accuse Brian of anything that would have him banned from the pet shed, because that would destroy Star. 'But we're not really sure, and he's always been such a kind snake, so it would seem very unlikely . . .'

'That bitch!' screeched Honey. 'I knew something like this would happen,' she spat. 'It's ridiculous that you allow a snake in the pet shed, Sister,' she railed. Which is a bit rich given that Star's father had paid for a centrally heated pet shed for all the pets and a separate glass aquarium area for Brian and Hilda to be housed in.

Without waiting for permission to leave, Honey stormed out of the room, and that was that. Sister Constance and I were now alone. We sat for the next few minutes in silence, breathing in the aromas of frankincense, old books and an open box of butterscotch, which was beside a statue of Mary on her desk. Finally the bell went, at which time she told me I could go to class and return with the others after supper.

TWENTY-FIVE

Daddy's Plastic Girls

Honey's righteous fury over Brian's attack on Absinthe should have been short-lived but for the fact that Honey adores being right and furious more than cats enjoy stalking mice and licking cream. Enjoying the combination of both emotions together was too delicious for her.

Even I felt ashamed for having blamed Brian when what had really gone wrong was all Honey's fault. Poor Absinthe had caught her paw in one of the enormous hoops Honey had pierced her ears with and had torn her own ear when she tried to move.

'You're too tragic to even speak to,' Star told Honey when she came into our room before supper.

'I don't want to believe that people like you even exist,' added Indie as she trailed in after her.

There wasn't much I could add to that. Also I was in the bed next to Honey's and had my mattress to consider.

Portia put down her magazine and smiled in her regal way at Star and Indie, who smiled back, and then we all huddled on the floor for a confab on Georgina's fate. Honey was looking at herself in the mirror at the time and didn't deign to respond, let alone grace the floor with her presence.

'So no one's seen Georgina since she was left to wait for the vet earlier in the day?' Indie asked.

'You don't think they've expelled her?' Portia asked in a low whisper as the vet was ushered in by Miss Bibsmore.

This vet was really fit looking for a grown-up, although his dress sense was tragically retro. He was so adorable though, the way he delivered his diagnosis on Absinthe in the gentlest, kindest voice you can imagine. He looked as genuinely saddened by the whole affair as we were, apart from Honey. She was furious.

'You mean you expect *me* to pay *you* for disfiguring my pet?' she shrieked, her head spinning around on her neck – well, not really, but it looked like it was about to. 'How dare you treat my rabbit without the permission of myself or my guardian!' she screamed. 'What am I meant to do with a rabbit with half an ear?'

'Well, I was called to the school, so I just presumed . . .'

'Ugh!' she grunted. 'That's the trouble with people like *you* and your sorry red brick university degrees! You presume too much. If *I'd* been consulted I would have told you to put her out of my misery.'

Portia, Star, myself and even Indie were used to Honey-isms such as this. All in a day's Honey. But as we looked up at the poor vet with his angelic tousled locks in an attempt to convey our solidarity with him, I could tell he didn't have a clue what he was up against.

'You mean *her* misery,' he corrected. The poor, sad, deluded sod. He really had no idea. He sat down on Honey's bed as if he wanted to comfort her. 'Sorry, Honey, isn't it? Perhaps I haven't explained myself clearly,' he persevered. 'Absinthe will be just fine. She'll make a full recovery. She's only torn part of her ear, but it will heal, and the main thing is she's retained full hearing capability. I'll drop by in a few days to remove the stitches and she'll be right as rain, I promise you.' He gave her shoulder a comforting little pat.

I caught Miss Bibsmore popping her head around the door and listening in on the scene as it played out, but Honey didn't.

Honey turned to him, her eyes flashing like machine gun fire. 'And I'm meant to take precisely *what* comfort from the news that I now have a disfigured pet? Are you suggesting that I throw good money after bad to keep a hideous half-eared rabbit alive? I could be spending your vet bill on a pair of rabbit-trimmed Gucci stilettos! You monstrous, money-grabbing pleb. Now get off my bed, you pervert.'

At the accusation of being a pervert, the vet dived off the bed and looked around at all of us. His plan of breaking the good news to a sweet teenage girl that her pet was going to be okay had crashed against the barriers of Honey's unspeakable nastiness.

He opened his mouth to reply, but Honey cut over the top of him. 'Well, hop to it!' She clapped her hands. 'Down to the pet shed, and put the wretched thing out of my misery.'

But the vet didn't look like he was going to 'hop' anywhere. His whole demeanour changed before our eyes from fit, kindly, older man to a dangerous force of authority. I swear a cool, chilling breeze was blowing around him as he said: 'Miss O'Hare, the only misery I know of is the lamentable attitude you and your friends have towards your pets. People like *you*,' he began, but I think he was too angry to go on because he started spluttering.

I felt sorry for him. Apart from Honey, I think we all were, so as he turned to leave, I began to blurt, 'Can I just say, that, erm, well, it was super of you to come and help Absinthe and, erm . . . well, seriously, actually I think. Yes, that's it, personally, and I think an enormous amount of people would agree, you've got a really cool and original dress sense for an old, I mean a grown-up. Yes, those retro corduroys are, well, well, they're on trend this season, aren't they? So that's really cool, isn't it?'

I wasn't exactly waiting for applause, but when my blurt stopped, the entire room was silent. Everyone was looking at me blankly as if I was mental. I mean, his dress sense was seriously horrendous but it *was* original in a retro sad sort of way.

He had already put his hand on the door handle at

that point, but he turned back to face not Honey but me.

I knew my speech wasn't as polished as it could have been, but I was shocked by the venomous look on his face. 'That's all you spoilt girls care about, isn't it?' he asked me directly. 'Cool clothes and accessories, Daddy's plastic and Mummy's contacts. Well, none of that will help you once I've filed my report.'

My face stung with the unfairness of his attack. I was only trying to cheer him up. 'I don't like your clothes, really,' I assured him.

Dig, dig, dig, Calypso, a voice in my head was heckling. So I grabbed the shovel. 'I was just, well, I was just trying to be nice to you, to cheer you up. Not that your green flares aren't cool in a retro (I think I actually said 'sad,' but I hope I didn't) sort of way. It's just that they're not my sort of thing. See, I wanted to say something kind after what Honey said to you. Besides, my mummy, that's Sarah, doesn't have any contacts, and my daddy, that's Bob, doesn't even *believe* in plastic!'

The vet clicked his tongue at me in disgust. That was so going to be the last time I ever complimented an older man, however fit and kind he might seem. Because that's the thing – you never know when grown-ups are going to turn on you. One minute they're all, 'Let's be pals and I really, really, really care' and the next it's all, 'Time for bed, lights out, blues all round, and I'm filing a report.' Star's right: grown-ups exist only to subjugate us.

'I shan't be sending a bill,' he told Honey in a grand voice he hadn't shared with us earlier. 'I can assure you, however, that I will be making a full and detailed report about this school and your treatment of animals.' He made the word 'report' sound like a weapon of mass destruction.

We were all cowering as he glared around the room at Portia, Honey, Indie, Star and myself as if we were Honey clones, when really we were as appalled by Honey as he was. The difference was, we'd suffered Honey for so many years we were virtually immune to her toxic psycho toff take on life.

'I can't believe he went off at you like that,' Indie said after he'd gone. 'I thought you were really nice to him,' she told me gently, rubbing my back.

'I even complimented him on his flares,' I added, shaking my head at the injustice of life.

Star said, 'It just proves what I've always suspected. Grown-ups are not to be trusted.'

TWENTY-SIX

The Feverish Age of Reports

Supper was fish fingers, my favourite, but not that night – I had no appetite. None of my friends with pets did. A rumour had swept through the school that the pet shed was to be closed, pending an investigation, and that the vet had spoken sternly to Sister Constance about the animal rights issues of allowing girls to pierce rabbits' ears and place large, heavy hoops in them.

We were in a complete state and none of us could eat our food. It wasn't just the pet shed we were upset about, either; we were more worried about Georgina's fate. Sharon, the lady on tray duty that evening, took our names and said we were all going on report for not eating.

'Fine, report yourself, stupid,' Star told her as she slammed her full tray into the slot with a crash.

'Don't you take your food issues out on me, dearie, or I'll report you for disrespecting a dinner lady innit!'

But Star had already stormed off.

'What is it with everyone and their reports today?' Honey asked gaily, skipping along beside us happily – just to wind us up, I suspect. 'Report, report, report. Is it the word *du jour* or something?'

Now was not a time for skipping and I told her so. 'You can imagine how panicked Star and I are about the fate of our own pets,' I told her as we headed off to Sister Constance's office after supper. 'And we're also worried about Georgina.'

As we waited on the bench outside Sister's office for our summons, Honey taunted us for our 'sickly sentimentality,' which, in case we hadn't heard, was soooo last millennium. Then she blabbered on about not being in the least bit fazed about the possible closure of the pet shed, as she was soooo over pets.

'Oh, shut up, will you, Honey!' Star snapped – only Honey looked shocked, and she's never shocked by Star telling her to shut up. Also, she was looking at me. That was when I realised that I, Calypso Kelly, unshielded by Daddy's plastic and Mummy's contacts, had just told The Ultimate Psycho Toff to shut up.

'Sorry, Honey,' I muttered.

Honey merely ignored me and began studying her manicure.

Star was abnormally silent. She was glaring at Honey, and Honey was glaring back at her as Sister Constance finally cried out, 'Enter!'

When we wandered in, we weren't invited to sit down.

Sister Constance didn't even look us in the eye. She looked stricken. The serene calm that characterised our Mother Superior seemed to have been drained from the inside of her soul, and her face seemed to have shrunk into her nun habit.

Star and I stood there with Honey between us. I felt Star nudge her, because Honey fell into me theatrically, as if Star had used superhuman force. Actually, knowing Star, she might have. Normally I would have done nothing, but hating Honey as I did at that moment, I nudged her myself – really, really hard – and she fell right back into Star's elbow.

'Ow!' she complained. 'Sister! Did you see what they just did to me?'

Sister Constance didn't look up, let alone reply.

'I have a preternatural tendency to bruise,' Honey whined, rubbing her arm. 'I wouldn't want to have the nurse look at me and jump to conclusions regarding abuse,' she muttered, knowing that no one gave a damn what she did at that particular point in time.

Again, Sister refused to comment.

Eventually Star asked about Georgina.

'Georgina has left the school,' Sister Constance replied. We waited for a bit for her to go on, but all she did was take a butterscotch from the box on her desk and begin to suck on it really loudly.

'What? For good?' Star asked.

Sister Constance nodded. 'Miss Castle Orpington has

left the school grounds of her own accord,' she explained, the butterscotch rolling around in her mouth. 'She, along with Tobias, fully accept responsibility for the flask of vodka, but other than that, her father has refused to discuss her future at Saint Augustine's. He's in Morocco at the moment and cannot be disturbed.'

'But *you* will let her back?' Star demanded to know.

Sister sucked hard on the sweet, which made the most revolting noise. 'That is a matter for the school board, Star. More to the point is the spiritual bankruptcy that led her to seek refuge in alcohol.'

Honey rolled her eyes. 'I think she probably just wanted to get drunk, Sister.'

Star and I both had to suppress a giggle.

'Girls!' Sister warned.

But Honey continued, 'I think you're blowing this out of proportion. Why, Eades boys wander about their school sucking on flasks all the time and no one bats an eye. A boy from Marlborough I know said they can even buy it at the school tuck shop. And by the way, now that we are on the topic of tuck shops, all the boy's schools seem to have the most enormous shops. That is soooo unfair, Sister. They can even buy clothes and order Saville Row suits at their schools, whereas our tuck shop is just a windowsill that's only open once a week, and even then we can only buy sweets. We can't even buy phone credit! It is soooo babyish.'

Sister Constance, daintily taking her butterscotch out of

her mouth between thumb and forefinger, replied, 'Miss O'Hare, you do say the most ridiculous things. And the older you get, the less tolerance I have for your ridiculousness. So, for the love of Mary, will you just shut up!'

All our jaws collectively dropped to the floor as Sister popped the sweet back in her mouth and sucked on it loudly.

After a few minutes of rude sweet-sucking noises, Sister spoke again. 'Georgina isn't my only concern, though. I had the vet in here earlier, and he has grave, grave concerns about the attitude some girls have towards their pets, which I must admit I fully share. He furthermore expressed doubts about the viability of the pet shed after the unfortunate fate of your rabbit, Miss O'Hare.'

'Fine, shut the pet shed,' Honey said. 'I'm so over animals anyway. Unless we're talking those little fur-trimmed Gucci shoes. I think I'll have them in mauve. I know, maybe if I give them Absinthe, they'll give me a discount,' she added, giggling at her awful joke.

That was when Star thumped her across the back and Honey fell theatrically across Sister's desk and got a bit of a nosebleed – not because of how hard Star had hit her, but because of her theatrical fall. Plus, after you've had as much cartilage removed from your nose as Honey has, your nose tends to bleed quite easily.

Sister ignored Honey and the spot of blood on the end of her nose as she sucked serenely on her sweet for a moment. I thought she wasn't going to say anything about it at all, but then she did. Not to Honey, just to Star and me. 'Take Honey down to the infirmary,' she instructed me. 'Star, I have called your father.'

Star remained strangely silent, but I couldn't stop myself. 'Sister, that's soooo unfair! You saw what happened. Honey launched herself, and besides there is barely a drop of blood. If we take her to the infirmary, there might be a, well, a report or something!'

Sister gave me a look that spoke volumes – volumes as in, 'Don't push it or you'll be the next one launched.'

TWENTY-SEVEN

Friends Don't Steal Other Friends' Boyfriends

On the way down to the infirmary, Honey, in keeping with her Honey-ness, immediately dialed the police. 'Hello, officer? I have just been attacked by a ferocious girl. A famous rock star's daughter, and I've been badly injured. . . .'

I snatched the phone off her and pressed the END button.

'What?' she asked, blinking with innocence. 'This' – she pointed to her completely bloodless nose – 'is GBH; that's Grievous Bodily Harm. Star will *have* to be charged and I hope incarcerated.'

The only grievous thing about it all was Honey, and I told her, 'You've hardly even been hurt. The bleeding was totally negligible and you used Star's mild whack to launch yourself onto the desk intentionally. Besides, it didn't even bleed properly, it was just a spot, and there's no sign of blood now.'

'Don't be ridiculous,' Honey snapped, pinching her nostrils together as if stopping a torrent of blood. She called the police again.

It wasn't the first time the police had been called by Honey to have a fellow student arrested. Once she'd tried to have Star done for having red hair – in Honey's eyes a crime against aesthetics! And anyway, Star's hair isn't even red, it's strawberry blonde – after several sprayings with *Sun-In*, anyway. The point is, Honey's frantic call about GBH didn't have the police hopping around the way she'd hoped. They arrived but wandered into the infirmary in a bored sort of way, accompanied by Sister Constance. They didn't seem even mildly keen on the idea of charging Star or anyone else. Honey had to implore them even to open their pads and write something down, and even then they only wrote down her name. By this stage, there was no evidence that Honey had even *had* a nosebleed, and Sister Constance, whom they justifiably considered a reliable witness, said it was all just a storm in a teacup and offered them butterscotches. They were more than happy to accept both Sister's version of events and her butterscotch and wander off back to their police car.

Just the same, a rumour had swiftly spread that Star had been led from the school grounds in handcuffs for assaulting Honey. The truth was, her father, Tiger, had picked her up and taken her home along with Brian and Hilda, because as he told Sister Constance, he didn't consider Saint Augustine's a safe environment. He wasn't so easily bought by the offer of butterscotches, apparently. Either that or Sister had downed them all herself by the time he arrived.

For me, Georgina and Star leaving was like the theft of my two closest friends, although I felt sorriest for Indie because now she'd have to go to bed and wake up alone in an empty room.

'It's worse for you,' I told her. 'You'll have no one to chat with at night.'

'You could always come and stay with me,' she suggested hopefully. That was when I first realised that Indie and I had become proper friends in our own right, as opposed to two girls with shared friends. 'Otherwise I'll sneak into your room,' she promised.

'Why don't we have a moonwalk?' I suggested as the idea suddenly occurred to me. 'We can escape after lights out and take our duvets, vodka and tuck stashes down to Pullers' Wood. It's a Saint Augustine's tradition.'

Indie clapped her hands. 'George and Star have told me all about them,' she replied excitedly. 'Let's!'

The first time Indie came into our room on her own, only Honey and I were there. She hissed at Honey, 'You are such a bitch!' exactly like Star would have.

Honey, who was checking her mobile, looked up nonchalantly and replied sarcastically, 'Thank you so much for all your tea and sympathy, darling. I'm the one with the broken nose who'll probably have to spend the rest of my life having corrective surgery.'

Then I noticed that it wasn't her mobile she was fiddling with at all. It was mine.

'That's if you have any cartilage left after all your other nose jobs,' shot back Indie.

'Honey, what are you doing with my phone?' I demanded crossly.

'Just reading your messages,' she responded shamelessly, before turning back to Indie. 'At least I've *had* a nose job! You should think about surgery yourself, Indie. I mean, most people are probably too polite to say anything, but honestly, darling, take it from someone unafraid of the truth. Surgery is a necessity in your case rather than an option, if you see what I mean.' Honey held up her Chanel compact to Indie's spectacularly stunning face.

As Honey hadn't responded to my demand that she give me back my mobile, I snatched it from her and began to check my messages.

'Oh, like the surgery you had to remove your brain, you mean?' Indie replied, snatching the compact from Honey and tossing it into the bin.

There were no messages. 'There are no messages,' I said to Honey, holding up my phone.

Portia walked in at that moment, but she only said 'Hi' to Indie, ignoring both Honey and me.

'Oh, well there were a few. I read them. Several in fact,' Honey replied idly, shrugging her shoulders. 'I must have deleted them accidentally. Soz, darling, but your phone is soooo ancient. They were all from Billy, as usual. Probably best you didn't see them, actually. Billy's got a very pervy turn of phrase, and I know how politically correct you Americans are.'

I stood there opening and closing my mouth both at her audacity and her news that Billy had been txt-ing me. I had been hoping for something from Freddie, but this turn of events had me frantically wondering what was going on.

'I didn't know things had heated up quite that much between the two of you,' Honey continued, now smirking. 'I suppose I always thought of you as a little mouse . . . but you're quite the seductress, Calypso.' She laughed loudly at her own turn of phrase.

I just stood there, blinking. So did Indie.

'So you're admitting you just deleted her personal messages?' Indie clarified.

'Hardly! At least not on purpose, obviously,' Honey gasped indignantly.

'Rubbish,' Indie said crossly.

While this exchange was going on I was wondering whether this was the first time Honey had *accidentally* erased my messages. It would certainly explain a lot!

Honey commenced brushing her hair, which involved flipping her head over. 'Why don't you scuttle off to your own room, Indie; things are getting a little crowded in here, don't you think, Portia?' Honey asked.

'I don't think you want to hear what I think,' Portia replied as she focused on sending a txt message from her own mobile. I tried to gauge her expression, but as ever she was as inscrutable as the Sphinx.

My eyes were burning with desperation to see whom and what she was txt-ing. 'How many times have you tampered with my mobile, exactly, Honey?' I demanded, turning my attention back to Honey before I shamed myself by craning over to peer at Portia's screen.

'Oh, Calypso, talk about self-centred!' she snapped, flipping her head back up. 'Why does it always have to be about you, you, you? You can't always take centre stage like this. Don't you think it's poor Georgina and Star we should be worrying about, darling?' she implored, her lower lip dropping as if she truly cared.

'You're incredible, Honey,' Indie said as she flopped on Honey's bed.

Honey fluttered her eyelashes. 'Thank you, darling. I'm sorry I can't return the compliment.'

Indie leant back on Honey's bed, making herself comfortable by rearranging her pillows. 'All Star did was give you a bit of a slap and after the way you've been behaving, I can't believe she was so restrained,' Indie told her. 'If I were Calypso I'd give you another slap for deleting Billy's txts.'

'Calypso doesn't seem to mind, so why do you?' asked Honey as she grabbed at her pillows. 'Now get your filthy feet off my bed and go back to your own room.'

'I *do* care, as a matter of fact, Honey,' I corrected her as Indie left the room.

'Oh, then it must be *me* who doesn't care,' she replied with the ease of a someone completely comfortable with her role.

I was so angry I stormed out of the room. When I passed Clemmie and Arabella's room they called me in. Of course I told them all about what Honey had done.

'What a bitch,' Arabella agreed.

'She's done it before,' Clemmie added casually.

'All par for the Honey course,' they both sighed.

'I know she's done it before now. I don't know if Freddie or Billy have tried to contact me before and, well, I've been so confused about how I feel because I haven't been getting many txts at all.'

Seeing how upset I was, they both gave me a cuddle. Their other roommate, Rosie, had been in the en suite having a shower, but as she came out she remarked, 'I thought you and Billy were an item?'

I briefly looked up at Rosie, who was still in her robe. She smiled and went back into the bathroom. I turned to my friends. 'I think I only started liking Billy because of all the complications with Freddie, mostly because Freddie wasn't txt-ing me. Well, actually neither was Billy, but he was doing his A levels, so that was understandable. The real issue was that Freddie was going to the ball with Portia. Wait a minute. Why did Rosie think Billy and I were an item?'

The girls looked at one another. 'Honey told us, I think,' Arabella said, looking to Clemmie for confirmation. Clemmie nodded.

Now I was really confused.

'When you say Freddie is going to the ball with Portia, do you actually mean going with as in *going with*?' asked Arabella.

I shook my head. 'I don't know. That's the thing. Honey's got me confused.'

Clemmie put her arm around me. 'So, it's Freddie you *really* like?'

I nodded.

'Seriously, serious?'

I nodded again, because as easy as it would be to like Billy, after seeing Freddie at fencing I knew that I felt something much stronger for him. He might be inconvenient, but he was the one I wanted to pull.

'Okay, well, you're not going to like this, then,' Arabella warned me, shaking her head, 'but Honey told us that Freddie and Portia were an item.'

I looked from Clemmie to Arabella. 'What did she say, exactly?'

'Just how mad for one another they were,' Arabella replied vaguely.

'Yes, but it is Honey we're talking about, and as she's our only source I wouldn't put much stock by it,' Clemmie added.

I nodded. 'I know, but . . . well, Portia hasn't helped.'

'Portia wouldn't be a bitch,' Arabella said firmly. 'I've known her all my life and one thing she isn't is a back-stabber.'

'Oh, it's such a mess,' I groaned, putting my head in my hands with the frustration of it all.

'Honey is a witch,' Clemmie said, 'but Portia stealing Freddie, I don't buy. Have you spoken to Portia about all this?'

The tears sprang to my eyes at the obvious sense in this remark, and Clemmie and Arabella took me in their arms for a cuddle. It felt good to finally share my plight with others, and all my doubts and suspicions about Portia came tumbling out, as well as how horrible I'd been towards her, and how I couldn't go to the ball because I had nowhere to stay in London, and how even if Portia hadn't been trying to steal Freddie I wouldn't blame her now if she did.

Clemmie and Arabella were really comforting. Arabella offered me some sweets, and Clemmie said she wouldn't even mind if I ate a Jelly Baby, as Sebastian was growing up now and hardly resembled their little faces at all.

I smiled through my tears. 'Indie and I were thinking of having a moonwalk tonight, if you want to come,' I told them, drying my eyes.

'Hoorah, a moonwalk!' they squealed, bouncing on the bed with excitement. 'We haven't had one since last term.'

'I know, it's been so cold, but the stars are bright and the moon's full and I know I won't get to sleep tonight anyway. I'm too worried about Star and Georgina.'

They were already gathering sweets, fags, Body Shop Specials and duvets as I left their room. On the way back to the Saint Ursula room I was determined to try and sort things out with Portia once and for all. Talking things over with Clemmie and Arabella had given me the confidence that I could.

TWENTY-EIGHT

The Girl in the Iron Beak

I arrived back at my room, intending to invite Portia to the moonwalk. I had a picture in my head that once under the stars, stuffing ourselves with sweets and vodka, I'd have the bottle to apologise for being so horrible and put things back on track. But things had changed in the room in my absence.

Portia was reading *Nun of Your Business* – last year's copy – but I didn't have a chance to speak to her about moonwalking or making up because Honey dived on me like I was her best friend in the world.

'Darling!' she said as she threw herself on me enthusiastically. 'I am soooo seriously sorry about deleting the messages from Billy. Please forgive me,' she begged, seemingly genuinely contrite. 'I'm almost certain I remember what they all said.'

What could I do? Apart from hug her back? 'Of course I forgive you,' I told her, not just because I was surprised and curious – although I was – but because I was totally weirded out by what she was wearing on her nose. I guess there is no nice way of putting this. Honey was wearing a big, black metal sharp-pointed beak.

'What have you put on your . . .'

'Oh, this?' she asked, nonchalantly tapping the monstrosity perched on her face. 'Sister thought it was best. It's a nose guard.'

'Sister Regina?' I asked, shocked that the adorable, lovely little Florence Nightingale of the infirmary would stoop to such artifice.

'Sister Dumpster,' Portia said from behind *Nun of Your Business*.

This is my chance, I told myself as I approached her bed. How hard is it to say sorry? It's only one word. I only got as far as her bedside table, where the photograph of her family stared out at me.

'So Portia, do you fancy going for a moonwalk this evening?' I asked lightly.

'Her name is Dempster, actually,' Honey snapped at Portia – that is, she was trying to snap, but her words echoed inside the iron beak.

Portia didn't reply to my suggestion; in fact she didn't even look at me. I looked at her mother staring out from the family photograph, then looked at Honey, the ultra aristo-psycho toff. She looked like a monster, a victim of torture. The Girl in the Iron Beak. It was completely bizarre.

'Daddy said I should sue,' she sighed. The metal nose made her sigh sound really nasal and common.

But I didn't laugh.

Portia huddled further towards the wall. I think *she* might have been laughing.

'Poor you,' I remarked, more or less for the sake of it because even though I was furious with her for deleting my messages, and for the trouble she'd brought on Star, she was Honey. 'So Honey, what were those txt messages from Billy that you deleted?'

'I told you, just heavy breathing, a little smutty for your wholesome little American taste.'

'Heavy breathing? Smut?'

'Darling, you *really* don't want to know.'

'Oh, but I do,' I told her firmly.

Then Portia's voice added, 'So do I.'

'Oh, darling, what's that top you're wearing?' Honey suddenly squealed, which made me jump six feet in the air as the words echoed about her nose. 'It's divine!'

I looked down at the stretched-out-of-shape white-ish t-shirt I was wearing. 'Erm, Top Shop; I think it was in the five-pound bin.'

'Oh, don't you just *adore* Top Shop?' she enthused. 'It's so tacky and yet so happening. Wrong, but deliciously right and darling on your figure. You make it look like something Lee whipped up.'

'Lee?'

'Alexander McQueen, darling; everyone who knows him calls him Lee.'

Portia loudly flicked the switch on her mobile charger. Honey rolled her eyes dramatically in Portia's direction, and the look, combined with the iron beak, was really quite alarming. I found myself feeling sorry for poor Bob and Sarah, forgoing the pool and the other luxury treats they sacrificed so that I could live in a room with something the carnival had kicked out.

'Sorry, what was that you said, Honey, I missed it?'

'I was saying, Mummy, Poppy and I sat in the front row at his last show in Paris and he totally adored us. Well, me more than Mummy or Poppy.' She giggled. 'They were tearing their false nails out with jealousy.' She laughed her hyena laugh, only the iron beak made it sound like an exhaust pipe exploding on an old car.

'He's got a boyfriend, hasn't he?' I hazarded.

'Oh, Calypso,' she hooted. 'Even gay men like girls like *me*.'

'Of course they do,' I replied as I wandered into the en suite to take a shower and smother my laughter.

'I did mean it before though, Calypso. I am genuinely sorry, about, you know, deleting your messages from Billy.'

I came back into the room. Honey had just said the word 'sorry' again, and more relevantly she increasingly sounded like she actually meant it. I was so shocked I said, 'Okay, it's fine,' even though I didn't mean it. 'But in the future I'd rather you didn't help yourself to my mobile, Honey.'

'I was surprised that there weren't any messages from Freddie, darling,' Honey added, looking pointedly at Portia, who was tidying up her area.

I glanced at Portia as I replied, 'Oh, I suspect he's seeing someone else.' I was trying to get a reaction, to test the waters, but Portia went on folding her clothes and putting them away in her drawer as aloof and regal as ever. So I tried harder. 'Besides, I've gone off him, really. Billy and I have got something more special.'

This time Portia looked up, but only because she was noticing that one of the evil fluorescent lights was flickering. She pulled over a chair, stood on it and tapped the tube back in place. Then calmly she went back to the task of tidying her area. It was maddening.

Indie came running into our room and, totally ignoring a bitchy remark from Honey, handed me her phone – a tiny little purple jewel with her name picked out in diamonds around the face.

'Calypso?' It was Star's voice. 'Your phone isn't working. Georgina's tried to call you as well and she said to check that your SIM card is okay.'

'My SIM card? Why?' I asked.

'I don't know, she didn't say, but she's really insisting you check it.'

I looked over at Honey, who was studying her nails with a suspicious amount of intensity. 'Okay, I will, but I'm more worried about you. I hate it here without you. We all do. You *are* coming back, aren't you?'

'Of course I'll be coming back. Daddy just wanted to make a point to Sister. But after this week, it's half term anyway, which means you won't see me unless you come to my place for the party.'

I tried not to whine but I couldn't help myself. 'I *really* want to go to La Fiesta though, Star. I've never been.'

'No, you don't, Calypso. Believe me, they are tragic!' she assured me. 'And full of plebs, and we're too old for that rubbish anyway. Even the Year Eights go now.'

'But the cashmere tops and the skirts – and the shoes. We bought the whole outfit,' I pleaded desperately.

'They're just clothes, darling! Please say you'll come; everyone else is coming. We can wear the outfits at my place. We can wear them all week if you like. Imagine it: we could waft about in them like stunning figurines from the nineteen-thirties. Daddy said we can use the recording studio for the last track. I want you to be part of it, Calypso, you know, on the CD? It was Indie's idea.'

'But I can't sing for toast.'

'No, on instrumentals.'

'And what instrument would that be, exactly?' I asked, a smile beginning to spread across my face.

'I don't know . . . triangle?'

'Triangle?'

'Don't mock the triangle, darling. It's a very underrated instrument.'

'It does sound fun,' I agreed, almost, but not quite tempted. Well, not enough to forgo my dream of La Fiesta anyway. I knew I should get over myself, but a dream is a dream, and Bob is always telling me to hang on to my dreams.

'So you'll come?'

I was noncommittal. 'Well, the thought of wafting about in bejewelled cashmere like nineteen-thirties figurines and playing the triangle does have a certain appeal.'

The truth was I saw myself as a tragic Cinderella who had forever been barred from the ball. Calypso, the proverbial underdog (that's me) was finally and firmly determined to put a stop to all those who would prevent her from attending the ball, be they Draconian parents or my closest friends.

And though I know Star loved me, she didn't really understand. She'd been to loads of balls whereas I'd never been to one. An irrational part of me was even a bit cross with Star for not understanding and being so stubborn when she knew how long and how much I'd wanted to go to this ball. We'd spoken of little else in LA, and Georgina and Star were the ones who'd persuaded my parents to let me go.

Star stuck the emotional thumbscrews on me. 'Kevin's coming to stay and so is Billy. Loads and loads of Eades boys are coming, coach-loads of them, and I'm inviting some of the fit boys from the village as well.'

'Billy will be there?' I said it out loud so Portia would hear, but she merely walked into the en suite and turned the water on loudly.

'Yes, he's spending the whole week, and Freddie's going to the Annual Euro Royal Bash Thingamee, so please come.'

'Maybe I will come,' I agreed. The truth was though, it was all a pose. Hearing Kevin's and Billy's names together only reminded me of Freddie, and that just reminded me that he wouldn't be at *my* ball but at the wretched Annual Euro Royal Bash Thingamee with Portia. And as lovely and fit as Billy was . . . he wasn't Freds.

'How is Georgina? Is she coming back? There are all sorts of rumours going around.'

'Of course she's coming. Everyone who matters is coming. Indie is coming straight after the ball.'

I wished I could go after the ball too, but the train fare from London was about a hundred quid or more, and all I had was thirty-seven pounds left to last me until after half term.

I changed the subject back to Georgina. 'No, I mean, is she coming back to school?'

Star seemed surprised by my question. 'Why wouldn't she be coming back?'

'It's just that everyone's saying she's been expelled for having that flask of vodka.'

I heard her giggle echoing down the phone. 'Oh yes, I can just imagine. Saint Augustine's waving goodbye to Tobias's school fees as well as hers. Tobias doesn't require a bed and doesn't eat, so it's a 25,000-pound drop in the coffers as far as the school is concerned. And don't forget, Calypso, Tobias was caught with the vodka, not Georgina. They can't pin it on her. Tobias has been suspended for a week for having vodka; Georgina has only been suspended for helping a fellow student conceal vodka.'

'Seriously?'

Our conversation was interrupted by Miss Bibsmore. 'Mobiles! After nine? Hand me that mobile immediately, Miss Kelly.'

I gave Indie a regretful look as I handed over her jewel to Miss Bibsmore. I expected Miss Bibsmore just to plop it in her pocket, but instead she turned it over and over in her hand, marvelling at its beauty.

'Well, perhaps you best hang on to this one, Indie. I wouldn't want to be responsible for something so lovely.' She handed it over to Indie and blushed.

'Thank you, Miss Bibsmore,' Indie smiled.

'But you can 'and yours in, Miss O'Hare, right now.'

'What about everyone else?' Honey hooted through her iron beak. No one else had mentioned her iron beak whatsoever – but everyone knew full well that she was only wearing it for attention and to try and make a point about Star injuring her.

'I'm not talking to everyone else so mind your own beeswax.'

'Beeswax? Sorry, no idea what that might be Miss B,' she said, her attempt at sounding innocent rattling through her beak like a coin dropping down a drainpipe. 'I don't speak *pleb* slang.'

'It's the gunk inside your head that you use for a brain, Miss O'Hare. I don't claim to be intelligent and I might well be what your type refers to as common an' all, but at least I don't gad about with a bit of tin plonked on my nose.'

'Ugh!' Honey screamed in outrage. 'I was told to wear this nose guard after being assaulted by a dangerous criminal who has yet to be brought to justice.'

'Well, as far as I can see you're on the loose an' all, so unless this other dangerous criminal has a mobile as needs handin' in, I'm not interested.' Miss Bibsmore stuck her gnarled wrinkly hand out for Honey's mobile.

'I'm soooo going to complain to Daddy.'

'I've no doubt you will.'

'I don't know what could be holding his solicitors up. I really don't. A person like you shouldn't be allowed to take valuable possessions from people like me! It's outrageous. How do I know you're not going to ring up all your hideous plebbie relatives on it?'

'You don't, but I'll be taking it just the same an' all, thank you. Though if I were you, Miss O'Hare, I wouldn't go planting ideas like that in a plebbie head like mine,' she cackled.

Honey slammed her mobile in Miss Bibsmore's out-stretched hand but didn't let it go. 'Before you take it, I actually need to ring that vet to make sure he's put that hideous, deformed rabbit out of my misery.'

Miss Bibsmore clenched her hand around Honey's hand. 'No need. I've spoken to the vet, and a nicer man I've yet to meet. I told 'im I'll be looking after that poor creature from now on, and 'e's more or less agreed to drop his report as long as the likes of you are prohibited from keeping pets at Saint Augustine's.'

'Oh, that's really sweet, Miss Bibsmore,' Indie told her, and Miss Bibsmore rewarded her with an awkward little cuddle.

'You're a lovely girl, you are, Indiamaca – a *real* princess. A girl that certain other girls should look to for guidance. But off to your own room with you now. It's lights out soon. Hail Mary . . . ,' she began, and we joined her in a few Hail Marys before she switched off our light and shuffled off.

Alone with Portia and Honey in the dark, I turned on my torch and opened up my mobile to check on the SIM card, and there it was, safe and sound.

I went into my mobile's phone book so that I could txt Georgina and reassure her all was fine on the SIM card front, but when I went into my address book it was empty.

'This is weird. My address book is empty?' I said out loud.

'I don't see why she didn't take *your* phone,' Honey whined.

'Probably didn't think it was worth taking,' I told her.

'I was speaking to Portia, darling,' said Honey.

Portia didn't reply.

After a while Honey said, 'Besides, your phone is such a brick. Your SIM card is probably dying.'

'I guess,' I agreed, while not entirely convinced. It wouldn't have surprised me if Honey had deleted my address book. I shone my torch light in her face, but she didn't look the least bit guilty or worried. I pressed the point anyway. 'You didn't interfere with my address book, did you?'

'Moi? Darling, what a horrible thing to suggest. What sort of girl do you think I am?' she cried out indignantly.

I didn't dwell on my broken phone for long though, because Clemmie and Arabella, cuddled up in their duvets, crept into our room. They were followed closely by Indie, cuddled up in hers. 'We've got Body Shop Specials and loads of tuck, so just grab your duvets,' Arabella ordered. 'Oh, and your fags and torches.'

TWENTY-NINE

Moi? Self-Centred?

I t wasn't as easy to sneak out of the main building as it was when we were housed in Cleathorpes. Even though we were only two floors up and had the benefit of scaffolding to climb down, we'd definitely be splattered on the lawn below if we slipped and fell. The climb wasn't going to be easy holding torches, sweets, Body Shop Specials, duvets, fags and pillows.

'Let's wrap it all up in a sheet and I'll climb down first,' I suggested gamely. 'Then when I'm safe, toss me the bundle and the rest of you can climb down.'

'I'll climb down with you,' Portia said as civilly as ever. 'The bundle will be too heavy for one of us to catch.'

'This scaffolding is freezing,' I remarked to her as we started down, hoping to draw some warmth from her cold civility, but she didn't have a chance to reply even if she had wanted to, because no sooner had we touched our toes on the lawn than Indie threw the bundle down and we had to grapple with that. Portia was right, I would never have managed it on my own.

Indie was the next down, followed by Arabella, Clemmie, and finally Honey, whose iron beak kept chinking on the scaffolding. We made our dash across to Pullers' Wood in super fast time, because even though it was a mild night, the grass beneath our trainer-clad feet was freezing.

We made our nest in a little clearing, spreading out our duvets and setting up our tuck. It was just like last year, only without Star and Georgina. Even the moon was full, which meant it was so bright we didn't need the torches once our eyes adjusted.

Indie told me that Star had called again. 'She's insisting that you to go to her place for the half term break.'

'Well, as I've nowhere to stay in London, I'll have to, I suppose,' I conceded.

Honey sat up and prodded me with her foot. 'But I said you can stay at my house. We'll have the whole place to ourselves, apart from the servants, obviously.'

'They're called staff now, Honey,' Indie snapped. 'You have absolutely no respect for the people who work for you, do you?'

Naturally, Honey ignored the remark. I hadn't even had a chance to get my head around the prospect of staying at Honey's famous Chelsea mansion. I suppose I hadn't actually thought she'd meant it.

'Oh, look, there's a shooting star,' cried Arabella, pointing with her cigarette up at the heavens. 'I'm going to wish that I pull Alfred at Star's party,' she announced.

'I wish I could go to Star's place with rest of rest you,' Indie added, cuddling under a duvet with me.

'Given the choice I'd rather go to the Euro Ball,' I sighed wistfully as I spotted a shooting star of my own.

Suddenly Portia spoke. 'You should be grateful you even have a choice.'

I was stung by what I saw as a direct attack on me. 'But I don't have the choices I want. Unlike you, Portia, I haven't been invited to the Royal Ball.'

The vodka stash concealed in the Body Shop bottles was being passed around. 'Do you know, Calypso,' Portia remarked lightly, as if about to explain weather systems, 'I actually used to look up to you? I actually used to admire you. Last year, when you set up *Nun of Your Business* and raised all that money for charity, all I wanted was to get to know you better. I was so thrilled when I discovered that you and I were sharing this term. I saw it as a chance to get to know you properly. But you're nothing like I thought you were. In fact, as far as I can tell, you and Honey are *the* singularly most self-centred girls I've ever had the misfortune to know.'

I took a big gulp of vodka and almost choked. So much for my plan to make up with Portia under the canopy of the stars. I felt like I'd been slapped across the face. Instead of making up, all my pent-up resentments about Portia going to the ball with Freddie just exploded out of me.

'That's easy for you to say, Miss I-Was-Born-with-a-Silver-Spoon-in-My-Mouth.'

Honey did her hyena laugh, which sounded more peculiar than ever echoing through her metal beak.

'Don't ruin tonight, you two,' Indie pleaded, nudging me in the ribs with her elbow. 'This is my first moonwalk at Saint Augustine's. I don't want any arguing.'

'Yes, have another drink,' Clemmie urged, passing the Body Shop Special flask to me.

'Yes, stop it, both of you,' Arabella added, passing another Body Shop Special over to Portia. 'Balls and parties simply aren't worth falling out over.'

'Exactly,' agreed Clemmie.

I took another long slug of vodka and passed it to Indie, hoping the confrontation was over.

'A silver spoon in my mouth didn't save my mother's life though, did it?' Portia replied emotionlessly.

She was right, and in that moment I realised what a tragic piece of work I was, obsessing about a couple of boys when what really counted was being here with my friends and knowing that on the other side of the world Bob and Sarah were working hard to give me all this. I remembered how I'd not even bothered opening the e-mail from Bob and Sarah when there was an e-mail in my in box from Freddie. I'd been obsessing about all the wrong things. 'I'm really, really sorry, Portia,' I told her as the tears sprang to my eyes. 'Please, Portia, I'm sorry.'

But she continued, her voice pleasant but cold, 'People like *you* will never understand that money and position don't instantly deliver your dreams. Sometimes, you have to do things you'd rather not do. Sometimes you have to put other people before yourself. Do you think I want to go to this stupid ball any more than Indie does?'

I felt the blood rush to my face at her words. For a start I was shocked that she hadn't acknowledged my apology, and then I began to feel angry because even though she could see I was tearful, she was still going for me. Behind her aloof demeanour, which prevented her from showing her true feelings, was the simple truth: she disliked me.

'People like you . . . ,' she continued.

'Oh, just have a sweet, you two, and lighten up,' Clemmie groaned. 'I didn't risk my life climbing down that bloody scaffolding to hear you two arguing.'

Still, her outburst worked for a moment, at least until the silence was interrupted by Honey. 'You really, really hate Calypso, don't you, Portia?' she said with a reverent awe in her voice.

But I barely listened to Honey. The fragile sense of belonging that I'd built up last term was under attack. 'Anyway, Portia, what do you mean by people like *me*? People without money? People without title and privilege?' I lashed back. 'Just because I'm American and titleless, and not as rich as you . . .'

Portia groaned. 'How typical that you make this about

your country rather than looking at yourself. I'm not talking about your nationality, Calypso. I'm talking about the fact that self-centred, manipulative people like you and Honey make the world a colder, more miserable place for the rest of us.'

'Me and Honey?' I repeated. I looked over at Honey in her metal beak and her eyes met mine in shared horror. 'Honey and me!' I said it again because it wasn't easy getting my mind around our two names linked together like that.

'How *dare* you!' Honey squawked through her beak. I don't suppose she wanted to be grouped with me either.

'Um, this is getting a bit heavy, guys. Can we just chill a bit?' Indie pleaded. 'They're *both* just stupid balls full of stupid boys we'll loathe by next year. None of it means anything.'

'At least you're invited, though,' I reminded her.

Arabella interjected. 'Well, I'm glad I don't have to go to the stupid Royal Bore. I can't think of anything worse than dancing with all those old farty men. Yuk.'

Indie giggled. 'That's what it is, actually, a Royal Bore.'

'Exactly. It all sounds positively evil to me,' Arabella groaned. 'No, I'm looking forward to pulling lovely fit boys at Star's house party and riding quad bikes around in the mud.'

'I wish I could,' added Portia. 'I'd much rather be spending time with Star and the . . . boys. Just chilling.'

The image of Madam Deportment 'chilling' made me laugh. 'Chilling? You, Portia? You're so cold I'm surprised bits of you don't snap off,' I blurted before I could stop myself.

Portia was right: I *was* becoming like Honey. Help!

THIRTY

Honey World: 'You Can Check Out Any Time You Like, But You Can Never Leave'

I spent the rest of the week in Indie's dorm, mostly because I was too uncomfortable to be around Portia.

Honey, on the other hand, stuck to me like glue, which was creepy, not just because of the iron beak, but because of the associations the other girls might have made about us hanging out together. Indie hated Honey and wouldn't let her in her room, so at least I was safe there. Indie was really kind. She told me not to worry about what Portia had said and urged me to make up.

'But I've tried,' I reminded her, and she threw it back in my face.

'Give her time. You know what Honey's said to you

about Portia, but you don't know what she's said to Portia about you.'

'I don't think Portia listens to Honey,' I told her, quite certain I was right.

As far as Honey was concerned, it was now written in stone that I was spending the half term week at her place, and out of desperation, I let myself be talked into it. Although I dreaded the thought of spending time with Honey, I was still determined to go to the ball.

On Friday, the day we left school, I had to go back to my room to pack my bag. I hoped Portia would be gone already, but despite my careful timing, I was just in time to see her placing the last item in her bag and zipping it up. Dressed in old jeans and a t-shirt, a cashmere hoodie tied casually around her waist, her long dark hair tied up in a ponytail, she walked past me without acknowledging me in her special regal way. Honey high-fived me, and I high-fived her back, because, well, I couldn't just leave her hand hanging in midair when I was going to be stuck with her at her house all week!

That was when it hit me. Portia had said she'd much rather be spending the week at Star's when we were on our moonwalk. And what's more, she'd sounded like she actually meant it.

'She said she'd much rather be spending the half term break at Star's,' I announced as if coming out of a dream – or perhaps it was a nightmare.

'Who cares what Misery Briggs prefers?' Honey

shrugged. 'We'll have the best time at La Fiesta; I've arranged caviar and champagne for the ride back to London. . . .'

'Yes, but don't you see? Freds is going to be at the Royal Bore, not at Star's; so if she's so keen on Freddie, why would she want to be at Star's?'

Honey shrugged again, then turned her back on me and went into the en suite, slamming the door behind her.

Had I been a complete idiot, allowing Honey's suggestions and poisonous whispers to seep into my consciousness? Indie was right, I had to sort this out. I charged down the stairs, which were packed with girls and their luggage, all of them making their half term plans to catch up on the King's Road. By the time I fought my way outside, I was calling out Portia's name as loudly as humanly possible without losing a tonsil. But her chauffeur-driven Rolls-Royce was already crunching down the gravel driveway.

In the limo on the drive back to her place, Honey produced those tiny little bottles of Veuve Clicquot that you see runway models drinking at after show parties. I had never even tried champagne, not that I was going to admit this to Honey or anything. I was actually quite curious to see what the big deal was. Sucking up the contents of our mini-bottles through matching orange straws, driving down the hedge-lined country lanes, I watched in shock as Honey suddenly threw her iron beak out the window.

'What about your nose?' I asked fearfully, because after a

while Honey's lies sort of seep into you. Of course I knew all this, I'd known her for coming up on five years, which begged the question . . . what was I doing, sitting in the back of her limo with her, like we were close girlfriends? And then it got even worse. As the bubbles of the champagne charged up through the straw and into my mouth, I looked down, and she was actually holding my hand.

She squeezed it warmly. 'Oh, I don't need it now, I was only making a point. If Star thinks she can get away with hitting me, she's about to get a nasty surprise. Daddy said I needed the infirmary to quantify my injuries.'

We had come to a T-junction, and as we took the turn to London, I realised that I was the one who had taken a wrong turn. Instead of heading off to stay with my best friend, Star, in Derbyshire like a sane girl, I was in Honey's limo on the way back to Honey's mansion in Chelsea, where I would be spending the next week. A whole week in Honey World!

There was no chance of escape now, though. I sucked on my straw, hoping the champagne could make me feel more optimistic, but all it did was make me feel like screaming hysterically and tearing at my clothing the way those women do in Alfred Hitchcock movies.

'I've got loads of bleach at home, so don't worry about your hair, okay?' she said faux-kindly, giving my head a pat.

Of course she had bleach. No doubt she also had arsenic and cyanide and a whole host of other poisonous toys to try on me as well. I felt like her little pet, which is probably how she saw me. With Poppy and her mother in LA, Georgina and all the other girls who tolerated her at Star's estate and her rabbit now in the possession of Miss Bibsmore, I was all Honey had left. Maybe *I'd* end up being turned into a pair of designer shoes!

Looking at it from the other angle, I did have choices, as Portia so accurately pointed out. I could have been at Star's with all the other girls. I could have been riding quad bikes by day and pulling fit boys by night. Okay, Freddie wouldn't be there, but I could have met other fit boys, danced, pulled, moved on. But instead I was in Honey's limo en route to Honey's mansion, where bleach and god knows what else awaited me.

It was about five o'clock when we finally dived out of the limo on Cadogan Gardens, a garden square behind Harrods in Knightsbridge, where even the plants have trust funds. The door was opened by my old friend, and Honey's crippled manservant, Oopa. He was dressed in the usual valet garb, morning coat and striped trousers. He didn't smile but merely wandered out to the limo and started to bring in the bags. The rest of the staff were lined up as if to meet the queen, curtsying and doffing their caps to Honey. It really was like we were in another century.

'Bring up some champagne, Oopa. Dom, I think, don't you, Calypso?' She asked me as if genuinely interested in my opinion.

'Oh yes, always Dom,' I agreed, even though I didn't want any more champagne and I definitely didn't want to be alone with a seriously châteaued Honey. Nonetheless, I scuttled up the marble stairs after her, trying to reassure myself that I would be okay. It was only a week after all, and at least Honey was being nice to me . . .

She opened the door on a bedroom so palatial that you could get lost in it. She had her own phone and one of those intercom systems so she could contact the staff in any room of the house. But there was something rather sad about it all, as if all this luxury could in some way compensate for being alone. As much as Honey went on about her Daddy suing everyone, he'd never actually attended any of the school functions for parents. I started to feel a bit sorry for Honey. I would hate to go home to LA to a house with no Bob and Sarah – even if I did have loads of people to do things for me and lots of lovely things. The best thing about holidays at home with my parents was being with them – as mad and wholemeal as they were. I was the most important person in the world as far as they were concerned. They loved me.

'We'll have a glass of bubbles and then I'll take you to your quarters,' she babbled away excitedly, flopping on her antique four-poster bed. 'Chopin once made love to George Sand on this bed,' she moaned as she writhed around ecstatically.

I muttered something lame like 'How splendid,' but I wasn't really paying attention. Everything in her room was so unexpectedly tasteful, and I was envious that she actually owned a bed that Chopin and George Sand had made love in, even though that image was a bit gross. I wasn't a great fan of George Sand, but she was still an author and, more importantly, she was brave and wild-spirited, like Star.

'Why didn't you go to the premiere in LA with your mother and sister?' I asked her.

'I don't think that's any of your business,' she snapped at me in the way people do when you've touched a raw nerve. But she soon gathered herself together and added, 'So, I've called in Stephan to do our hair and Mimi to do our nails, and then I thought we could just drink champagne, eat sushi and pop out to Calm-a-sutra for a bit of a laugh.'

'Calm-a-sutra?' I enquired as I gazed at the sad, vast gorgeousity of her bedroom.

'The nightclub in Kensington,' she explained, looking at me like she just realised what a big mistake she'd made in bringing an unsophisticated nobody like me into her world.

'Oh, sorry, of course I *love* Calm-a-sutra, it's really cool, isn't it?' I gushed. I'd never been there in my life, obviously, but like everyone, I knew of it through the social pages. I almost said, 'But it's a club and we're only fifteen' – well, I was only fourteen and ten months actually, but I tried not to remind the other girls about that.

'So show me what you're wearing to La Fiesta, darling,' Honey demanded.

'Oh, we bought these adorable outfits in Los Angeles,' I told her enthusiastically. 'You know, when Georgina and Star were out there.'

I thought I saw a look of irritation flash across Honey's face at the mention of Star and Georgina being in LA with me, but it disappeared quickly as we heard a knock at the door.

'Come,' Honey called, and Oopa staggered in, buckling under the weight of a heavy silver tray bearing an ice bucket, a bottle of vintage Dom and champagne flutes.

'Shall I be of the pouring man?' he asked in heavily accented English.

'Just do what you're paid to do, you wretched little ungrammatical cripple. I'd hardly ask for champagne if I didn't want to drink it, would I?' she snapped.

I bet she would, I thought to myself, already beginning to wonder how long I could keep my hatred of Honey secret. I was starting to think the price of going to La Fiesta was going to be very costly indeed. A week seemed like an impossibly long time to spend in the sole company of the most toxic psycho toff in the world. And with Honey knocking back the champagne at this rate, it would be even worse. I began to make escape plans. The Ball was on Sunday night, so there was the possibility that I could make an excuse and leave on Monday to join Star and the others, except that I had no money of course. Maybe I could call Star and plead with her to send one of her father's roadies to pick me up. Star would understand. She had probably anticipated my call pleading for rescue, knowing Star.

Oopa did as he was bid and then backed out of the

room, tugging his forelock (not really, but I bet Honey wished he had been).

After Honey had downed another glass of champagne (I'd taken care to take only a sip of mine), she showed me my quarters. It was a room in the basement, a quarter the size of hers but still very nice with a massive king-size bed, a fireplace with a plasma screen above, and an en suite bathroom even nicer than the one at school.

'This is soooo cool,' I told her, looking around.

Honey wrinkled her nose job. 'Anyway, let's go back to mine and work out what we'll wear tonight,' she said, grabbing my hand and leading me back upstairs.

It was actually quite fun preparing for Calm-a-sutra. We put MTV on, and Honey encouraged me to try on all her cool designer outfits, and we danced about gaily and jumped on her bed. At eight o'clock the sushi, Stephan and Mimi arrived at once. I'd had loads of manicures and pedicures in LA with Sarah but I'd never had my hair dressed!

Stephan and Mimi guzzled the rest of the champagne and picked at our sushi and fawned and chatted away to us as if we were really grown-up clients. After they left, Honey and I helped one another put on our make-up. 'You've got madly long lashes, darling,' she remarked approvingly as she applied a mile of mascara to them.

'Thank you,' I said, even though I was worried I looked a bit overdone.

I stood up and did a twirl in the full-length mirror

stand, thinking I looked amazingly grown-up, but Honey threw another strappy dress at me. 'Try this one, actually; it might be a better fit.'

It was a sort of dark green colour with a copper thread running through it so it spangled, only not in a tacky way. It was longer than the tangerine one I was wearing but completely backless.

I held it up against my figure. 'This is stunning, Honey.'

She glanced at it before turning back to her wardrobe for another rummage. 'It's not a label or anything. I just found it at Vanilla, rummaging around one day.'

I slipped off the dress I was wearing, which was worryingly short, and tried the non-label on. 'I love it.'

Honey nodded. 'Keep it. I'm never going to be tall enough to fit into it.'

'Wow, are you sure?' I asked, uncertain about accepting a gift from this girl who until recently had been so cruel to me.

'Don't be mad, it's nothing. Besides, that other dress made you look like a slut.'

'Thank you,' I told her. 'I mean about the dress, not the slut thing.'

She dismissively waved off my gratitude and turned her attention to the pile of jewellery on her dressing table. 'These earrings or these?' she asked, holding up two pairs of wildly glamorous chandelier drop earrings.

They were both fabulous. I pointed to the ones in her left hand.

'Typical. They're the cheap crystals from Accessorize; you can wear those if you want. These are the diamond ones,' she explained, holding up the others. 'One of Mummy's husbands bought them for her at Graff. I *always* get her castoffs,' she sighed, as if receiving expensive diamond gifts was one of the many crosses she bore.

We arrived at Calm-a-sutra around midnight, tottering out of the limo in our impossibly high Christian Louboutin shoes.

The doorman recognised Honey instantly, and we were ushered to one of the private booths, which were really large white beds with soft white faux fur throws and matching pillows. A flock of fit Eades boys from the Upper Sixth immediately came over and started to chat to us. I recognised Charlie, Sebastian and Peregrine from the pub in Windsor and got the impression they were expecting us. I looked at their cocktails worryingly, anticipating the boys tipping them over one another later in the evening.

I agreed to a try a sip of Peregrine's mojito, which tasted really nasty. Honey of course said it was delicious and demanded Charlie get her one of her own. I was bored very quickly, as Honey focused her attentions of heavy flirting with Charlie. All the other conversations at our bed seemed to centre on other trustafarian teens I didn't know and glamorous places I'd never been to.

'Do you ski at Klosters or Val-d'Isere?' Peregrine asked me in a generous attempt to include me.

Honey dragged herself away from Charlie to answer for

me, 'Oh, don't ask her, darling, she probably doesn't even know how to ski.'

'I do know how to ski, actually, but . . . erm . . . well, I live in America.'

Sebastian, who was soooo seriously châteaued by this stage that he couldn't focus properly, told me I was 'a babe.'

'That's sweet of you,' I said moving even farther away from him in the bed, which practically placed me on Peregrine's lap. He was very nice about it though and not at all sleazy. When he asked if I wanted to dance, I saw it as an opportunity to get Honey away from Charlie.

'Excellent idea, let's all dance,' I agreed, forcing Honey, Charlie and the others to join us.

Honey's dancing practise by mirrors actually seemed to have paid off, and soon she was in another world, thoughts of pulling Charlie, and seemingly everything else, far from her head as she closed her eyes and danced in mesmeric movements to the music. In fact the two of us ended up dancing together while Charlie, Sebastian and Peregrine did that sort of English public school boy dance – you know the one – it looks a bit like old men with Zimmer frames attempting a rugby scrum.

After a few dances we started to head back to the bed booth when Peregrine took me aside and asked, 'Are you and Freddie an item or what?'

'Or what,' I replied, wishing I had an answer to give him. 'Why?'

'Well, I don't know him that well but he asked me if I saw you, to tell you to call him.'

'Let me get this straight. *He* asked *you* to tell *me* to . . .'

But I didn't get a chance to clarify what Freddie might have wanted Peregrine to tell me because Honey grabbed my arm. 'Come on, we're leaving. The car's outside,' she shouted in my ear, and that was when I realised how wasted she was. Her eyes were glazed and her speech was slurred.

'I have to get Honey home,' I told Peregrine.

Charlie and Sebastian offered to see us out, and noticing the paparazzi gathered around the door in force, they were really responsible and had security help hold back the paps so we could climb discreetly into the limo. The last thing I needed was another episode in the tabloids.

'Make sure she drinks loads of water when you get her home,' Charlie advised, but I wasn't paying attention. Honey was slumped with her eyes closed at the other corner of the limo. I opened up my phone. It was too late to call Freddie, but I decided a txt-flirt would be okay. That way he would get it when he woke up. I smiled at that thought. I still had no address book, but that didn't matter because I knew his number off by heart – and that heart was pounding as I punched in my message.

Just spoke to Peregrine. Call me! C

I pressed SEND and waited, but the message came back: NO SERVICE. I checked the signal, but that was fine, and I knew I still had credit left.

I jabbed Honey with my foot to wake her. 'Honey, can I borrow your phone to send a message to Freddie? My phone isn't working.'

Even though she'd looked me in the eye as I'd asked, she suddenly collapsed back into her seat and started snoring loudly.

'Honey!' I yelled, but she resolutely refused to budge, apart from when I tried to nick her phone from out of her bag, and then she hit me.

'Sorry, darling. I thought you were a pikey trying to steal from me,' she explained before drifting back to sleep.

'No, I just really need to make a call and my phone is out of . . . ,' I tried to say but it was pointless.

She was still snoring when we arrived back at the mansion. I gave Honey same water and asked her again if I could use her phone, but she firmly dispatched me to my quarters.

I was feeling sleepless, so I took a bath in the luxury of the large black marble Jacuzzi that had steps leading up to it. The Aveda products smelt heavenly, and the towels were all fluffy and enormous. It was like being in a movie, only not one I wanted to stay in. To be honest I'd have preferred to bathe in pond water if it meant I could have a mobile that worked.

THIRTY-ONE

Honey's House of Horrors

I was awakened by a buzzer going off in my room the next morning. I looked for where the noise was coming from and saw a red light flashing above a sign with the words

Honey's Bedchamber

written underneath in swirly-whirly writing.

I clambered into my jeans and t-shirt and rushed upstairs, expecting the worst – perhaps she'd got trapped in her duvet or was being strangled by her eye-mask.

'Open my curtains,' she screamed hysterically. 'I can't see a thing.'

I stumbled in the dark over to the curtains and tried to open them, but they wouldn't budge.

'Use the button by my bed, you idiot,' she howled from another side of the room.

So I crawled over to her bed, found the switch on her bedside light, found the button for the curtains and let the grey autumnal light flow in.

Honey was lying crumpled in a corner by her bathroom door.

'Are you okay?' I asked when she didn't get up. I could see a little bit of blood coming out of her nose.

'I was trying to go to the loo,' she sobbed. 'I bashed my nose on the door.'

And that was when it happened – when I finally lost my ability to hold in my secret hatred for Honey a moment longer and burst out laughing. 'It's a shame you threw that beak away – it was obviously really handy.'

'You bitch,' she snarled. 'Maybe you'd be more comfortable upstairs with the servants.'

'Sorry,' I said, kicking myself for losing control.

But there was no going back. Oopa was instructed to remove me from my quarters to the servants' floor upstairs, where I was confined. I wasn't actually locked into a cell, but as good as. I didn't feel comfortable leaving the room in case I ran into Honey, so I lay on the camp bed in the tiny box room. It was so small the bed was too long to completely fit, which meant it was a bit buckled in the middle, and I couldn't stretch out completely. I spent the day meditating on the mess I had made of things, and I don't mean with Honey. I mean with everything – with Portia, with Freddie and most of all with the choice I'd made to choose a stupid ball over my friends. I'd been naïve to think that it would be any fun at all at La Fiesta without Star and the others. In the pursuit of a childish dream I'd gone – in the words of my father – too far.

I couldn't remember the exact directions to Star's estate, but if I could, I swear I would have jumped out of the fourth-floor window and walked there, even though it would have taken two weeks.

Sunday was better, as Honey needed to re-bond with me for the ball. She came into my room and woke me up with a lovely cup of tea she'd made herself. 'Sorry about being such a bitch yesterday,' she said. 'Oh darling, look at this room, it's uninhabitable,' she cried out as if genuinely alarmed and ashamed at how I'd been treated. 'The bed doesn't even fit in the room!'

'I know, I had to sleep with my legs up in the air!'

'Oh, poor Calypso, will you ever forgive me, darling?' she asked, her lower lip wobbling.

'And this blanket seems to have brought me out in a rash,' I told her as I scratched at the bumps that had come up all over my body during the night.

'Ghastly! That's soooo Oopa's fault, darling. He's an evil old devil. That blanket belongs to Mummy's dog, Chanel.'

She went to hug me, but I pulled away, scratched and said. 'I'll forgive you if you lend me your mobile to make a call.'

'Of course, darling,' she gasped. 'Anything. You know that.'

I couldn't believe it. 'Really?'

'Absolutely. Who do you want to call. Are we missing Billy darling? Are we missing our boyfriend?'

'No, actually, when we were at Calm-a-sutra on Friday, Peregrine gave me a message from Freddie. He wants me to call him.'

Honey's face clouded over. 'Darling, you can definitely use my phone but, well, I didn't want to tell you, but as you're clearly deluded, I guess I'll have to. Freddie and Portia are an item.'

'No.' I shook my head firmly. 'No, Portia said she'd rather go to Star's. I need to call Freds, Honey, really. I really do,' I pleaded.

Honey took my two hands in hers and looked into my eyes. 'Darling! For all my wicked flaws and silliness, you know how much I care for you, don't you?'

No. 'Yes, of course I do, but . . .'

'Misery Briggs hates you, Calypso. She never stops going on about how much she *loathes* you with every fibre of her aristocratic body. The simple fact is, she's a snob.'

However muddled my feelings for Portia were, she wasn't really one for bitching. 'That doesn't sound like Portia.'

'Have you already forgotten her outburst on the moon-walk? I almost slapped her for you, darling.'

'No, I haven't forgotten anything,' I said, choosing my words carefully, 'but if I could just borrow your phone and . . .'

Honey held her hand up to silence me. 'No, Calypso.

It's for your own good. I'm your *real* friend, probably your *only* friend these days. If I don't look after you, who will, darling? Leave Freddie and Portia to get on with their royal fling. We've got a ball to prepare for. You need all the self-esteem you can get, and I've promised myself I'm going to make sure you get it.' It sounded like a threat more than a promise.

Had I really sunk so low that Honey was now my only real friend? I wondered later as I took a long, cool bath in the hope of getting rid of the ghastly rash. My body was like a relief map. Honey gave me some calamine lotion to put on it, which soothed the itching but made me look like strawberry mousse.

We spent almost the entire day getting ready, and by six o'clock, when Honey called Nobu for sushi, I was actually starting to feel excited about the ball again. And although Honey opened up the Aladdin's cave of her wardrobe to me again, I couldn't find anything nicer than the skirt and bejewelled cashmere top I'd bought in LA.

'What bag are you taking, darling?'

I held up the little Gucci bag Sarah and Bob had given me last Christmas, but Honey wrinkled her nose job. 'Darling, that's not on trend, nor is it old enough to be vintage. Try this,' she insisted, passing me a tiny little bejewelled fur Fendi.

'Oh, Honey, I can't – it must have cost thousands and thousands!' I protested.

'Only four or five,' she insisted. She pressed the bag into

my hand, even though I didn't really want the responsibility of such an expensive bag, especially as I planned to
spend the night dancing and would have to leave it in the
cloakroom or on a chair. But I didn't really have a choice.
Honey had a marvellous knack for getting what Honey
wanted.

'Darling, it looks perfect with the rest of your outfit. I'm
going to do my eyes and just use a dab of lip-gloss, what do
you think?' she asked as if she really cared about my
opinion.

I leaned over to examine her palette. 'I love the browns;
I think they're really sultry and old-movie glamour.'

'Exactly, let's do old-movie glamour, darling,' she
agreed, smiling up at me. 'But first you'll have to put
some make-up on that rash of yours; with all that calamine
lotion you look like you've got measles.'

I took the foundation she passed me and despite my
doubts, I went into her en suite to apply it. When I
returned, Honey was holding my phone. 'What are you
doing with that?' I demanded crossly; I didn't want her
deleting any more messages.

She looked surprised and hurt as she put the phone into
the fur Fendi she was lending me. 'I was just swapping all
your stuff from one bag to another,' she explained.

'Sorry,' I said, but she didn't reply.

We were back on speakers by the time we climbed into
the limo, thank goodness. I even accepted another one of
the tiny Veuves from the fridge and sipped it through the

straw. My heart was racing as to what the evening was going to be like. Honey tried to get me to see the humour in the acute discomfort in which I'd spent the previous night, but I was still all bumpy with the rash.

'Oh darling, don't be mad. The foundation has totally covered them up; you're so paranoid. No wonder you have such bad luck with boys, darling. Besides, who'll be looking at you when I'm there?' she asked, faux-jokingly. Then she pinched me, only not in a playful way.

'My skin has the texture of a relief map, Honey. I look diseased.'

Honey laughed uproariously until not only did the collagen in her lip bubble up, but after a choking fit, she did a little vomit, which she spat in my handbag.

'Sorry darling, it was the first thing to hand. Don't worry, I'll buy you another one tomorrow.'

I was beyond caring, though. I found myself saying, 'That's okay,' and 'Thank you, that's so sweet of you,' and 'Actually no need – I mean, in fact it's really your handbag anyway.' She looked a bit cross then.

On our arrival I stood with Honey on the long snaking queue outside the Hammersmith Pallais, caked in foundation, holding my bag of vomit and trying to summon the feelings of excitement I had felt earlier in the evening. It wasn't easy. I wondered how the party at Star's was going. I imagined fit boys and all my friends lounging around Tiger's chill room with the Angel of Death peeing Jim Beam over the black Japanese stones. I imagined them dancing to Star and Indie's music, and then I looked down the queue at the hordes of Year Eight and Nine girls and boys Star and the others had tried to save me from. There was the odd tragic parent on the other side of the road, sitting in their Range Rover, waiting to see their daughter get into the party safely.

This is when I had my epiphany. I think *hubris* is the word. We had studied the word both with Ms Topler and during Ancient Greek lessons. *To presume that one is greater than the gods.* Well, the gods were having a good old laugh now. I looked up at the sky as a few drops of rain fell on my foundation-coated body.

Honey's phone rang.

'Hi, darling, yaah, we're here now about to go in. We had the maddest night at Calm-a-sutra on Friday. I pulled Charles, remember we met him . . .'

I tried not to listen in, but then Honey shoved her mobile hard against my ear. 'Here, she wants to speak to you,' she said in a really pissed-off way.

It was Georgina on the other end.

'Hi, Georgina, how is –' I started.

'Demand Honey give you back your SIM card immediately!' she insisted firmly.

'My SIM card's in my phone, I already checked.'

'Believe me, that is not *your* SIM card.'

'I don't understand . . . ?'

'So just trust me because I know Honey a lot better than you do, okay? We always used to nick the SIM card out of one another's mobiles in Year Ten. Well everyone's mobile, actually, you know, just so we could check who was receiving txts from whom. It's easy to do. We always kept a whole collection of the various pay-as-you-go cards and replaced them.'

'That's horrible.'

'Yaah, I know. Sorry. I don't do it now!'

I whispered into the phone with my back turned on Honey. 'Honey's a complete bitch, Georgina. I'm having a horrible time!'

'Calypso, you didn't just work that out? Anyway, we don't have time to discuss this now; just ask her for your SIM card back, *now*.'

Turning around, I casually said, 'Honey, can I have my SIM card back, please?'

Honey rolled her eyes.

'What did she say?' Georgina asked. I could hear a party in full swing on the other end of the line.

'She rolled her eyes.'

'Repeat these three words out loud, then: Village. Pleb. Shag! And then say you know and you'll tell everyone if she doesn't hand it over this very moment.'

I turned to Honey, who was looking at me beadily. 'Village. Pleb. Shag!' I said, enunciating each word carefully, slowly and loudly so I wouldn't have to repeat them. 'I know everything and I'll tell everyone,' I warned her with a bravado I didn't feel.

'Fine.' Honey rolled her eyes. 'It was for your own good,

if you must know,' she sneered. But she took her phone back, shut it and, after a scramble in her bag, passed me over what must have been my real SIM card.

'But why?' I asked, confused.

'It amused me.' She shrugged her skinny sun-kissed shoulders.

'It amused you?'

'Yes – do you know how sickening it was, watching Portia becoming best pals with a pleb like you! Treating *me* as if *I* were the freak! It was just soooo *wrong*,' she said as if she was being madly logical or something.

'So, you stole my SIM card and deleted my txts to redress the social balance?'

'Yes. I mean no, I borrowed your SIM card occasionally and then put it back occasionally. I didn't delete the messages, well, not strictly speaking, anyway. I forwarded the messages to my SIM and just deleted them from your SIM, so you see they're not really deleted. I was just borrowing txts from your txt library, really. Think of it that way.' She smiled sweetly.

I was aghast at her total lack of shame – I don't know why.

'And it was going to be a surprise but you may as well know I did you the most *enormous* favour. When you were putting the body makeup on I forwarded all the messages I borrowed back onto your SIM so everything is just as it should be now. Don't get so worked up about it. I always nick SIM cards, like any normal person does. Even your precious friend, Georgina does. In fact, it was her idea,' she added.

'Her idea to steal my SIM card?'

'Not *your* SIM, obviously. But when she was *my* best friend we used to steal everyone's, apart from yours because we wouldn't have had much fun with your SIM before this year, would we, darling?' She laughed. 'We used to do it together before you came along and ingratiated yourself into *our* world and ruined everything!' she explained crisply as she shuffled forward with the moving queue.

As we moved ever closer to the entrance, I tried to absorb what her game had meant to my relationship with Portia as well as with Freddie and Billy. Without Honey's interference how would the half term have played itself out? I reflected on the first time we went to Windsor, and I bumped into Billy on the bridge. I remembered leaving him alone with Portia, the two of them chatting away happily. Was that when they realised they liked each other?

'And don't think *you're* so special,' continued Honey, gathering outrage as she ranted. 'I nicked Portia's SIM too. Only of course I had to put hers back more frequently because she has a family that loves her and she gets loads of txts. When I first found out you were txt-flirting Billy and Freddie, I thought it might be amusing. Then once I discovered that Billy was keen on Portia, I couldn't resist. Darling, it was like watching a gripping soap opera unfold.

You can't blame me, not when you pushed in on my world, stealing Georgina and chumming up with Portia.'

'I bloody well can blame you and I will,' I told her furiously, realising now that she must have deleted that txt Billy had asked me about. All the time I had been considering pulling Billy as a second-best, less complicated boyfriend, Portia had already pulled him. Actually, rather than her stealing Freddie, I had been stealing Billy – at least that's how it must have appeared to Portia.

I felt sick.

Honey smiled at me and poked her tongue out. 'So sue, sweetie,' she shrugged. 'I still love *you*!'

At that moment we arrived at the head of the queue and Honey handed her ticket to the door gorilla and skipped in to join the warm dry throb of the party.

I followed, handing the door gorilla my ticket.

'Stand aside, luv. That's not valid.'

'But my parents bought it online,' I told him desperately.

'Like I said, you isn't valid, move aside.'

'But can't I go in with my friend?' I begged – using the term 'friend' loosely, you understand. 'It's raining.' I did my special little-girl-lost face, but it didn't work.

'Stand aside, you're blocking the door,' he repeated without so much as looking at me as he continued to check and take tickets from others on the queue and allow them through. 'You isn't valid.'

'Honey,' I called out, 'he won't let me in.'

She didn't come out but spoke to me from behind the door gorilla. 'Never mind, darling, just wait there for me. I'll be out at two when Oopa is picking us up. The servants have the night off or I'd suggest you wait for me at home. Big kiss!' With that, she shrugged and disappeared into the noise and bright lights of the ball.

I took shelter with one of the tragic parents standing nearby under an umbrella and watched the girls and boys as they filed into the party. They all looked soooo young! Eventually the parent who had offered me shelter under her umbrella waved desperately as her little girl finally disappeared into the party. She apologised to me but said she and her umbrella were leaving. I almost pleaded with her to take me home with her, but I resisted the temptation.

So there I was, the tragic American Freak who had actually imagined that Honey, the toxic psycho toff, had liked me. I wiped a tear before it could fall down my face and ruin my make-up, before realising there was no need to worry about that now. I wasn't going anywhere. Why shouldn't I cry my heart out?

I stood in the rain with my SIM card in one hand and my clutch bag of vomit in the other. I opened up the Fendi and tried not to breathe in as I found my phone and wiped it free of vomit. It was a bit of a struggle, and I dry-retched a few times, but eventually I managed to swap the SIM cards and start my phone up.

My message bank was near to full. The first few txts

were from Freddie, just the usual flirty txt. The next was from Billy, and even though I wanted to delete it and scroll down to see if there were more from Freddie, it was quite long for a txt, so I began to read.

> I know this is a shity wy 2 tll u. but after I saw u in W I kind of pulled Portia. I feel really bad but I guess that dusnt help? Sorry. B.

It was sent the day I'd kissed Freddie in the rain under the awning in Windsor. Which meant the same day I'd decided Portia was stealing Freddie from me, Portia was actually pulling Billy. I felt stupid as I remembered flirting outrageously with Billy the next time I saw him with Portia. To think – I'd interpreted his embarrassment as a sign that he was desperately keen on me when actually he was desperately keen on Portia!

It was hard to absorb the full enormity of how not receiving that txt from Billy had destroyed my friendship with Portia. I scrolled down to the next txt, which was from Freddie.

> sorted the euro ball. Where will I pck u up? Txt me or do u stll wnt me 2 bugger off? Freds x

The tears were streaming down my face, and I didn't care that every time I wiped them away I was smearing my eye make-up even more. Freddie had wanted to take me to the Royal Bore after all. My crying jag was interrupted by a suited door gorilla who came up to me and tapped me on the shoulder. I expect he wanted to offer me a tissue, so I waved him away. Only unlike your average door gorilla, he spoke really nicely to me. 'Excuse me, miss, are you Calypso Kelly?'

'Yes, I am and I need to get into that ball,' I told him, resisting the urge to throw myself into his big comforting-looking chest. 'I am totally drenched —'

'I understand you had trouble entering the party. Sorry about that, miss, but His Royal Highness didn't think we'd manage to find you in there, and . . .'

I looked around. 'Is Freddie *here*?' I asked.

He gestured toward another man in a suit, only this suit wasn't a door gorilla; this suit was Freddie, my Freddie. Freds.

'Freds? What's going on?'

How romantic was this? How utterly fairy fable-ish, I thought as I swooned with excitement — right up to the point where Freds wrinkled his nose and asked me,

'Have you just vomited on yourself, Calypso?'

THIRTY-TWO

My Royal
Wake-Up Call

I began to explain about Honey and how she'd vomited into my handbag, but Freddie started to laugh. 'It's not *that* bad,' he teased. 'At least not as bad as your skin, which appears – if I'm not mistaken,' he added, peering closely at my arm, 'to be peeling off you.'

And then he did the coolest thing! He took his hand and ran it down my arm. Only it wasn't cool when he looked at the gunk on his hand and grimaced.

'That's the make-up she made me put on to hide the rash from the prickly blanket. . . .'

He put his arm around me. 'You can tell me all about it on the boat. Right now we have a ball to get to.'

'You mean the Royal Bore? I mean, the Annual Euro Royal Bash Thingamee?'

'Yes, now put this on,' he instructed, handing me a motorbike helmet and leather jacket. 'Quick spin down to the river and we take a boat straight to the castle pier.'

I wanted to pinch myself as I climbed onto the old Norton behind Freddie and we sped beneath the Hammersmith fly-over. I clasped my hands around him tightly as we rode Bond-like down some old stone steps. I swear my heart was in my mouth by the time we got to the little strip along the Thames called the Lower Mall. I could see the jetty and a giant boat with security guys hanging about it, waiting for us.

Two men in chinos who were chatting into mouthpieces were there to take the bike from Freddie. We handed them our helmets and jackets and walked down the jetty hand in hand. I had to carry my lovely shoes, though, because they kept slipping through the slats.

Just before we climbed onto the boat, Freddie wrapped his arms around me and kissed me, only not for very long as he pulled away to ask, 'Is there actually anything valuable in that bag of yours?'

I looked at the fur Fendi Honey had lent me and shook my head. 'No, I washed my phone in the rain and now it's in my . . .' I looked down at the phone wedged in the elastic part of my bra where my cleavage would have been – if I had any.

Freddie looked too and grinned. 'So, no passport? No valuable item of jewellery, no wallet, no government documents of vital importance, no driving licence, car keys?'

'Nothing. The only item of value is my Lancôme Juicy Tube lip-gloss.'

'In that case,' he said, removing the bag from my hand

and tossing it into the Thames, 'I think we can dispense with it.'

'Oh,' I said sadly as I watched it sink to the bottom of the river. 'I was really quite attached to my Lancôme Juicy Tube lip-gloss.'

'Sorry,' he said, putting his arm around me. 'I was lying about the spew thing, though. It really did stink. Besides, I'm planning on kissing you quite a bit, and I hate lip-gloss.'

I smiled. 'It was actually Honey's bag.'

'Really?' He rubbed his jaw in a madly sexy way, appearing to ponder the situation for a split second and then smiled as he announced in a Sean Connery piss-take, 'Well, my dear, the bateau awaits us!' Then he bowed down, really, really low, and ushered me onto the bateau.

On the boat he directed me to the shower, where I scrubbed the make-up from my body. It was like being in a really cool dream – only one I'd never even dared to dream, although I still regretted losing my lip-gloss to the Thames. Being without lip-gloss always makes a girl feel slightly vulnerable, but then I reminded myself that a prince had just whisked me off on a motorbike and now we were en route to a ball. A *real* ball – and not just any ball, the Royal Bore!

There was a knock on the door as I was about to climb back into my soggy clothes. I opened it an inch. Freddie was standing there, only he was facing the other way as he passed me the most stunning ball gown I had ever seen. It was black silk taffeta spangled with tiny multi-coloured diamonds and thousands of sparkles. It looked like a long ballerina's dress, like a summer night sky sparkling with stars.

'Oh, Freddie, it's so lovely. How did you know what size I was?'

He scratched the back of his head. 'Well, see, that's where I had to solicit the help of secret agent Portia. I took her out for pizza that day I first saw you in Windsor. You girls can eat pizza till it comes out your ears, can't you? She told me your size and suggested where I'd find such a dress. I almost got her a gating, I interrogated her for so long.'

'Oh,' was all I could really muster for fear of blurting about all the horrible, suspicious things I'd thought and how mean I'd been to her about everything. 'But how did you know you were taking me? I thought it was complicated.'

'Complicated doesn't even come close. Mother quizzed me to no end about you before she agreed to send off for the dress.' By this point I was getting cold so I took the dress from his hand and closed the door to change.

When I came out, he passed me a box that contained black Jimmy Choos with satin ribbons that laced up the leg.

I wanted to say something cool like, 'Oh, I can't,' but I didn't have the mettle. Instead I virtually snatched them from his outstretched hands. He helped me sort out all the bows and ribbons as we tied them up my leg. I really did feel like Cinderella being claimed by her prince. I only wished I could stop feeling shame over being so ghastly to Portia.

When we arrived at the ancient stone battlements of Windsor Castle, fireworks were already being let off. Freddie and I dashed up the stone steps of the pier and straight through security, through the throngs of glamourous dancing Euro Royals, marvelling at the fireworks display.

I looked up at the exploding heavens above us, but Freddie insisted we leg it, as we were late. As we entered the first of the castle's many anterooms en route to where I was to be presented to his parents, Sister Michaela's first history lesson from Year Seven started coming back to me – only not the bit where her habit got caught in a nail sticking out of the floor and ripped and we got to see her bald little nun head. No, I mean the part about the castle's history. Even though I saw Windsor Castle all the time, having been schooled not two miles away, for me it had only ever been a landmark, a marker for a nearby pizza place or tea shop. Now I was seeing it as one of Freds's castles, one of his homes. His parents' official residence, in fact. But most of all I was thinking, Calypso Kelly, you are stepping inside nine hundred years of history – and I was thinking in the voice of Sister Michaela.

There, among all the glorious chandeliers, ball gowns and dancing couples, my eyes fixed on the masterpieces by Rembrandt, Rubens, Holbein and Van Dyck. They lined the walls the way framed posters of old films line the walls of my house in Los Angeles. Bob calls them vintage. But Freddie didn't give me time for wonder as he led me rapidly to where I was to be presented to his parents. My head was swivelling, my heart was racing and before I could take it all in, there they were – his parents: the King and Queen of England. I was so happy I had spent all these years at an English public school and knew the proper etiquette on forms of address.

And then it got even better! I caught a glimpse of approval pass between Freddie and his mother and father. And then his father asked *me* to dance. We did a lovely waltz, and afterwards he thanked *me*, and before I could tell him that some of the sparkles from my dress had dusted off on his tux, I was whisked off by some old prince – an uncle, I think. Whoever he was, my dress gave him the same treatment as the king, and then it was the king of Spain's turn to get the special Calypso sparkle treatment. I kept praying they wouldn't notice, but then when I danced with Freds's father again he whispered discreetly in my ear, 'Your dress seems to be spreading its magic all over the ballroom.' The king of England actually said this in a nice tease.

I spotted Indie in a rich pink taffeta silk gown and tiara that no one but Indie could have carried off. As she waltzed by with some elderly bald man I sort of recognised, she gave me a little wave and a wink. I was so happy I could burst . . . right up until I saw Portia dancing with

Freddie. I've never felt so confused about anything in my life, because while I was so grateful to Portia for all she had done, I hadn't actually danced with Freddie myself.

I waved at them, but only Portia saw me – and she didn't wave back. The prince of Sweden was whisking me around and my sparkles were dusting his dinner jacket, so it was easy enough to put it from my mind, especially when he started dusting the sparkles off and apologised to me for his dandruff problem.

Later on, Indie and I stood outside in the cool night air for a bit, sipping on our champagne and looking up at the ink-black sky. We laughed about all the odd people we'd had to dance with. 'Now you know what I meant when I told you how terminally dull these things are,' she teased.

'Royal Bores, they're all the same,' I said grandly, as if I went to these things all the time, and we both laughed. Secretly, I was having the best night of my life – if you ignore the spew and runny body make-up thing. Even my sparkle disaster seemed perfect.

And then Indie ruined my feel-good fantasy. 'Have you spoken to Portia yet, Calypso?'

'I waved,' I told her, which I knew sounded feeble, even as I demonstrated the friendly little wave I'd sent to Portia. 'But she ignored me.'

'I think you have to sort things out with her, don't you?'

I nodded.

'You know she's madly keen on Billy, don't you?'

'I do now,' I told her. 'I only found out after she left the school on Friday, though. Honey had stolen my SIM card, and I don't know . . .'

'You got jealous?' she suggested.

'Yes,' I agreed.

'Well, I know how that feels,' she said, taking a sip of her champagne and looking out over the Thames. And as I watched this beautiful princess in her glamourous gown I realised that I hardly knew her – well, not half as well as I wanted to, at least.

'I was so jealous of you when I first started. All Star and Georgina talked about was Calypso, Calypso, Calypso.'

'All they talked about to me was Indie, Indie, Indie.'

Indie smiled and took my hand as a lump formed in my throat at the shame of my own behaviour these past weeks. Because as much as I wanted to blame it all on Honey, what sort of stupid girl was I to be taken in by a girl who had so consistently made my school life miserable? Also, there was no getting away from the fact that I'd been horrible to Portia without any help from Honey whatsoever. No wonder Portia was so wary of me.

Honey was just being Honey, the quintessential DPG, the psycho toff supreme.

I had no excuse.

'I invited Portia to come to Star's place, but she refused,' Indie told me.

'How come?'

'Her father. She doesn't want to leave him alone now that her mother's dead.'

'Poor Portia.' I looked up at the black sky and remembered our moonwalk and her blunt appraisal of me as a self-centred Honey clone. 'I've been so horrible to her,' I admitted to Indie desperately. 'I don't know what I can do now to make things okay again, though.'

Indie held me by the shoulders and looked me in the eye. 'I do. Make her come to Star's. I know she thinks her father needs her now, but make her come to Star's. She needs it more, and the best way to cheer her father up is for her to be happy.' Then she gave me a cuddle and I cuddled her back. 'Promise you'll try, Calypso?' she insisted as she pulled away.

'I'll try now,' I assured her, but as I watched Indie disappear back into the throngs of bejewelled, tiara-clad women dancing with men in sashes and medals, I couldn't think of how I was even going to approach Portia. I felt so utterly useless.

'So, had enough of all this Royal Bore business yet?' Freddie asked, coming up behind me and wrapping his arms around me.

I nodded, still staring up at the sky, frightened I might start crying or something tragic like that. He took my chin and turned me around and planted a kiss on my nose. 'May I have this dance?'

'I'll have to check my dance card,' I teased as he took my hand and led me back into the ballroom.

He was splendidly graceful as he led me around the floor, and then, just as I was about to burst with happiness, the waltz came to an end and he whispered in my ear. 'Our carriage awaits us.'

I couldn't bear that the night had to come to an end. 'I feel like Cinderella about to turn back into a pumpkin,' I told him, sticking out my lower lip.

He kissed it, 'I think you'll find that it was the carriage that turned back into the pumpkin. Cinderella turned back into herself – only without the meringue-like ball gown.'

'But I don't want to turn back into a girl that smells of vomit, and I definitely don't want to go back to Honey's,' I told him, realising as I said the words just how much I *didn't* want to go back to Honey's. In fact, I would rather sleep under the Embankment with the homeless than go back to Honey's House of Luxury Horrors.

Freddie wrapped me in his arms and kissed the top of my head. 'We're going to Star's! It's all sorted. So come on, let's hit the road. We've got a party to go to, people who need us, and quad bikes calling out our names. Actually, one of them is calling out your name.'

I looked at him quizzically.

'Star's named one of the quad bikes *Calypso*.'

I looked long and hard at this beautiful prince who seemed to genuinely like me, and in that moment I realised I wanted to be a better person, which in a nutshell meant I never wanted to be compared to Honey ever again.

'Can I borrow one of your security guys for just one sec?' I asked.

'It depends what you want to do with him,' Freddie joked.

'There's someone I need to say goodbye to, and I need to go alone, and I doubt I'll be able to find my way out to the car without him,' I explained.

'And I can't help?' he asked.

'No, it has to be a security guy,' I told him firmly. 'I'll see you in the car.'

I rushed through the ballroom, trailed by my rather large security guy, who wasn't exactly what you'd call nimble or light on his feet. As we ducked and dived our way through dancing couples and chatting groups in my search for Portia, he kept falling over and bumping into people. Eventually I found her dancing with the vaguely familiar bald man Indie had been dancing with earlier.

'Portia,' I panted, 'can I have a word, please?'

She looked at me impassively. 'Sorry, Calypso, now's not a good time,' she replied with perfect civility.

'But it can't wait. Please, Portia . . . please. It won't take a moment.'

'What do you want to say, Calypso?'

I looked at the bald guy and the bald guy looked at me. He looked very, very sad, and in that moment I recognised the eyes of Portia's father. His face had changed so dramatically that he didn't even look like the same man Portia's mother had fallen asleep on in chapel. In fact, the last time I'd seen him, he'd had hair!

I looked at Portia. Her own long raven hair was piled up in an elegant chignon and crowned with the oldest-looking tiara I'd ever seen. She looked truly regal. 'Mostly, I want to say I'm sorry,' I explained. 'But . . .'

'It's all fine,' she replied, even managing a slight smile, but it was only a slight one and it didn't quite reach her eyes. I noticed then that she was holding her father's hand.

'No, it's not all right. I've been horrible. Honey stole my SIM card and yours too, actually, and started playing mind games with me, and I fell for it.'

'Why?'

'I don't know. I was totally insanely obsessed that you were stealing Freds and . . .'

'Stealing what?'

'Look, can we just leave it that I behaved badly, madly and even a little dangerously? The point is, at the start of term we became really good friends, and I can't bear to think that it can't be like that again. I know it was all my fault, but it was all over boys, and do you really want to think boys are that important?'

'Hardly,' she agreed.

'Then come with Freddie and me now to Star's.'

She let go of her father's hand and ushered me to a quiet area.

'I can't, Calypso.'

'Why, because of me?'

'No, because Daddy needs me.' I watched her eyes as they travelled over to her sad father. I watched him return her smile with his own watery one, and even though I was ashamed of how I'd treated her, I no longer felt like the most self-centred, selfish girl in all the world because I was determined to make things right.

'I know,' I told her, and then, risking total rejection and humiliation, I cuddled her and kissed her cheek. 'But Billy is sitting in one of Star's wardrobes up in Derbyshire, refusing to come out until you arrive. Star's beside herself! She's had to resort to sliding buttered toast with Marmite under the door, she's so fearful of him fading away from lack of food.'

Portia smiled a proper smile as she whispered in my ear, 'Calypso, have you noticed . . .'

'That I can be a jealous witch? Yes, but I still want you to give me a second chance, because, well . . . because that's the sort of girl you are, Portia!' I looked her in the eye, feeling proud of my little speech. I seemed to have developed into quite the orator in the last few moments. Perhaps when I grow up and fence in the Olympics and win I shall be asked to make a speech and I'll even do it without blurting. Maybe I'll even be all composed, and . . .

Portia interrupted my little fantasy. 'No, Calypso,' she said, pointing around the room. 'Look around you. All the guests are covered in Calypso dust.'

I looked around at the glittering crowd – which was in fact glittering with *my* glitter. 'Oh buggery bollocks!' I exclaimed loudly as Her Serene Highness of Somewhere-or-Other waltzed by, and then I pressed my hand against my foul-mouthed New-World lips.

'Calypso!' Portia chided as she giggled.

'I'm soooo not bred for this sort of occasion. Sorry, I'd better go, Freds is waiting. I'll say hello to Billy for you though, okay?'

'Not so fast,' she said, grabbing my hand. 'How can I trust you not to steal him?' Portia asked, eyeing me up beadily.

I couldn't believe that I'd tried so hard to make up, only to have her mistrust me again. Seriously, these aristos are a bloody tricky lot! 'Portia? I'm going up with *Freds*!' I told her indignantly. 'The whole Billy thing was just a misunderstanding . . .'

'I still think I should come up to keep an eye on you just the same,' she told me, only now I could see she was suppressing a grin. 'Everyone knows what a ferocious txt flirt you are.'

I went bright red with shame, and my brain started up its *Dig! Dig! Dig!* chant again.

Portia kissed her finger and placed the kiss on my forehead. 'I was only teasing. I'm coming up to Derbyshire tomorrow.'

My head spun around on my shoulders. 'What?'

'Fred's sorted it all out with my brother tonight. Tarkie's going to stay home for half term. Besides, what sort of girl would I be if I left Billy to wilt away in a wardrobe with nothing but Marmite toast for sustenance? He doesn't even like Marmite.'

'But Indie said . . .'

'Bugger what other people say,' my enigmatic new friend declared – and quite loudly too.

I laughed as people turned around to stare at the two of us. That was all the encouragement I needed to grab her in a cuddle and smother her in sparkle. Then I kissed her father goodnight, dusting him in sparkles too. 'Sorry,' I blurted, 'I appear to have sparkled you.'

And then her father took my hand and brought it to his lips and kissed it. 'I assure you, young lady, the pleasure is all mine,' he told me, and smiled.

I grabbed Freddie's security guy, who was lingering discreetly out of earshot, took off my shoes and legged it to the car.

Freddie was waiting by the open door and ushered me into the vehicle like an ostentatious butler. He could probably get a job working for Honey with that bow.

'My lady!' he said, doffing an imaginary cap.

I climbed inside the black Mercedes. 'Thank you, Jeeves, that will be all!' I told him.

He dived in after me. 'I very much doubt it, my lady!'

I giggled as he wrapped me up in a big princely cuddle and then strapped me safely into the seat belt.

'Oh my god, I've left all my stuff at Honey's!' I cried as we drove out onto a country lane.

Freddie waved my fears away the way he'd waved Kevin away when he kissed me under the awning in Windsor. 'I'll have someone pick it up tomorrow morning first thing. It'll be with you by the afternoon.'

'And you?' I asked flirtily. 'Will you be with me?'

'To quote Sartre, one of my favourite idlers of all time, "I'm here now, aren't I?"'

'And to quote his miserable mistress, Simone de Beauvoir, "What about tomorrow?"' I shot back.

'Did she say that?' Freddie asked, surprised by my awesome literary knowledge.

'I don't actually know,' I admitted, unable to delude him. 'Probably not. But I did,' I told him. 'And I'm here now, aren't I?'

He smiled and ran his hand through his jet-black hair. 'Okay, well I'm not sure Sartre said, "I'm here now, aren't I?" But I'm pretty certain that Shakespeare – *Macbeth* in fact – said, "Tomorrow and tomorrow and tomorrow." Which is how long I'm staying up at Star's place. Although let me txt Kevin and check that it was *Macbeth*. He's the literary one.'

'No one's txt-ing anyone!' I told him firmly as I grabbed his BlackBerry and tossed it to the floor. I was so over mobile phones . . . at least for a bit. Then I wrapped my arms around Freddie's neck and pulled him in for a big snog-age session. Kissing Freddie is . . . well it's . . .

Well, I'm not going to tell you, actually.

Of course I'll tell Star, though.

Calypso's fencing terms and English words

FENCING TERMS

attack *au fer*: an attack that is prepared by deflecting an opponent's blade

bout: one single fight, usually lasting around six minutes

compound attack: an attack incorporating two or more movements

corps-à-corps: literally body-to-body – physical contact between fencers during a bout (illegal in sabre)

disengagement: a way to continue attacking after being parried

en garde: the 'ready' position fencers take before play

épée: another weapon used in fencing

flèche: a way of delivering an attack whereby the attacker leaps to make the attack and then passes the opponent at a run. French word for 'arrow'

flunge: an attack specific to sabre – a type of *flèche* attack in which the legs don't cross

friendly: a game played for practise

lamé: jacket made of interwoven wire and fabric

parry: defensive move, a block

parry of quinte: in sabre, a parry in which the blade is held above the head to protect from head cuts

piste: a fourteen-metre-long combat area on which a bout is fought

plastron: a padded under-jacket to protect the torso (where most hits land)

point: the tip of a weapon's blade

pool: a group into which fencers are divided during preliminary rounds to assess ranking

president: a registered referee or arbiter of the bout

retire: retreat

riposte: an offensive action made immediately after a parry of the opponent's attack

sabre: The only cutting fencing blade. Points are scored both by hits made with the tip of the blade and by cuts made with the blade, but more commonly by cuts. The sabre target is everything above the leg, including the head and arms. For this reason the entire weapon, including the guard, registers hits on an electrical apparatus even though hitting the weapon's guard is not legal. This means the sabreur is totally wired − unlike fencers using the other weapons. Before play begins, the sabreurs must check that all parts of their electric kit are working. This is done by the sabreurs tapping their opponents on the mask, the sabre, the guard and the metal jacket so that all hits will be recorded.

salle: fencing hall or club

salute: once formal, now a casual acknowledgement of one's opponent and president at the start of a bout

seeding: the process of eliminating fencers from their pools, based on the results of their bouts

Supermans: a fencing exercise − a holding stance used for warming up, so called because the fist is raised like Superman's before he flies.

trompement: deception of the parry

ENGLISH WORDS

arse: *derrière*. To make an arse of yourself means to embarrass yourself

As: exams taken in the Lower Sixth as a precursor to final exams

blag: to talk your way into or out of something, or to fake something

blank: to not register someone; to look through them

blue: blue paper given to write lines on; a minor punishment

bottle out: chicken out, lose your nerve. 'Bottle' is another word for 'nerve,' so you can also 'lose your bottle'

champagne socialist: a rich person who claims to have left-wing politics while enjoying a luxurious lifestyle (i.e., champagne)

common: slang for vulgar, of low social status. Note: you can be rich and still common

cosh: a heavy stick or bludgeoning implement. To be 'under the cosh' is to be under pressure

cut: to ignore someone, to look right through them; see *blank*

Daddy's plastic: parental credit cards

Domesday Book (Norman): compiled by William the Conqueror in 1086 as a survey created for taxation. Though unpopular in its day, many of England's oldest families take pride in their ability to trace their lineage back to this book

DPGs: Daddy's Plastic Girls; girls who are defined by their limitless credit card privileges

dressing down: telling off

en suite: bathroom attached to bedroom

exeat: weekend at which pupils attending boarding school go home, usually every three weeks

fag: cigarette

fit: cute, hot, attractive. Girls and boys use the word to describe the opposite sex. Note: a girl wouldn't refer to another girl as fit – she'd say 'stunning')

fruuping: all-purpose expletive

gating: a punishment in which one is not permitted to leave the school grounds on weekends

gypo: derogatory slang for 'gypsy'

High table: the superior or senior table in communal dining

Hon: as in The Honourable Georgina Smart-Arse; child of a life peer, baron or viscount

hoodie: sweatshirt with a hood

house mother or house mistress: female head of a boarding house

HRH: His (or Her) Royal Highness

It Girl: society girl with a large media profile

Jelly Babies: soft, brightly coloured sweets (candies) shaped like babies

kit: equipment and outfit for specific event or activity

Lady: daughter of a duke, marquis or earl; female life peers or wives of hereditary peers are also Ladies

listens: mobile phone messages that you let others listen to

loo rolls: rolls of toilet paper

Lower Sixth: year before the final year at school (16–17 years of age)

mad: eccentric, crazy or unreasonable – out there

Marmite: a black salty spread for toast or bread made of yeast and high in Vitamin B – you either loathe it or love it

neck: to gulp, as in 'neck your vodka' (juice, etc.)

NA: Narcotics Anonymous

nouveau: new money

NQOC: Not Quite Our Class

OTT: over-the-top, outrageous or extreme behaviour or style

pikey: an insulting reference to someone's lack of background or education; see *pleb*

piss-take: to tease or to make fun of someone, either maliciously or fondly; a joke

pleb: short for plebeian – a derogatory term suggesting lack of class

prat: idiot, fool

pull: to make out, score, kiss, etc.

public school: exclusive boarding school

quad bike: a four-wheel motorbike, good for rough roads and fabulous for driving around your estate

queue: line; 'to queue' is to wait in a line

quid: slang for pound (British currency)

readies: slang for folding money; actual banknotes

refectory or ref: large canteen where meals are served

rinse: to totally decimate your opponent in sport or debate

rip: to ridicule, tease; equivalent to 'take the piss'

rubbish: garbage; also slang for tease or take the piss

rusticated: suspended from school without being given schoolwork to carry on with – meaning that on return, the pupil is further disadvantaged by having to catch up

safe: 'okay'; an expression of agreement; see *sorted*

scrum: rugby term for a pile-up of bodies

slack down: to disrespect someone, ignore their instructions

slapper: slut

Sloane: posh, snooty girl (named after Sloane Street and Square, an upscale area in London)

slut: can mean either a slapper or someone who is madly untidy

smart: sassy; can also mean fashionably attired

snog-age: (rhymes with 'corsage') to tongue kiss

social: interschool dance (girls and boys)

sorted: an expression of approval; 'no problem'

soz: sorry

speakers: speaking terms, as in 'We're on non-speakers'

spliff: marijuana; a joint

spots: pimples, zits

stick: a hard time; to give stick is to tease someone

suspended: sent home from school with schoolwork (a punishment less harsh than a rustication)

term: Three terms make up a school year: winter term is before Christmas; spring term is between Christmas and Easter; summer term is between Easter and the summer holiday

ticked off: told off, reprimanded

toff: snobby aristocrat

torch: flashlight

trainers: sneakers

tuck: snack foods you are allowed to bring to boarding school; junk food

wind up: to tease either gently or nastily

wholemeal: whole wheat, used to describe decent middle-class people

Year: Girls start boarding at age 11 in Year Seven, and the 'Years' go up to Year Eleven (age 15–16). The final two years are referred to as the Lower Sixth and Upper Sixth (ages 16–17 and 18, respectively)

Zimmer frame: a metal frame on wheels used to assist elderly people walking

Acknowledgements

No author can claim *all* the credit for her work, because apart from being very greedy it would be a complete and utter porky. So gushing praise all round for my backup team of Laura Dail (the most serenely bright agent a girl could wish for) and my top-notch and much-adored editors, Melanie Cecka and Victoria Arms, and all the rest of the brilliant Bloomsbury USA team, not least Michael Storrings for his stunning cover design. Add still more applause to my darling Mummy and Daddy, Veronica and Bernard O'Connell, for sending me to such a lovely school and putting up with my difficult teen years which they are still patiently waiting on to end. Mad amounts of 'Hoorahs!' for the cracking team of teenage girls and boys at boarding schools all over the UK, especially my own sons and daughter and all their lovely, generous friends for their wit and wisdom. Then of course there are my own grown-up-ish friends, Alicia Gordon, Eric Hewitson, Niki de Metz, Malcolm Young and Simon Peter Santospirito, who add an alchemical mix of sense, madness and laughter to my après-writing activities.

O'CONNELL, TYNE.
    STEALING PRINCES

RING
09/08